things in glocca morra

PETER COLLIER

Encounter BOOKS
New York • London

First American edition published in 2021 by Encounter Books, an activity of Encounter for Culture and Education, Inc., a nonprofit, tax-exempt corporation.
Encounter Books website address: www.encounterbooks.com

Manufactured in the United States and printed on acid-free paper. The paper used in this publication meets the minimum requirements of ANSI/NISO Z39.48-1992 (R 1997) (Permanence of Paper).

FIRST AMERICAN EDITION

LIBRARY OF CONGRESS CATALOGING-IN-PUBLICATION DATA

Names: Collier, Peter, 1939–2019, author.
Title: Things in Glocca Morra / Peter Collier.
Description: First American edition. | New York : Encounter Books, 2021.
Identifiers: LCCN 2020011264 (print) | LCCN 2020011265 (ebook)
ISBN 9781641771344 (cloth ; acid-free paper) | ISBN 9781641771351 (epub)
Subjects: LCSH: Kennedy family—Fiction. | Kennedy, John F. (John Fitzgerald), 1917-1963—Fiction. | GSAFD: Biographical fiction.
Classification: LCC PS3553.O47465 T48 2021 (print) | LCC PS3553.O47465 (ebook) | DDC 813/.54--dc23
LC record available at https://lccn.loc.gov/2020011264
LC ebook record available at https://lccn.loc.gov/2020011265

To my son

Andrew Louis Collier,

With love always

New York – January 31, 1981

Hollywood – September 1945

New York – March 30, 1981

Hollywood – October/November 1945

Boston/Washington – Aftermath

New York

*

January 31, 1981

ONE

We're condemned to live our lives forward and understand them backward.

That's how Ted Sorenson, expert ransacker of *Bartlett's* and word man par excellence, dumbed down the gem from Kierkegaard in one of his speeches for Jack. Today the maxim is displayed on marquees outside high schools all over the country at graduation time, but in 1961 it was still fresh and very much in synch with the faint whiff of existentialism that mysteriously attached itself to the Kennedy presidency. A dedicated Ciceronian himself, Jack loved the heft and balance of the phrase, but acting on its mandate was another thing altogether. For him, as for all the Kennedys, the unexamined life was not only worth living, but a necessity.

That I myself am understanding backward in this form, at this time, is the result of a visit from an archivist named Daniel Goldman a week ago. When the Kennedy Library called to ask if I would meet with him, I knew word had reached Boston that my actuarial tables had been turned and it was time to suction out whatever privileged information I still possessed about *the President* before my heart, which sometimes beats as fast and feebly as a hummingbird's, decides to call it a life.

I told them I would talk to this Mr. Goldman but probably not say anything.

I was watching the sparrows grubbing in the dirty snow of my window box when he got out of the cab on Fifth Avenue three stories below and hunched into the wind chill's blast. I identified him by the industrial-strength briefcase and the brisk librarian's walk. It was three minutes until two; by the time he reached my apartment he would be exactly on time. I thought of telling him that one of Jack's favorite aphorisms was "Punctuality is a virtue of the mediocre."

Goldman emerged from the elevator and became distorted in my peephole, his fingers combing strands of hair from the side of his head over a balding crown. He was probably not much over forty, but his jowly face had already capitulated to gravity.

I opened the door on the first knock and gestured him to the sofa, where he sat as demurely as a deb, spine straight and knees together. A photo above the highboy showing Jack and me as teenagers getting ready to zoom into life in his Ford Roadster caught Goldman's eye like flypaper.

"That's you and the President."

"Yes, when we were a work in progress."

"Taken at the family home?"

"Hyannis, yes."

He studied the image closely, then gave an unctuous smile: "People always speak of yours as a somewhat unlikely friendship."

The passive aggression in "unlikely" was irksome. But he was right, of course. One of our patrician Choate classmates once said to my face, "It is as odd of Kennedy to choose a mooncalf like you as his best friend, Billings, as it was of God to choose the Jews."

Later on, the New Frontiersmen too were baffled by my privileged position. Who was this clown who was always the first one pushed into the deep end at the Kennedy pool parties; the onetime literature major able to recite "Dover Beach" on cue while everyone else in the administration was speaking in prosy realpolitik; the "extra man" for unaccompanied women at important dinners; the big guy with the high-pitched voice and Coke-bottle glasses who could always be counted on to drink out of the dribble cup in front of Haile Selassie or plop down unawares on a whoopie cushion at the state dinner for Malraux?

And why was this doofus allowed to sit in on important meetings and even have overnight privileges at the White House?

Then someone in the know would tell them: Billings has been around forever; nobody knows why, but he's the President's second self.

"The two of you first met at prep school." Goldman was still warming me up.

"That's right."

"That's a moment you must remember well," he said with fine-tuned aggression.

I noticed that he was jiggling one foot rapidly to ward off urination or worse.

"The facilities are that way if you need to use them." I pointed to the bathroom down the hall.

"Thank you. A long trip from the airport." He immediately hustled off.

* * *

Of course I remember. It occurred at exactly 4:17 on the afternoon of September 8, 1930. I had arrived at Choate by taxi about an hour earlier, a social misfit who'd already been expelled from two other prep schools, less for infractions than as a result of an obtuse inability to fit in. I was sitting on the unoccupied bed in our dorm room picking at the cracked and bleeding eczema on my elbows that testified to how deeply I was rejecting myself those days and staring at my wristwatch in the hope that time would fly me out of the life I had led up until that moment.

It was 4:17 when I happened to look up and see a skinny boy with gray-green eyes in a white T-shirt and khakis leaning against our doorjamb with the filtered backlight picking up the honey-colored accents in his hair.

"What are you doing in my room?" That blunt-force Boston accent hit my ears for the first time.

"They put me here."

"Oh, so you're the new kid."

I resumed staring at my watch, but I knew that he was evaluating my precocious size—six feet tall and 150 pounds at the age of thirteen.

"Do you play football?"

"I'd like to," I mumbled hopefully, unaware that I had just sentenced myself to decades of hiking the ball and blocking for a variety of Kennedys who alone were allowed to pass and run in our games.

"What's your name?"

"Lemoyne Billings."

"Lemoyne?" A sly smile bloomed in time lapse on the triangular face. "No, that doesn't sound right. You must mean LeMoan? Of course: LeMoan Billings. Now there's a distinguished name."

"Lemoyne," I repeated.

"That's what I said," he eyed me. "LeMoan."

The rest of that day—the rest of our lives together, really—Jack continued to chew on my name. After LeMoan, it was Pneumoan. Then Lemon. Then Le Monde. Then Lerman. Then Lemur. Then Lemmer. Then Lemming. And so on, until I came to feel that I was whoever he wanted me to be at any given moment, which I suppose was exactly his intention all along.

When we returned that evening from a silent meal in the dining hall, I went to a corner of the room and changed into my pajamas with my back to him. He turned on the radio, stripped to his underpants, got in bed, and began leafing through his worn modern English version of *Le Morte D'Arthur.* Then, as Paul Whiteman's "Willow Weep for Me" came on, he jumped up and began foxtrotting to the music with his arms around an imaginary partner. When he knew he had my attention, he stopped in the middle of the room and turned his back, then slowly bent down until his head was upside down near his knees and he was looking at me from under his crotch.

"What are you doing?" I pulled the covers up tighter around my neck.

"My exercises," he replied. "I have walking leukemia. At least that's what the doctors call it. They've told me that I'd better learn to kiss my ass goodbye, and that's why I do my spine exercises every night."

That last comment pushed my on-button. Feeling like Lazarus called forth from the dead life I'd led until then, I promptly signed on as Jack's companion and connoisseur; his accomplice and all-purpose yes man; second fiddle in his one-man band.

He had just begun his guerrilla campaign against Choate (or "Chode," as he naturally called it, having located what he regarded as the perfect pun for the school in the term describing that obscure area of transition between the genitals and anus) for trying to scrub off him the last stain of shanty Irish that might yet cling to the Kennedys. He assumed as a matter of course that I would join him in his minor anarchy, and I did.

For two weeks, the two of us emerged after lights off to flush cherry bombs down the toilets; drench the cook's sanitary napkins in strawberry preserves and put them on display in the cafeteria; salt the head custodian's hemorrhoid cream with itching powder; and generally wreak havoc.

It all ended the minute Choate's imperious headmaster George St. John sent a haughty letter of complaint to the Kennedys.

"The Old Man is pissed, Lemuel," Jack told me after fielding the scorching call from home. "He said for you to come with me to Thanksgiving so that we can get things straightened out."

At this time the Kennedys were living up in Westchester County in the town of Bronxville in a twenty-room brick colonial originally built for Anheuser-Busch. The Old Man was creating the items on his CV faster than a secretary could type them: the Big Bear prowling for tasty scraps on the floor of the Depression; momentary Hollywood mogul; political insider climbing the greasy pole of the New Deal; not to speak of his scrupulously redacted extralegal activities, alluded to later in a story told by Paul Ricca at a lunch arranged by Bobby (who had distantly befriended the aging Chicago Mob boss while investigating him as attorney general) in which Ricca described a locally famous shootout between the Old Man's Irish thugs and the tough Jews of Detroit's Purple Gang during Prohibition over rights to smuggle Canadian whiskey that left "three Hibernians and a pair of Semites done for," as he put it.

When we arrived, Jack headed straightaway to the Old Man's office, towing me along by the invisible cord that already connected us.

He knocked on the door and a raspy voice within yelled "Come!" We entered and I caught my first sight of the founding father himself. His suspenders were off his shoulders and hanging below his waist, and his red polka dot bowtie was unknotted at his neck. He was tilted back in his chair with his feet up on his desk shouting into the speaker of the candlestick telephone he held with one hand while jamming the receiver to his ear with the other. Behind him was a stunning woman only a few years older than Jack and me. She wore a purple kimono and bangle earrings that flashed like fishing lures within the cotton candy swirl of her bright blond hair.

Because Jack always referred to him as "the Old Man," I had formed an image of Mr. Kennedy as a forbidding Pentateuch patriarch. But in the flesh, his thinning strawberry blond hair and freckled face made him look youthful and almost innocent, at least until you looked into the gelid blue eyes behind the rimless glasses. They told the truth: here was a man whose golden rule was to do unto others before they did unto him.

"Hi, Jack." The blonde vamped us while the Old Man continued to rage on the phone.

"Hi, Wanda," Jack grinned.

Just then the Old Man snarled, "Listen you prick! You get that goddamn stuff into the warehouse tonight or else!" Then he slammed the receiver back into the cradle and stared malevolently at the phone for a moment before turning to us.

Jack froze. A fluttering sensation took wing in my stomach when the Old Man looked me over as if wondering how I would taste for lunch.

"Get this, Jack!" he finally spoke. "I don't want you ever to do anything that will give that son-of-a-bitch headmaster of yours the right to chap my ass again!"

"I won't, Dad." Jack was meek as an altar boy.

"You know I mean what I say," the Old Man growled.

"I know you do, Dad."

"Okay. Now get the hell out of here while I talk to your friend."

Jack smirked at me as he made his escape.

Mr. Kennedy appraised me again before asking, "What the hell is your name anyway, Billings? Jack calls you everything under the sun."

"Lemoyne."

He considered it the way someone in the old country might have bitten a coin. "Not something I'd name a kid of mine, but no matter. What size shoe do you wear?"

"Eleven," I gulped.

"Perfect!" He gave an economical smile.

Then he nodded to Wanda: "Run over there and get me that shoe box, will you, Sweetie?" She sashayed to the corner of the room.

"Wanda's my secretary," he said in a way that dared me to disagree.

She rummaged around and brought him the box. The Old Man opened it and pulled out a pair of beautiful new cordovan wingtips.

"Put these on," he commanded.

The shoes' gleaming leather had the smell of money. But they were tighter than a bench vise when I laced them up.

"Gee, thanks, Mr. Kennedy," I stammered.

He shot me a suspicious glance, then looked at Wanda and barked out a laugh sharp enough to cut air. "He thinks I'm giving them to him! Like I'd give thirty-dollar shoes to some goddamn stranger!"

He took two quarters out of a glass ashtray on his desk and handed them to me. "They're my size, ten, but they need breaking in. I'll give you four bits to wear them while you're here. And whatever you do, don't scuff the fucking toes!"

Jack was waiting for me when I exited the office.

"Whew," I exhaled.

"I know exactly what you mean," he said, squeegeeing imaginary sweat off his forehead with an index finger.

The rest of that afternoon I watched with numbness creeping up my ankles as the other Kennedys performed in character. Joe Junior, "the hair apparent," as Jack contemptuously called him, maliciously dug at a nerve on the side of Cork, the family terrier, making the animal thrash its hind leg idiotically. Rosemary wandered around with a face like an untethered balloon. ("Rosie? Oh, she'll be okay once she gets her grades up," Jack shrugged.) Eunice trotted through the house holding imaginary reins and making whickering noises. Bobby ran into the living room periodically with a look of panic to tell us that the Old Man would be very mad if we didn't turn down the record player, causing Jack to snarl at him, "Drop dead, you little kiss-ass." Pat and Jean made faces because of Teddy's poopy diapers.

The only one of them who staked a claim on me besides Jack himself was Kathleen. With inset emerald eyes, bisque skin and a pretty, bottom-heavy face, she was as clearly the pick of the female Kennedy litter as he was of the males. The nickname "Kick" perfectly captured her effervescence. She wore a red hooded coat and an ermine hand muff when the two of us walked around the compound in the chill of that first afternoon and I encouraged myself to fall in love with her on the spot.

The next day, Wanda and I and a silent family priest watched the family members shout at each other all through Thanksgiving dinner in the rich argot of ers, ahs, and ums that functioned as the Kennedy equivalent of glottal clicks. Rose, outfitted in one of the cerise dresses she wore as a distant pun on her name, stared at Wanda for a long time in that cold avian way of hers and then, addressing her as "Dear," condescendingly described at great length the religious retreat she and the girls were leaving for the next morning. Wanda tried to pay attention, but seemed to be in physical distress, repeatedly clearing her throat as if trying to dislodge a bone.

I saw Jack purposely let go of his fork and bend down to retrieve it from the floor. He came back up and whispered, "Drop your napkin or something and while you're down there take a look."

When I did, I saw four things underneath the canopy of tablecloth: Wanda's dress was hiked up; she wasn't wearing any panties; her pubic bush was black, not blond; and the Old Man was fingering her to beat the band.

"Welcome to my world," Jack said under his breath when I came back up. Because I was already established as sidekick for life, had fallen for his sister, and, perhaps equally importantly, my feet were big enough to stretch the Old Man's shoes, it was now my world too.

* * *

When Daniel Goldman re-entered the living room, propelled by the toilet flush, he was looking over his shoulder as if fearful that something might be gaining on him.

"As you know," he sat down with the look of someone finally ready to take care of business, "the Kennedy Library is fortunate to have a wealth of materials about *the President*, but there are still periods in his life we don't know much about."

"Hard to believe," I replied. "I thought you had him laid out on the biographical mortuary table, all dissected and examined and stitched back together again."

"Far from it," Goldman replied sternly. "There are still many lacunae in the record."

Lacunae was obviously a tasty condiment in his mouth, and he paused for a second to let me appreciate its use before continuing.

"Take the fall of 1940, for example," he was now reading from notes on a yellow legal pad he'd taken out of his briefcase, "when he was at Stanford for a summer session. That's an episode about which almost nothing is known. It's one of those blanks we hope you might be able to help us fill in."

"Afraid I can't be of much assistance there," I replied honestly. "Jack and I were a couple of years out of college then and I was working at my first real job. I think he went out to Palo Alto on a whim. His brother Joe Jr. was still the focus of the Old Man's attention then, so Jack was free to remain in his cowboy–Indian chief–fireman phase without having to worry about where he was headed."

Goldman listened with a skeptical look and then cleared his voice before offering a deal: "You can be perfectly frank with me in your responses, Mr. Billings, and not have to worry that anything you say will become public before you're ready. Our interviews are very secure. Some of our subjects seal their oral histories for thirty or forty years after their death before anyone, including scholars, can see them. Their wishes are scrupulously respected."

I forced myself not to ask him what the half-life of plutonium is.

"I just want to make sure you know," he continued patronizingly, "that you can speak freely without worrying that what you say might cause unpleasantness during your lifetime."

"Which we know will not be all that long," I said.

Goldman rolled his eyes in a feigned rebuke of my ghoulishness as his index finger moved to the next item on his page.

"Or the time at the end of the war when he was out in Hollywood for several weeks. What about that? This is the longest period of his adult life where we lose sight of him altogether. You certainly must know about this because materials in the files indicate that you were out there with him."

Remembering that Jack always said my face registered lies like a polygraph, I bent over to retie my shoe.

"It was so long ago," I came up after taking a deep breath. "These days, I'm lucky to remember what I had for breakfast."

"But you were there during that time, right?"

I nodded.

"What exactly did the two of you do?" Goldman was in full prosecutorial mode now.

"Same old thing. Jack chased women and I held his coat for him when he caught one."

"That's it?"

"It was only a few weeks."

The archivist plowed grimly ahead: "What about his father? Calendar entries I ran across in our files indicate that he was in Hollywood at roughly the same time the two of you were."

"It wasn't a family outing. As you probably know, Mr. Kennedy had been involved in the movie business during the late Twenties and early Thirties, and often spent time in Hollywood afterwards."

"How were he and the President relating then?"

"*Relating?* Come on, Mr. Goldman, as a student of this family you've got to know that whether he was fourteen or forty and whether he was in Hollywood or Hyannis, the greatest problem Jack Kennedy faced, almost until the day he died, was not the Cuban missile crisis or the civil rights movement or Berlin or Vietnam. It was his father and how to keep him at bay."

"Thanks for all this—very valuable," Goldman said insincerely as he put his yellow pad back in the briefcase and moved to Plan B. "The other thing I hoped to discuss with you during this visit is primary source materials—letters and other items we know you accumulated during your long relationship with the President."

I was not surprised that rumors about my little archive had reached Boston, probably via Jackie, who always spends some time rummaging around in it when she drops by to encourage me to adopt what she calls, in that breathy voice of hers, a "healthier lifestyle."

In fact, I have been cataloguing and cross-cataloguing my letters from Jack since November 22, 1963, when overnight the past became the jail I keep trying to break back into. I have segregated them into batches marked "dirty" and "clean," and annotated each one with a typed gloss explaining the context in which it was written. I tell myself I am serving history. In truth, I manufacture excuses to handle these pieces of paper because they provide the tactile jolt that keeps my heart from giving up.

"I do have some correspondence."

Goldman lifted his briefcase onto his knees and rested his forearms on it, leaning forward avidly. "I know you're probably not ready yet to consider gifting them..." I began shaking my head, and he made a course correction: "... but for now, can you give me a sense of the nature of your holdings?"

I stood up, and after the vertigo subsided I walked over to my file cabinet and extracted a couple of manila folders. In the mirror I saw Goldman surreptitiously pull a small tape recorder out of his briefcase.

"You don't mind, do you?" he said nervously when I turned around.

I shrugged and sat down with the letters. He slid close to me, holding the mike like an Olympic torch.

"This is dated April 13, 1936," I picked a letter at random. "Jack had left

Harvard for a couple of weeks to go to the family's second home in Palm Beach to recover from a bout of his mystery illness. I was in my second year at Princeton and he'd asked me to come down and keep him company. He wrote it when I was driving back to New Jersey." I read:

> Dear Lemon: The seat of your car must have had a delectable smell after having you sit on it for twenty-four hours. When I get back to school, I'll have to do some pretty stiff cramming to get ready for exams. Speaking of which, I suggest you cram up your chocolate speedway all that stuff about being too busy to meet me in New York for May Day.

The cloacal references made Daniel flinch, so I selected another note, written a few weeks later from Cambridge and more in keeping with what he probably regarded as Jack's normality.

> Dear Lemmer: It's coming to the point where I can get tail pretty much as often as I want now, which is definitely a step in the right direction. With luck, I'll be demonstrating the beast with two backs in person when you arrive this weekend, which will probably be as close as you'll ever get to the fertile crescent yourself. Just finished a statistics seminar, by the way, in which we learned that one out of every ten men at Princeton has the syph.

Daniel's minimalist smile was replaced by proprietary interest when I added a couple of sentences from a hurried postscript ordering me to line up a place for us to stay during Army-Navy game weekend and concluding with the warning: "I'll have the hottest thing ever with me and I don't want you running into my room every five minutes to find out how my bruised cock is doing."

"Who was she?" Daniel asked.

"Who remembers? Who could keep track? By this time, as I'm sure you know, Jack had already gotten the idea that it was transfusions of sex that kept him alive. That's why he was always on the lookout for new blood. For him it was quite literally a matter of I Fuck Therefore I Am."

"Yes, quite the cocksmith." Daniel obviously liked the man-to-man stuff.

I thought his picture needed to be more complex: "But for all that, a passive seducer whose technique was to display all his assets and leave women standing there with their mouths watering as he danced off. And never one to worry about inflicting orgasms or otherwise obsess over a girl's sexual well-being as if she was a car always needing to be polished or have its engine tuned. On the contrary, he was happy to be a wham-bam-thank-you-ma'am kind of guy who couldn't wait to get into a woman and couldn't wait to get out. 'Jack B. Quick,' he sometimes called himself. It wasn't because he was some kind of pernicious narcissist, as some of his biographers have claimed, but because however much he needed the boost sex provided him, he dreaded the contact itself."

Daniel tried to take all this in.

"Shouldn't surprise you," I continued loading him down. "You of all people must know that Jack Kennedy had been picked at and prodded and hurt and humiliated by physicians since he was a boy. This made him *noli me tangere* to the core. The problem he faced all his life—metaphysical, that is, not situational—was how to fuck without touching."

Daniel blinked a couple of times and then resumed his look of doggy expectancy as I read a few more excerpts that illumined a few tiny stars not yet seen in the Kennedy galaxy. But the hungry way he lunged at every small fact began to grate. So I put the manila folders down, forced a yawn and shook out a couple of Inderals from the vial on my end table.

"Time for me to get my heart rate steady enough that I can get through my afternoon nap without a major incident," I explained. "I warned the people at the library that this would happen."

"Oh yes, I was told that you might tire." He gathered his things. "I guess I'd better grab the shuttle and head back home."

He ejected and pocketed the used tape cassette, loaded a fresh one, and then placed the recorder on the coffee table, shooting a greedy look at my filing cabinet: "Perhaps I'll leave it here in case you might want to read a letter or two into the machine every so often and give a little commentary like you just did."

"Not going to happen."

"Stories," he wheedled as he headed toward the door without picking up the tape recorder. "Just tell stories. That's all I'm asking."

As if it's that easy; as if we tell stories rather than them telling us; as if the past is not constantly shape-shifting and interrogating those who think they hold it securely in their hands; as if some stories don't have the power to consume the wick of the teller's life in their flame.

What he was asking awakened the bitch in me. "So you want me to just lay down on my couch here and free-associate into your machine?"

"That would be great," he was proud to catch the allusion. "Just say the first thing that comes into your mind."

I sprang the trap: "Actually, Jack hated psychoanalysis, you know."

"How so?" Daniel was alert to the prospect of another tidbit.

"Like others back in those unenlightened times, he thought it was 'too Jewish.'"

He blanched: "I knew that his father had some anti-Semitic inclinations, but..."

"Yes, you're right," I soothed. "Jack wasn't really prejudiced against Jews."

A look of relief came over his face, and I struck again: "But he was curious about them. You ask for stories. Here's one you may not have heard. The two of us were having lunch in the Choate dining hall shortly after we met when one of the handful of Jews at the school, a boy named David Levy, sat down with his tray across from us. I remember him as having curly black hair and big brown eyes and he seemed to be a nice fellow. But Jack stared at him all the time he was eating his meal. Never said a word; just stared. Levy finally blushed and put down his fork and asked why he was doing this. Jack replied, quite pleasantly, 'Because I've never seen a Jew eat before.'"

Daniel blinked rapidly, then raised his shoulders in a shrug that implicated his eyebrows and was out the door.

* * *

This morning I awoke to another thick snowfall that silenced New York and gave it an implausible façade of purity. The fat flakes were drifting down so slowly outside my window that it seemed almost possible to see the distinctive pattern in each one.

I scanned my shelves for a book to snuggle up with, but then my eye lit on the tape recorder still sitting where Daniel put it a week ago. I picked it up for the first time, turned it on and went through the usual routine—"Testing-one-two-three." Stop-rewind-playback. "Testing-one-two-three." I knew that the microphone I held, like memory itself, was an instrument of betrayal.

Just tell stories…

That had always been my role. Jack himself was a conversational counterpuncher, someone who liked a good tale but wanted to avoid the jeopardy of the telling, so he was always ordering me to give command performances. "Hey Lemuel! Tell about the time we sailed to Europe on the *Normandie* and I saw Primo Carnera's name on the passenger list and arranged the surprise wrestling match for the two of you …" Or: "Come on, Lemur, tell how Zip the Pinhead and Mignon the Penguin Girl both came on to you that day we were wandering through Times Square and stopped at Hubert's Flea Circus…"

But while he loved a good story, no one was more aware than Jack of the dark powers of narrative. One summer day in 1963, a couple of months before Dallas, we were sitting in the Oval Office, just the two of us, and he was musing about what he'd do after the second term he now felt sure he would win. How to make his post-presidency unique? That was one question. But more importantly, how to deal with all the digging around in his life, his intimate life, that was bound to take place once the office and the glamour he had brought to it no longer protected him?

After staring out the window for a while, slowly tapping his front teeth with his index fingernail, as he often did when ruminating, he said, "There will be good books about me and bad books about me, but the best books about me will be those that never get written."

I got his point: my silence, far more than anyone else's, would be golden in the days to come.

It is still a powerful injunction even now. But I've carried this burden with me for too long. Night is coming and it's time to lay it down once and for all.

Hollywood

✳

September 1945

TWO

Late in the afternoon of Labor Day 1945, Jack's Lincoln Zephyr sedan was inching its way down Hollywood Boulevard. The traffic was stop-and-go because everyone was out celebrating not only the holiday, but the end of gas rationing and the end of the war that began six years and two days earlier with the invasion of Poland and formally concluded the previous morning when the Japanese signed the instrument of surrender aboard the USS *Missouri.*

"Mother always makes a big deal of Labor Day," Jack said, revving the motor to encourage the car in front of us to move forward a foot or two. "Last day of the year to wear white or seersucker."

I had been watching the Zephyr's temperature gauge for warnings of vapor lock, but its big V12 continued to thrum confidently in the rolling standstill. Jack had recently bought the 1941 classic with money from the newspaper job he'd had for the past couple of months. He got it for $685, about half the original cost, from a man in Redondo Beach who had driven it less than five thousand miles in four years because of the wartime fuel shortage. It was as close to a new car as you could get at a time when automakers were still almost a year away from full conversion back to domestic production.

We were caught in the middle of the Highland intersection when the signal changed. While drivers on our right and left laid on their horns, I watched the people streaming in and out of the stores. They were not yet buying, but looking with fierce determination, trying to convince themselves that the spoils of victory were really theirs—a new dress or suit; a house in one of the dozens of Southern California tracts already on the drawing board; membership in the middle class; power and glory; dominion. They had just inherited the world but weren't sure what to do with it.

Then we started up again, stuttering toward the Egyptian Theatre, which was still playing *Anchors Aweigh* weeks after its release. Jack looked across me at a pair of Betty Grable lookalikes in short shorts and halter tops keeping pace with us on the sidewalk. They were Vargas-girlish with bloody lipstick and sandy hair pompadoured in front and bobby-pinned above their ears. Their walk, stilted by high heels, churned their buttocks in a way that made him laugh out loud with pleasure.

"Now *that,* my friend, is what they mean by The Shape of Things to Come! Bare Midriffs! Mile-High Thighs! Good God, will you look at that."

Trying to do my part, I leaned out the window and panted, "Hub-ba-hubba."

"That's the way they make them out here in Lotus Land." Jack kept looking hungrily at the girls' long-legged strut. "Can't you just feel your finger running up the leg from the ankle to the back of the knee and then all the way up to the gates of paradise?"

The girl nearest to us turned around with a coy smile. I had forgotten that teeth could be so white.

She sent an air kiss over her shoulder and Jack slapped his cheek to let her know she had hit her mark.

"No doubt about it, they're fine," his voice fell into a register of fatalism. "But you have to remember that sooner or later, every one of them, however gorgeous, is going to be a giant pain in the ass for some poor guy."

We picked up pace and got as far as the Pantages before coming to a standstill again. Men in crisp military uniforms were sauntering out of the theatre at the end of a matinee.

"Looks like a dress rehearsal for a film about demobilization." Jack took on the persona of hardened combat vet he'd already flashed a few times that day. "Were these people out here in Shangri La ever really at war? Or did they just stash their Nipponese friends and neighbors in concentration camps after Pearl Harbor and figure, okay, now we've got things under control, let's get back to normal?

"Listen to this: I'm coming down on the train from San Francisco the other day and there's this Army second looey sitting across from me.

When he told me he'd been stationed here in Southern California for the duration doing staff work, I asked if he'd ever felt he was in any danger. He thought for a minute and said, 'Well, there was that time in '42 when a Jap submarine surfaced up near Long Beach and lobbed a couple of shells onto the sand. That had us going for a few days.' *Had us going!* Can you believe that crap? We're out there ducking fifty calibers, and they're back here stateside worrying that their beach time might be interrupted!"

Flattered as I was to be grandfathered into the ranks of men who'd actually borne arms against the enemy, my own opinion was that Southern California had been at war with nature for so long that the war against Japan had probably been anticlimactic. Conjured out of desert by magician entrepreneurs, Los Angeles always seemed to me just a few days of water deprivation away from returning to hardscrabble and horned toads. For the past few hours, since stepping off the *Super Chief* train from Chicago, I'd been imagining the fault lines grinding against each other below my feet, the pressure building, the cracks about to open into jagged chasms that would break apart and send this paradise out to sea like a new Atlantis.

But as usual, my anxiety was Jack's anticipation. One reason he loved it here was exactly this sense of imminence, the feeling that something might happen. He'd been coming to Hollywood since he was a kid when the Old Man was making a killing producing cheap cowboy movies while living in a rented cottage over on Gower Street and banging not only Gloria Swanson but also Constance Bennett, Marlene Dietrich and several other stars, including Ginger Rogers, who finally had to claim that she had syphilis to get away from him, and Miriam Hopkins, who said to me one tipsy night years later at the Stork Club, "Joe Kennedy was charming in an oppressive sort of way, I suppose, but he had the worst breath of any man I ever fucked."

As a result of his past visits, Jack knew Hollywood like a native. He'd already been out here for a week or so, now on general assignment for the Hearst papers after several weeks in San Francisco as their special correspondent covering the United Nations founding convention. But the only information gathering I'd seen since meeting him early that morning had been his feverish effort at a succession of phone booths to get us into the big Warner Brothers fortieth anniversary party later that afternoon.

Having finally secured the invite, Jack said "Let's kill time before it kills us" and gave me a little cook's tour. The first stop was the La Brea Tar Pits, where he sat on a bench reading the newspaper while I stood at the barricade watching the heavy bubbles break on the surface of the thick oily ooze and imaging the panicked cries of Cervidae falling into the suffocating muck in their rush to escape sabertoothed predators.

We got sandwiches and took them to the Hollywood Bowl, deserted at noon. Jack insisted that I get up on stage and do my rich darky imitation of Paul Robeson's "Old Man River" while he sat in the front row clapping derisively. Next was a stop at Grauman's Chinese Theatre so I could match my hands and feet with the prints left by Judy Garland, Mickey Rooney and other favorites of mine.

Then we crawled down postwar, pre-prosperity Hollywood Boulevard for almost half an hour, before finally turning onto Cahuenga and heading up toward a first draft of the Hollywood Freeway.

I was still pinching myself about being back with Jack after the winds of war had blown us apart, I thought forever. Almost exactly four years earlier, his older brother Joe Jr. had ordered us to meet him at Delmonico's for lunch and "a council of war." When we arrived, Young Joe, as he was known inside the family, was already at a table in the corner, Black Irish handsome in that slightly menacing way of his, nonchalantly weaving a silver dollar between his fingers from thumb to pinkie and back again—the first person I ever saw perform that trick.

He ordered us to sit on either side of him, pulled out a fountain pen and, ignoring scandalized looks from the maître d', began defacing the tablecloth with inky designs of likely troop movements and military engagements around the world while Fortress America looked on from a distance.

"Son of a bitch!" He drew arrows that pulled the U.S. toward the Continent. "War's coming and we've got to get in it. I'm sick and tired of these commie Brits and Roosevelt's Jews ripping Dad for being soft on Hitler when he was ambassador to the UK! We've got to restore his good name!"

"Right!" Jack said as Joe Jr. punched him hard on the shoulder.

"Right!" I echoed as he punched mine even harder.

When we went to enlist the next morning, Young Joe waltzed right into the Army Air Corps, but the recruiters, still choosy with Pearl Harbor three months yet in the future, flunked me because of my poor eyesight and Jack because of his bad back, which of course was actually only a presenting symptom of his other, more ominous malady.

Jack went down to Palm Beach for a health regimen of sit-ups and milkshakes before trying again, and for a while the only Kennedy I saw was Kick, then living in Washington, about an hour from my mother's house in Baltimore. I still had a slim hope that I might make the transition from "big brother" to something more, but she too wanted to get into the action and found a job with the Red Cross in London. I was the only family member there to see her off when the *Queen Mary* sailed for Southampton, waving until she was a microdot on the upper deck.

After several weeks in limbo, I volunteered as an ambulance driver for the American Field Service and was sent to North Africa. Jack finally wangled his way into the Navy with his father's reluctant help. He spent a few months as a desk jockey in D.C. and then headed to the Solomon Islands.

His first dispatch from there, which took six weeks to reach me, laconically described his early combat engagements in PT-109 and signed off with the usual jibe: "Incidentally, there are some of your fellow Princeton graduates stationed over here. It is said that they are doing very well under white officers."

A month or so later, another note from the war zone informed me that Kick, no less anxious than her brothers to extend the Kennedy writ, had met and married the very Anglican Billy Cavendish, who, as future Duke of Devonshire, would someday be one of England's richest and most powerful nobles.

I wrote an answer in one word, underlined: *"Devastated!"*

"She must have gotten tired of waiting for your balls to drop," Jack scrawled on my letter before sending it back to me. "Buck up, old man."

Not long after he rammed his boat into a Jap destroyer, a fiasco the Old Man's press assets miraculously transformed into a modern equivalent of the Crossing of the Delaware, Jack became ill again and was sent home early in 1944. A few months later, I too was released and was about to go down to Palm Beach to meet him when word came that Joe Jr. had been blown up over the English Channel while piloting a B-25 in a "suicide mission" against a V-2 missile site on the French coast.

It was the event that brought death into the Kennedys' world. Soon after came news that Kick's noble husband Billy, a major in the Coldstream Guards, had been killed by a German sniper in Belgium shortly after D-Day. At that point, Jack vanished into parts unknown—for a time unknown even to his father, who made it his business to know everything about his children.

It was a long time before a mutual friend told me that Jack had been sighted at a dude ranch in Arizona, of all places, apparently trying to exorcise his ghosts by riding horses down mountains at such breakneck speed that admiring ranch hands gave him the nickname "Apache John."

By V-E Day, the Old Man had lured him back into the fold by getting his pal W. R. Hearst to take him on as a reporter. For Jack it was a way to placate his father while testing a profession that had always vaguely interested him; for Big Joe it was a way of getting the name of the son he had always held in reserve in front of America. I had seen his byline on a series of stories about the architecting of the United Nations in San Francisco, but my letters to him went unanswered. Assuming that he had gone his way, I figured I'd better go mine. I got a job at an ad agency, moved out of my mother's house for good, and started thinking of life without him.

Then, out of the blue, an unsigned telegram arrived at my office. "All work and no play makes Jack a dull boy," it read. "In Hollywood now getting the lay of the land in the land of the lay. Join for Playtime?"

I quit my job on the spot, packed a bag and headed to Grand Central Station, joining furloughed men in uniform waiting for a ticket to Chicago. Once there, I boarded the *Super Chief* with the feeling that I too was finally going home.

After three days cutting through the inert plane of the American heartland, then falling down into the Mojave Desert from the heights of the Rockies, the *Super Chief* pulled into LA's Union Station at eight in the morning. As the warpainted engine emitted a final heavy sigh of steam, I jumped down into a series of tableaux vivants of soldiers clutching sobbing wives and mothers—images I knew even then would last until the end of our generation's time.

At the stop in Denver the previous day I'd telegraphed Jack with the arrival time. Knowing how allergic he was to getting up early, I found a spot on the terra-cotta floor of the station's Art Deco lobby, picked up a discarded *Los Angeles Times*, and settled down on my duffel bag for a long wait.

I happened to look up after a few minutes and saw him near the entrance of the lobby, looking around for me. He was wearing aviator's dark glasses, a white T-shirt and a leather flight jacket with the collar turned up, and was backlit just as he had been the day we first met.

I jumped up and ran toward him, but he stuck out his hand like a spear to prevent the possibility of a hug.

"How are you?" I held the handshake as long as possible, fighting back tears.

"Fit as a butcher's dog," he replied briskly.

"You look older," I stammered.

He stepped back to give me a blasé once-over, with one raised eyebrow: "You look the same as always, except more so."

THREE

The Santa Ana winds I'd heard so much about bent the sparse vegetation clinging to the hills above us and made the Zephyr shudder. Everything was so sere and shriveled at the end of summer that it was easy to imagine a cigarette carelessly tossed out of a car window touching off a domestic Dresden.

I tried to make small talk about the family, *our* family as I was allowing myself to think of it again, which was spread out all over the country—all over the world, if you counted Kick, now living as a young widow in London. Jack kept his eyes on the road; his terse answers to my questions made it feel like I was playing tennis against a wall.

Finally I started pressing him about what the Old Man was up to.

"Same old thing," he said. "Looking for ways to turn coincidence into destiny."

"Is he going to get back into politics?"

"Not as a candidate. That dream is dead."

"Because of the appeasement stuff?"

Here he tilted his chin down to give me a wry look over his dark glasses: "In the time you've been on your own, you appear to have forgotten that Joseph P. Kennedy wasn't an appeaser; he just looked like one because he was set up by the warmongering sheenies around FDR."

"He never forgave the President for ditching him."

"Right, even though it was Roosevelt who raised him up in the first place. But you know Dad: no grudge not worth bearing. The day of FDR's funeral, some newspaperman asked him if now he couldn't at last say something good about the President, and Dad's answer was, 'Yeah, he's dead.'"

"So no more politics."

He was silent for a moment, eyes on the road. "Yeah, there'll be politics."

"What do you mean?"

"I've been chosen," he said fatalistically.

"Chosen?"

"Jim Curley's leaving his congressional seat in Boston and Dad can hardly wait for Johnny-boy to give him the okay to begin parlaying a bad back and wrecked PT boat into political gold."

"You don't want it?"

"I'd just be shadowboxing with Joe," he said morosely. "It was supposed to be him. He would have been good at it."

In fact, Jack knew better than anyone that Young Joe wouldn't have been good at politics. He was shallow and inflexible; too much like his father and too circumscribed by the role he had enthusiastically accepted as prosthetic for the Old Man's thwarted ambition. He might have climbed a rung or two on the strength of the Kennedy money and connections, but he would never have made it anywhere near the top.

Jack had always been the one with the esprit and intellectual curiosity necessary to succeed in politics. And he knew it. But because of the double bind he faced—knowing he'd never be able to make it as his father's pawn, but knowing too that he'd have to be his father's pawn even to try—he had decided just to look for other possibilities.

"So what's your plan then?"

"Not sure," he said. "Maybe keep being a writer. Maybe not. Time will tell. But this much I know. When Dad realizes that I'm not going to be his Charlie McCarthy, there's going to be absolute hell to pay."

"Does he know you're out here?"

"No," he shot me a dire look, "and let's keep it that way."

He retracted into silence again as we exited onto Barham Boulevard and joined the line of cars going up over the hill to various destinations in the Valley. We were headed for Burbank.

Jack was still skinny though more substantial than before the war. He retained vestiges of his youthful ardor, but had finally come down to earth after all those years as the high-flying, doomy young man who had learned to bend the little time he thought he still had into such intense and appealing shapes that people wanted to be there with him. He had a specific gravity now and seemed ready to take the next step.

We were passing over the concreted-in Los Angeles River with its trickle of mossy water when he suddenly hit the brakes and muttered, "Jesus, Mary and Joseph," his grandfather Honey Fitz's favorite oath.

Up ahead, the area around the Warner Brothers' entry was a war zone. Thick black smoke was blossoming over a burned-out panel truck flipped on its back like a beetle at the edge of the sidewalk. Strikers carrying battery cables, baseball bats, broken bottles and other weapons were using it as a command center while staging feints against a handful of security men clustered around a heavy chain held taut to keep them off Warners property. Burbank city cops stood on the sidelines near their squad cars, nervously smacking their nightsticks into their palms. Jack turned into the churning mob and tried to force an opening through the studio's famous portal.

Placards pounded the roof of the Zephyr, fists drummed on the hood, and lurid faces loomed in the side windows. The car began rocking from side to side. When Jack looked over at me, his eyes, normally narrowed with irony, were wide with apprehension and his lips were as compressed as a ventriloquist's. Then a flying squad of Warners guards rammed into the bodies surrounding the car, gaining enough space for us to shoot into the studio's main street before the chain went up again.

Jack stopped in a small parking zone and yanked on the emergency brake. As we gathered ourselves, I saw several executives in light-colored suits a few yards away sullenly studying the chaos in the street. They all wore starched white shirts and ties knotted in perfect Windsors despite the wilting afternoon heat.

We got out of the car and Jack walked up to one of them, a man of medium height with a choleric flush on his face and a pencil mustache that looked plagiarized from Errol Flynn. He was rotating his neck as if to relieve vertebral pressure and compulsively flattening his thinning hair with both hands while he paced rapidly back and forth.

Jack held out a hand and said, "Jack Kennedy."

A look of recognition passed over the scowling face. "Jack Warner," he replied, offering a brief shake. "I'm surprised you got through. It's like fucking Iwo Jima out there. Why didn't you go to the back entrance over on Olive Avenue? We told the people coming to the party to go there to avoid this shit."

He nodded grudgingly at a slightly older man with a long, melancholy bookkeeper's face and the grayish skin of coronary insufficiency standing next to him: "My brother Harry."

At another time we might have seen evidence of the celebrated feud between the two men, the last of the original four brothers left standing after Sam died early and Albert retired young. Eventually a fight to the finish, this conflict between them was so serious that when Warners had introduced talkies with *The Jazz Singer* several years earlier and the company's stock shot up from 8 to 65 overnight, they ate at the same table in the studio commissary every day for months without ever saying a word to each other about their good fortune. The silence was finally broken one day when Harry chased Jack down a hall holding a sharpened pencil aloft and yelling, "I'll get you, you son of a bitch!"

Now, the chaos in the street had produced not only a truce but a distant camaraderie.

"Commie bastards!" Harry spit the words in the strikers' direction as we all jumped back to avoid the exploding shrapnel of glass from a volley of pop bottles.

"This business is getting ridiculouser every day," his brother said. "As we speak, the makeup artists represented by the IBTA and the hairstylists in the ASE union are at war with each other at Paramount over who is authorized to install falsies. I kid you not! Falsies!"

Just then the mob separated to allow a thewy man wearing a white T-shirt and dungarees and carrying a step ladder to approach the entry we'd just come through. He was blond and weathered-looking, with Popeye forearms and a big grin. When they saw him, the rank and file began to gather round and clap in a slow cadence.

Jack Warner considered himself a suave phrasemaker, having once famously introduced a mistress as "a girl with a heart of gold and a snatch to match," but now he was so enraged that words deserted him. "Commie fuck!" he yelled. "Bastard starts this shit on our fortieth birthday! Can you believe it?"

Harry elaborated: "Clive Selkirk. Came over here from Australia to destroy our world. We didn't pay attention when he organized the painters. But then he takes over the cartoonists and makes Disney eat it. Then the electricians and carpenters. And then the set dressers, no less! He got all of them to join his half-assed Association of Studio Employees. Now it's tomorrow-the-world time! He's trying to kick off the apocalypse right here on our property!"

"The prick!" Jack Warner sent the union leader a death stare. "Red as

Superman's cape. Where the hell does he think he is anyway, at the Winter Palace? Worst goddamn thing I ever saw."

There was so much noise and confusion that it was hard to hear what Selkirk was saying as he set the ladder down at the edge of public property and climbed a couple of rungs to rev up the crowd. But it was clear who he was saying it about. He kept pointing at the Warner brothers and their lackeys and then at the other side of the street, where twenty or so beefy men were milling around on a grassy parkway, some of them not bothering to conceal their brass knuckles. They had been standing in groups of two or three, nonchalantly eyeing the strikers, but now began to congeal purposefully around a squat man with a placid Buddha smile on his face.

"Who's that?" I asked.

"That Jew bastard Geist," Jack Warner replied, rolling his eyes in annoyance when he realized he'd answered the question of a nobody.

Harry, who read and spoke Hebrew, grimaced, "Jew bastard? I guess you've forgotten you were born Jacob Wonksolaser."

Then he relented: "Solomon Geist, a piece of shit criminal who muscled his way into the International Brotherhood of Technicians and Actors, the supposed union that's been raping us for years that the commies now want to replace with their Association of Studio Employees so they can rape us harder. The Outfit sent him out here from Chicago before the war to give a pink slip to the Mustache Petes and other amateurs who'd been running the rackets in LA since God was a little boy. Now he's the star of the show along with his psycho friend Bugsy Siegel."

"Don't forget Siegel's itchy trigger finger—that fucking dwarf Mickey Cohen," Jack Warner added. "A couple of years ago Geist and Siegel and Cohen tried to organize a union for extras. Can you believe it? They wanted to make us pay a bunch of *pisherkes* for every day they *don't* work!"

Harry nodded dolefully: "Like my bother says, there's a civil war going on in this town. Screen Actors Guild for Geist; Screen Writers Guild for Selkirk. Six of one, half a dozen of the other. Commies and criminals—scorpions in a bottle. Shake them up so they eat each other."

By this time, Selkirk had stopped his harangue and was waving his arms like an orchestra conductor to lead the demonstrators in a booming takeoff on the Hoagy Carmichael song:

You got to ac-cen-tuate the picket line,
E-liminate the scabby kind,

Latch on to that old picket sign
Till the producers see the light…

Right then, two buses pulled up and Jack Warner yelled triumphantly, "Sing your heart out, schmuck. The cavalry has arrived."

The bus doors hissed open and scabs armed with iron pipes and chains poured out. Like a pair of moiling peasant armies, the scabs and strikers met in a dense, compacted struggle while hand-to-hand clashes erupted on the periphery. In an instant I saw a man with blood sheeting down his face from a gash on the top of his head extracted from the melee by a squad of monitors wearing white air-raid warden helmets bearing the Association of Studio Employees logo. A woman in a Rosie the Riveter jumpsuit with her hair in a bandanna fell to the blacktop holding the skin on her leg around a compound fracture and screamed an aria of pain.

Across the street, Geist nodded to his men and they began slowly advancing.

"Watch this," Harry Warner said. "Each of those goons is getting ten dollars a day and they're about to earn their dough."

Their walk became a run as they charged into the battle, kicking up the violence by a quantum. Within seconds, blood was running down the side of Selkirk's mouth and dribbling onto the shirt of the thick man he held by the throat with his left hand while methodically smashing his face with his right. Everyone was in violent motion except for Solomon Geist himself, who remained standing in the same spot across the street, hands in jacket pockets, placidly watching the battle as if it were a sporting event.

Suddenly a series of explosions caused everyone to duck. The Burbank police had fired tear gas into the crowd and were advancing in formation to begin randomly beating people with their nightsticks.

"About fucking time!" Jack Warner snarled. "Kick the shit out of every one of them! Don't bother sorting them out!"

Then he said, "I'm done with this," and abruptly headed off toward some bungalow-style offices with his entourage trailing behind.

Harry had mechanically followed his brother, but as an afterthought he stopped and walked back to us.

"I know you guys came for the party. It's over there at Sound Stage Seven." He pointed at a huge structure a couple of city blocks away. "Take your time. It's just getting started. I'll see you there."

FOUR

Jack and I watched the cops' mopping-up operation a little while and then walked off toward the generic town the studio had built as one of its primary sets, a utopian midwestern neighborhood on a curving street with tidy lawns in front of façade houses with clapboard siding and wraparound porches. At the end of this pseudo block there was a pseudo business district with the shell storefronts of a bank, a five-and-dime, an ice cream parlor, and of course a movie theatre.

"Everything we fought for," Jack said as we peered into the windows. "All spic-and-span. No trash on the sidewalks. And best of all, no people to fuck it up."

The sounds of soft jazz were pulling us toward the immense sound stage looming up ahead when suddenly Jack stopped like a pointer and gaped. I followed his eyes to a picnic table a few feet away where John Garfield was sitting, his forehead earnestly wrinkled and his hands making robust circular gestures while he argued some point with Joel McCrea, who sat across from him and listened respectfully. Fredric March stood slightly apart, looking down at his feet with a scowl and shaking his head in disagreement. We were close enough to hear Garfield say testily to March, "... but if the U.S. keeps its head in the sand, Europe winds up living under the hammer and sickle, something you might not mind but not so good for the rest of us..."

"Where do they get it?" Jack whispered, mesmerized by the heightened reality the three men were creating out of an inconsequential discussion.

"Get what?"

"*It*," he frowned at me impatiently. "You know, the star thing. *It.* Look at them! They're just three guys shooting the breeze. But they're also bigger than life. Where does it come from? How do they make it work for them?"

"They make it work by working at it," I answered, aware even then that Jack had *it* himself, although he hadn't yet located the on/off switch or the volume control.

Sound Stage Seven looked to be three stories high with the square footage of a couple of airplane hangars. Jack was always a fan of Warners' lean black-and-white films with their tight plots, liberal values, and fast-talking guys and dames like Cagney, Bogey, Bette Davis, and the wisest guy of all, Bugs Bunny. When we entered the elephant doors, as the building's huge sliders were called, he gave a thumbs-up to a large glass case displaying the Best Picture Oscars the studio had received for *The Life of Emile Zola* and *Casablanca.*

The war zone we'd left a half hour earlier now seemed as far away as the Eastern Front. Waiters balancing trays of champagne and canapés circulated as smoothly as ice skaters. Ingenues in pastel bloomed across the floor like hothouse flowers.

I was scanning the crowd for stars when Harry Warner appeared arm in arm with a short, rumpled man with thick curly hair and a big-lipped floppy smile. Warner steered the man toward us, saying to him, "Here's your target audience. Irish as corned beef and cabbage."

Then to Jack: "This is Yip Harburg. He's a commie, but he's a good one, unlike the dreck you saw out there on the street. We forgive him all his fucked-up political ideas because he's the greatest songwriter around. He did "Over the Rainbow." That's immortality right there. Yip is working on a new show about the Irish called *Finnegan's Rainbow.* I told him you speak leprechaun so he should try it out on you."

"*Finian's*," Harburg corrected Warner as he shook Jack's hand. "It's my take on the Emerald Isle and all its neverland enchantments. I'm trying to get Harry to put up some money for it, but he's a cheap bastard and playing hard to get."

"That's because I'm not sure that there's a pot of gold at the end of this particular rainbow," Warner gave a long-faced look. "Anyhow, I'm not cheap, I'm thrifty just like the Irish."

"I think you mean the Scotch," Harburg said.

"Whoever." Harry watched Lana Turner and Hedy Lamarr walk by with their arms flung over each other's shoulders like tomboys.

Harburg dug into his briefcase and extracted a vinyl .78 record in a paper sleeve, like the V-discs that families had used to record messages for servicemen during the war. He handed it to Jack along with a business card.

"Here's a rough run-through of the big song of the show. We'll probably start working with a live orchestra sometime early next year and try to get it on stage maybe a year after that. Since you've got a touch of the Auld Sod in you, I'd be interested to know what you think."

Then Harburg looked into the crowd and grinned at Harry: "I see your brother over there. You'll have to excuse me so I can go tell him he can outflank you if he ponies up an investment right now. I'm sure that will cinch the deal."

As Harburg cut through the crowd like an icebreaker, Jack said to Harry, "By the way, I forgot to tell you *mazel tov* on your fortieth."

Harry raised an eyebrow: "When people of your tribe say *mazel tov*I always wonder if they think it means Go Fuck Yourself."

"It's a big achievement," Jack said. "*High Sierra, Key Largo, Maltese Falcon*—that's immortality right there."

"Actually, we cheated a little when we picked 1905 as the start date," Warner smiled. "That's when we began exhibiting other people's pictures. We had a lot of other beginnings after that. If we were being accurate our birthdate is probably 1923. That's when we stopped being Warner Brothers and incorporated as Warner Bros., drop the t-h-e-r, but my brother Jack says who wants to celebrate a twenty-second birthday? He likes to inflate things. He thinks life's all about perception. If he were standing here right now he'd probably be telling you how he was an Army colonel who should have been a general and how he singlehandedly brought victory into our grasp, though the only thing he did was head a film unit that made educational movies for the GIs on how to keep from getting the clap. He thinks forty is a historic number because it makes us older than Paramount and Universal. So we celebrate our fortieth. Anyway, end of the war, getting what we fought for, teaching all those other chickenshit countries how to live like human beings—that's reason enough to have a party."

Then Warner spied a woman with green eyes and a pretty heart-shaped face.

"Gene Tierney, cutest girl in the building," He called out to her, "Come over here, gorgeous, and meet a war hero."

Tierney came so close to Jack that I thought she'd bang her forehead into his chin.

"I'm deeply in love with Laura Hunt," he said, and then crooned the opening words of the Johnny Mercer song: *"Laura is the face of the misty night…"*

Tierney blushed with pleasure, and Harry Warner growled, "He's right. You were great, Gene. But I still don't know how Fox ever got *Laura.* It looks like a Warners movie. It sounds like a Warners movie. It feels like a Warners movie. Why the hell wasn't it a Warners movie?"

"Because you couldn't stand Clifton Webb, remember?" Tierney said archly.

"Right," Harry rolled his eyes. "How am I supposed to work with some *meshugener* who checks himself into the loony bin for three months every year in the hopes that the head shrinkers will teach him how to say no to his monster of a mother when she picks out his clothes every morning?"

"A girl like you should be wearing expensive jewelry," Jack examined Tierney's unadorned fingers, which he had kept holding after the handshake was over.

"A girl like me sometimes does," she returned his flirt.

The two were making deep eye contact when Sidney Greenstreet walked by in a three-piece suit with a watch fob stretched across his jutting gut.

"You're a fat hypocrite," Jack growled under his breath.

Tierney gasped, but then realized he was imitating Bogart's snarling insult to Ferrari, the black-marketer that Greenstreet played in *Casablanca,* and she giggled, causing Warner to stage-whisper to Jack, "You're on the right track, my friend. Scientific studies have shown that making a woman laugh is the best way to gain admission into her fun park."

While he was charming Tierney almost out of her panties, Jack's eye was snagged by a woman leaning indolently against the quilted soundproofing on a wall about thirty feet away.

She stood out even in a room of stars. Absently scratching at her left forearm and looking out blankly at the crowd, she was tall and had lustrous black hair that shone like a crow's feather. Her face was a remarkable construction—eyes perhaps a little too close together and the suggestion of a bump interrupting the line of her nose, but full sensuous lips and cheekbones that looked handcrafted. Her Modigliani neck was accented by a big-collared white blouse open far enough to reveal a sensual bone breastplate. High heels flexed her calves, and a simple black A-line skirt rebuked the sea of pastel party dresses.

A slender middle-aged man with a matador's face and dark hair graying at the temples stood a few feet away from her in a posture of ownership. He swept the room with a haughty vigilance, then shot his cuffs and gave an almost imperceptible head gesture that caused the woman to nod and obediently follow him toward an exit.

"That was something," Tierney said without resentment after the couple had gone.

"Who is she?" Jack asked.

"She just got here and I don't think they've given her a name yet," Tierney answered.

"Oh yes we have," Harry Warner had rejoined us. "It's Delphine LaReve."

Jack chuckled.

Harry shrugged. "I know, a little much but we think it might work for her. In real life, to the degree that it matters here in Tinseltown, it's Valentina. Valentina Morelli or Moselli or Moretti, or something like that. Whatever it is, it's too fucking close to Mussolini. After ten years of that big-lip clown strutting around in the newsreels, the last thing we need is more Italians. The French didn't do much during the war, but at least they were more or less on our side. So she gets a French name. Anyway, Italians, French, who even knows the difference? The French are just Italians in a bad mood."

"She's unbelievable," Jack said with an enthusiasm that caused Tierney—who would become one of his random conquests a couple of years later—to drift toward a nearby knot of people surrounding Farley Granger.

"And who was that guy with her?" Jack asked. "He looks familiar. Where have I seen him before?"

"Maybe on a wanted poster," Warner replied dyspeptically. "It's Fortunato."

Jack was suddenly alert. "Niccolo Fortunato?"

"Yeah. Nicky Fortune to his crime buddies and the rest of us. Rumor has it that he was sent out here by Chicago because Geist was in danger of getting beat by Selkirk. He's this girl's whatever you call a guy who has a protégé. Fortune and I are far from friends, but he's someone you want to do a favor if it doesn't cost you too much. So I said yes when he asked me to take a look at her test. It's homemade but interesting. Sold us on her. Want to take a look?"

"Sure," Jack said eagerly.

Warner signaled for a page and told him to set up the film, and then led us to one of the sound stage's side exits.

We walked a block or so to a squat stucco structure with vermillion bougainvillea crawling up its walls and descended an outside stairway to a basement screening theatre the size of a city movie-house balcony.

"My earliest memory of Hollywood is sitting in a room like this with my dad and my brother Joe watching a Red Grange movie," Jack said as we sank into plush loge seats. "I was maybe eleven years old."

"Red Grange," Warner smiled wearily. "Your old man had the smarts to see that a famous football star could also become a famous cowboy movie star. None of our gang would have thought of that. When he first set up out here—some mick picaroon who's doing the dirty with Gloria Swanson—we laughed. Another pussy hound from the world of high finance out here to show the pants pressers how to do their business. But pretty soon he's got that little studio Film Booking Offices or whatever he called it over on Gower. A chickenshit operation at first, but he's always on the move, and the next thing we know he's used it to help form RKO and is playing in the big leagues."

"I remember that first office," Jack nodded.

"Hole in the wall," Warner said. "The first time I met your dad he told me that his idea was to shoot a movie in a week and get it into the theatres in a month so he could get his money back right away. Nobody else in the business thought like that. I still remember the names of some of his epics. *The Dude Cowboy. Red Hot Horses.* No budget over twenty thousand. You never saw them in New York or Hollywood, but in Iowa and Nebraska they were bigger than *Stagecoach*."

Then the house lights went down and there was a clicking sound from the speakers. "The sound was so bad that we just turned it off," Warner whispered. "Maybe you can lip-read."

The broken numbers of the test pattern flickered in reverse order on the screen, leading to a gauzy closeup of the woman we'd just seen at the party. She was wearing a sliplike shift whose transparency acknowledged her sleek body as she walked alongside a bullet-pocked Italian wall, brushing the bricks with her fingertips.

Projecting the smoldering charismatic sexuality of Loren, Vitti, Verna Lisi, and other great Italian actresses to come, she stared directly at the camera without trying to ingratiate herself with it. The longer you looked at her, the more strongly she held your eye.

She wasn't Jack's type really. Too dark and serious; too much of a game played for keeps. But I watched him push all that aside as he stared at her without moving, his lips slightly parted.

The camera movement was jerky and the print was filled with light scratches. When the woman spoke, I struggled to decipher her words and match them to the emotions flickering across her face.

After three or four minutes, the film ran off the spool and the screen went white as the houselights came back on. We all sat there for a moment, still under her spell.

"Maybe too foreign looking," Harry Warner finally stood up. "The war's over but people still like blond pin-ups in sweaters."

"What was she saying?" Jack asked.

"Who knows?" Warner shrugged. "I think it was a scene from one of those Greek plays. Maybe the one about the guy who shtups his mother and then pokes his own eyes out to pay himself back for getting into her pants in the first place. Like I said, at first I looked at the test as a favor to Fortunato, but we think there's something there. How much, I don't know, but we offered her a part. Normally, my brother would have insisted on the usual audition by casting couch, but because Fortunato's involved he waived that requirement for fear of getting his throat slit.

"The picture is *Tomorrow Is Too Late*. It's about people who don't deserve it getting screwed when they come home from the war. It started shooting a month ago—a B that might do better than that if we can get it out before people start wondering what was the point of beating the shit out of the Germans and the Japs. This girl has a pretty big role for a nobody. Who knows what'll happen? Maybe she's the next Garbo, maybe she's on the next gondola back to the old country."

"She certainly looks like a star," I said.

"There's only one great actor in Hollywood," Warner replied morosely as he led us out of the basement and back up the stairs into the jarring sunlight. “You know who that is? Lassie. She never forgets her lines, she doesn’t bitch about her salary, and she doesn’t want to fuck around with the script.”

* * *

However much he needed women, Jack’s attitude toward them—although far more graciously expressed—was pretty much the same as his father’s: turn them upside down and they all look the same. But on the drive back to his place at Malibu, he kept talking about the woman in the film clip with an almost courtly awe.

“There’s just something about her,” he said. “She’s gorgeous but she has something that comes from the inside. She’s on fire, but very cool.”

“Oh, brother,” I said.

He shot me a dirty look and ran on about her for a few minutes. When he finally let up I asked him about Fortunato.

“Chicago crime figure turned war hero.”

“How do you know about him?”

“I had dinner with Wild Bill Donovan one night when I got back from the Pacific and he gave me the lowdown. He said Fortunato got his start in the Chicago crime scene as a teenager selling Jewish kids protection from other Italians at twenty-five cents a month. Then he got into numbers and other rackets. Apparently he was a smoother operator than the other knuckleheads he ran with, so Frank Nitti made him one of his lieutenants when he took over the Outfit after Capone went to prison, and Ricca promoted him to a colonel later on.”

Jack was a dilettante at heart, but when a subject grabbed him, as Niccolo Fortunato obviously had, he focused all his attention on mastering it.

“In Chicago it had pretty much been loan-sharking and gambling, until Fortunato convinced Nitti that unions were a growth industry. This opened up new vistas.

“Donovan said he could have dropped his teeth when Fortunato showed up unannounced at OSS headquarters right after the Sicily invasion and asked to be sent over there to work with the underground. He said the Italian crime figures were pissed at Mussolini for jailing hundreds of them to break their power and he might convince them to cooperate with our guys in the mainland campaign. So Donovan decided it was worth a try, and he smuggled Fortunato into Calabria when the Allies staged a small landing there to support the Salerno invasion in fall '43. Apparently Fortunato made some good contacts that paid off, but then he disappeared. Donovan said that he first thought the gangsters might have had second thoughts and thrown him overboard with concrete waders somewhere in Mare Nostrum. But early in '44 he turned up in central Italy working with the Resistance. Donovan said nobody knew why."

"Maybe he felt patriotic about Italy."

"Maybe. Whatever the reason, Fortunato was the real thing."

The real thing. In other words, one of those men of action who always fascinated the Kennedys because they worried that their own authenticity was cooked. Men they would entrust with their black ops in the Caribbean or Southeast Asia and then invite to dinner at Hyannis or Hickory Hill, to bask in the reflected glory of their derring-do.

* * *

It was dusk when Jack turned off the Pacific Coast Highway and aimed the Zephyr down a short driveway of packed sand leading to a bungalow wedged between two larger beach houses.

As we entered, he tossed me a spare key. *"Mi casa es tu casa,"* he said, adding sardonically, "as usual."

I would mechanically transfer this key from one chain to another over the next few decades, keeping it, I sometimes told myself, to help me someday unlock the full meaning of what happened those next few weeks in Hollywood.

The interior of the bungalow had the undercover elegance Jack always liked. Two facing sofas whose chocolate-colored leather was scarred with the perfect patina of wear faced each other in a living room filled with nautical objects: a gleaming sextant, an old anchor crusted with green corrosion, a woodcut of a giant stylized wave in the manner of Hiroshige—all of it organized around an immense plate-glass window staring out at the infinite horizon of the Pacific Ocean.

I whistled in appreciation.

"Yeah," he kicked off his shoes and did a back dive into one of the sofas. "It's a splurge, but during the time I had to bunk in that armpit of a PT boat I always told myself I deserved better."

After dinner we went outside, where the searchlight moon had turned the sand to snow. We sat silently on the deck watching the waves phosphoresce as they broke and began their long roll to shore. Then Jack went in and got the big box of his portable record player, connected it to an extension cord, and put on the disc that Yip Harburg had given us.

It was a scratchy demonstration cut sung a cappella by a so-so female voice and sounded like it had been recorded in a coffee can, but the words lit up the night. Jack only pretended to scorn Irish sentimentality; he allowed the song to cast a spell on him from the first note. He played it over and over again and was soon harmonizing the refrain:

How are things in Glocca Morra?
Is that little brook still leapin' there?
Does it still run down to Donny cove?
Through Killybegs, Kilkerry and Kildare?

After perhaps a half hour of this, he turned the record player off and stood for a long time with his hands in his pockets, looking out into the night. Finally he shrugged and said, more to himself than to me, "What's the point of being Irish anyway if you don't think the world will break your heart?"

Then he went back inside, poured himself a glass of milk, grabbed the phone and propped up his feet on the kitchen table. He gave a New York number to the long distance operator, and when he was connected he said, "Tell syndication that Kennedy will not be filing tonight."

FIVE

The clank of silverware rousted me out of my nest on the living room couch early the next morning. Jack was in his underwear at the kitchen table eating Wheaties and drinking orange juice from the bottle as he scanned the *LA Times*. Although he had been out of the Navy for well over a year, he still wore his dog tags.

"I've got to play the boy reporter today." He got up and stretched his spine, which was slightly serpentined from scoliosis. "You can be my copy boy. We're starting in downtown LA."

I followed him into his bedroom, where plates with moldering crusts of bread and dried wisps of ham and cheese sat on the dresser. An uncapped tube drooled Brylcreem onto his nightstand; shorts and socks lay on the floor in a little fabric Stonehenge where he had been stepping out of them for the last few days. It reminded me of the chaos he'd created at Choate, where I once found a four-month-old birthday cake, still in its box, under layers of magazines and newspapers and athletic gear in a corner of our room. The salutation had sunk like an intaglio in the petrified frosting: *Happy 15th Jack!*

"Why downtown?" I asked.

"Because that's where Selkirk the union guy has his office," he said, sitting down on the bed and setting about to examine his toes for athlete's foot.

"I thought you just did international stuff."

"I may not have worked for the *Daily Princetonian*, but I know a good story when I see one. And that little war we saw at Warners yesterday is a good story. I pitched it to New York this morning while you were in there with your snorechestra going full blast and they're gung ho. "Labor Turmoil in the Dream Factory," by John F. Kennedy! Guaranteed at least page three. Selkirk first, then Geist, then Harry Warner to expand on his scorpions-in-a-bottle theory, then back to the typewriter for an hour or two and roll the presses!"

* * *

The storefront headquarters of the Association of Studio Employees was sandwiched between a dry cleaner's and a locksmith on Spring Street not far from Pershing Square. When we opened the door we were immediately braced by two burly, crewcut men, both wearing naval bellbottoms and white T-shirts with cigarette packs rolled up in one sleeve high on the shoulder.

"That's okay," an Australian-accented voice yelled from an alcove in the back. "This is the writer guy I told you about. Bring him over here."

Clive Selkirk was a bulky presence whose big-featured face conveyed a disconcerting blend of sincerity and cunning. His close-cropped ginger-colored hair was pomaded so it stuck up in quills; his lower lip was mangled from the previous day's action. He was sitting at a desk strewn with scratch pads and newsletters, mugs half filled with a slurry of old coffee, and an overflowing ashtray the size of a chafing dish. The wall behind his chair was decorated with posters in the heroic Soviet socialist style showing muscular workers using heavy, stylized wrenches to smash stone swastikas. Several picket signs were stacked upside down in a corner.

"My longies," Selkirk nodded at the bodyguards, who hovered around until he released them with a nod. "They watch over me."

"Longies?" Jack frowned.

"Longshoremen. On loan from my fellow internationalist Harry Bridges. They are hell on scabs and Pinkertons and all the other..."

When he paused to sip his coffee, Jack goaded him by finishing the sentence: "...enemies of the people?"

Selkirk gave a hard look: "You took the words right out of my mouth."

"Speaking of mouth," Jack pointed at his lip.

Selkirk flashed a gold-capped molar and winced: "It only hurts when I smile." Then, more seriously: "You don't have to worry, we give as good as we get. A few months ago Geist dials Chicago, talks to the owners of his circus, and gets them to send out some of their torpedoes to terrorize us. These guys spend a couple of days driving around town in a big boat of a Packard with their jackets open so everyone can see the heaters flapping around under their arms. But a half dozen of my longies were waiting one afternoon when that Lincoln parks across from Paramount. They turned it over and beat the hell out of the wop bastards who climbed out of it and sent them back where they came from with their tails between their legs."

Jack was focusing on a framed photograph of Upton Sinclair on the desk. It was autographed under the inscription, "To Clive, one of the best Workers of the World. Unite!"

"Not bad to have the author of *The Jungle* in your corner, eh?" Selkirk exulted. "Become a mate of mine, old Upton. I visit him at his place over in Monrovia every week or two. Amazing house. He's getting on, but he's still got a mind like a razor blade."

"A rise-up light?" Jack mocked the Australian accent with phony innocence.

Selkirk squinted at him, and then said, "You think I talk funny? You ought to listen to yourself."

Jack frowned.

"Say America," Selkirk commanded.

Jack reluctantly obeyed.

"Now say Africa."

Jack said it.

"See!" Selkirk pounced. "You said *Americker* and *Africker*."

Always sensitive about his Boston accent, Jack grabbed the fountain pen in his shirt pocket and opened his steno pad. "So let's start at the beginning," he said in a refrigerated voice. "How did you get into the studio unions in the first place?"

Pleased to have gotten under his skin, Selkirk leaned back in his chair. "When I came over here, a friend of my dad's in the film business in Sydney got me a job as a scene painter at Paramount. I joined the local and wound up running for president after a couple of years because the fat asses supposedly representing me and my brothers there were actually sucks to the bosses. We did okay with the painters so we decided to form the Association of Studio Employees and began..."

"So it's better for Communists to control the unions than gangsters?" Jack interrupted.

Selkirk stubbornly finished his thought: "... began with Disney's cartoonists and had some good luck there and just kept going."

Then he eyed Jack and answered the other question. "We're a union, not the Communist Party. But as far as the Communists go, they're for world peace, for treating Negroes like human beings, for giving people a living wage. These things sound a little bit of all right to me."

"I'm sure Solomon Geist can also give an inspiring speech about how he's for the working man," Jack continued to bait him.

"Rhymes with heist," Selkirk growled, "and that's what we're dealing with here—a thug who steals the labor movement from the working man."

He paused a moment before asking, "You ever heard of the Balaban brothers?"

Hating to confess ignorance about anything, Jack gave a minimal shake of his head.

"They had a chain of movie houses in Chicago back in the early Thirties," Selkirk explained. "It was Depression time and they decided to up their profits by forcing their employees to take a 20 percent pay cut. Geist was a smalltime villain back then, but he knew an opportunity when he saw one. He makes an appointment with the brothers and says he needs two thousand bucks to prevent their employees from organizing. The Balabans laugh in his face. But over the next couple of weeks there are accidents in the projection rooms at all their movie houses. Film upside down and backward, breaking and melting and projectionists getting beat up. The Balabans decide to pay Geist off to get things back to normal and he uses the money to organize a projectionists' union anyhow. Charges each worker two dollars a month dues and does fuck-all for them while pocketing the money. When Frank Nitti and Paul Ricca hear about this, they're impressed by his ingenuity. They can do the math: hundreds of movie houses in Chicago, thousands in Illinois, tens of thousands nationwide. And the projectionists are just the beginning. After he takes over the Outfit, Ricca moves in on the International Brotherhood of Technicians and Actors, installs one of his stooges as president and sends Geist out here as the power behind the throne to get down to the real business—extorting the producers in return for selling out their workers."

"If this is true, why would the studios put up with it?" Jack couldn't repress his interest.

"Because when Geist gets established there, he makes a deal: wages won't rise and there won't be any work stoppages, and in return he gets recognition of his union and regular payoffs to himself and the guys who pull his strings. So Sam Goldwyn makes a trip to Geist's office every year with a paper bag with fifty K in it for the IBTA 'strike fund.' Ten rolls of a hundred $50 bills with rubber bands around them. Nick Schenck at MGM does the same thing. So does one of your friend Jack Warner's lackeys. And so on. Close to half a million every year for Geist and his friends back home in Chicago and well worth it to the studios.

"The working man doesn't have anywhere to go for help. The LA County DA Fred Howser is crooked as a dog's hind leg. Police Chief Horrall is so corrupt he sells detective badges for thirty dollars apiece. Both of them have their living rooms in the Outfit's pocket."

"Sounds like you're pissing into the wind, then," Jack needled, still smarting over the comments about his accent.

"Except for one thing." Selkirk jumped up, making his powerful body even bigger by self-parodying soapbox gestures, slicing the air with flattened palms, and brayed, *"Social justice! Social justice always bats last!"*

Then he laughed at himself and sat back down, resuming his normal tone: "We've got six thousand members now, almost as many as the IBTA, and unlike them we're clean. Our time has come."

Jack looked like he was about to say something, but Selkirk kept on the offensive.

"Come on, mate, it's 1945, time for this town to finally get its own New Deal. Everybody knows it. That's why the Warners and all the other captains of the entertainment industry are starting to think maybe paying blackmail is outdated and not just a drain on profits. They gag at the thought of us representing the set dressers or anyone else, but they're beginning to wonder if we might not be the lesser of two evils. So the big boys in Chicago are getting nervous. That's why they sent out one of their heavy hitters, some guy named Fortune."

"Fortunato," Jack perked up. "What's his role?"

"From what I hear, he's just consulting for now," Selkirk shrugged. "But maybe the bosses in the Outfit will decide that we're too hot for Geist to handle and they need someone with more juice out here. Then

Fortune could become the man. Who knows? Who cares? The bigger they come..."

For the next half hour Jack kept shooting out questions. He was a surprisingly astute and forensic interviewer, partly because he had learned that questioning others was a way of deflecting attention from himself all those years when he didn't want people asking about his health, but also because he was genuinely interested in the human comedy. Selkirk came right back at him, both of them enjoying the combat until Jack glanced at his watch and said he had an appointment.

"With Geist?" Selkirk guessed.

"Yes."

"Have fun bathing in that mongrel's bathwater."

He escorted us to the door, and as we were heading toward the car he called out: "When you're writing your story, remember this: When this thing is over, there'll be one man standing and that man will be me!"

On the drive to interview Geist in Burbank, Jack evaluated Selkirk's chances. "Dad has always believed that the human factor doesn't count. For him, life is mechanics—it's leverage and torque and pneumatics. And it's material advantage—how many shares you own, how many votes you can buy, how many politicians you control. My brother Joe saw things Dad's way. I always tried to argue that belief can be powerful too. It was never a popular position inside the family, except for my mother and her religious fanaticism. But think of Selkirk. Some of the things he believes in are wrong, but he believes and his belief has allowed him to build an army. That's why he has a chance."

"If he succeeds, Molotov will be over here making sure all the movies are set in tractor factories."

"This isn't about art," Jack reproached me. "It isn't even about politics. It's about who you can do business with. Who is most like you. What the studios hate about someone like Selkirk is not so much the Communist ideas, but the way these ideas keep him from making the easy deal."

He paused, and then shrugged: "But the problem with belief—in Marx or God or anything else—is that you wind up looking like a horse's ass if you're wrong. Who the hell wants that?"

* * *

Geist operated out of a bar called El Verdugo on Riverside Drive, about a mile from Warners. It was probably named for the land-grant family that once dominated this part of the San Fernando Valley, but I had enough Spanish to know that *verdugo* was also the word for "executioner."

It was dim inside and suffused with the faint maraschino smell of well drinks. When my eyes adapted, I saw an Indian sitting at the bar, along with two carny barkers, a gladiator, and a Civil War soldier. It took me a beat to realize they were extras who had run over here from Warners and Universal during lulls in the shooting to pound down a drink or two and then duck behind a heavy green curtain that only partly smothered the chinking payoff sounds of a half dozen illegal slot machines lined up in a small lounge.

As we were taking in the scene, Geist appeared, seemingly out of nowhere. He was a short man with a simian's body—long arms, short legs. His Buddha face was organized around eyes so narrowed they looked almost epicanthic. They seemed sleepy until you realized this was a con that allowed him to secretly study the impression he was making.

I was struck by how well put together he was in a hound's-tooth sport coat, dark shirt and darker tie, and alligator shoes—the uniform George Raft wore in *Scarface* and his other gangster films, which functioned as fashion shows for real-life mobsters to learn how to dress the part.

"How about a Manhattan?" he gestured with a glass holding a cola-colored drink.

Jack shook his head.

"Well, how about a Shirley Temple then? Shirley tastes good. John Agar told me so himself."

When Jack didn't bother to suppress a look of disgust, Geist flamed out at him: "Why shouldn't he taste her? They're fucking getting married next week. And your shit don't exactly smell like ice cream either, sonny."

Then he got control and tried to reset: "Enough about the silver screen. So how's your old man anyway? I knew Joseph P. a little bit back in the good old days when we were all so bad. Our circles sometimes looped over each other."

"His footprints are everywhere," Jack looked away, irritated that Geist had a handhold in his personal life.

"A shame he's not out here now to remind the studio guys what side of their bread has all the butter on it."

As the remark settled, Geist led us through a double door to a back room whose walls were filled with autographed photos of movie stars and shots of Chicago street scenes from the early 1900s. He sat down at a pub table and motioned us to straight-backed chairs. A black cat with a white mustache and boots jumped onto his lap, raising its tail like a ship's mast when he scratched the base of its spine. Two bulky sallow-skinned men in cheap suits suddenly materialized, assuming positions on either side of him. At first I didn't realize they were twins because one had a face so disfigured by a deep scar meandering from the corner of his eye down to his chin that he seemed of different lineage. They both stared at Geist with intense, almost drooling attentiveness.

"The Dragon Boys," he head-gestured at them. "They're my helpers."

"Dragon Boys?" I couldn't help asking.

Geist squinted at me. "Charley and Joe Draco. Dragon in Sicilian."

The scarred one mumbled something indecipherable except to his brother, who smiled and nudged him with an elbow and said something equally cluttered in return.

"You ought to get subtitles for these guys," Jack said to Geist.

This caused the unscarred one to frown and mutter something that sounded vaguely like "Beat your ass."

Jack gave him a smirking little bow: "And fuck you very much for those kind sentiments."

The bodyguard started forward but Geist stopped him with a hand on the sleeve.

"Your old man still have his helper?" he asked. "The spud with the girl's name."

"Molly Maguire?" Jack shrugged. "Yeah, he's still in the picture."

Geist nodded slowly. "I remember him. Big rawboned guy. He and Charley Dragon here would be a good match."

At this, the scarred twin mumbled something again and raised a fist. The gesture opened the front of his unbuttoned jacket momentarily and I caught a glimpse of the pistol holstered under his arm.

Geist saw my look and sent me a hooded smile: "Don't worry. It's like my friend Benny Siegel says—We only kill each other."

Then he raised a leg slightly as he squeezed out a petite fart and incongruously mumbled, "Excuse me." The cat jumped down and ran out of the room.

Jack got out his pad. "It was Paul Ricca who sent you out here, right?"

Geist hid behind his drowsy eyes: "Yeah, I got to know Mr. Ricca when I was a young man in Chicago, and yeah, he was interested in developments in the entertainment business."

"How come...," Jack groped for a way of saying it, "...why not another Italian?"

Geist gave a laryngitic laugh. "A chip off the old block—always wondering what the Chosen People are up to. The studios out here were being run by Jews, so maybe Mr. Ricca figured it takes one to know one. Maybe he knew my work and felt I was dependable, whatever tribe I happened to belong to. Maybe he felt that outside another Italian, a Jew is more Italian than anyone else. We sweat when we eat, we flap our arms when we talk, we love our kids and hate our enemies."

Jack ignored the hokum. "When you were in Chicago, did you know Fortunato?"

"Nicky?" Geist blinked a couple of times. "Yeah, I knew him."

"And?"

"And what? He was my gombah."

"Was?"

Geist considered the request for clarification, then plunged into a story.

"Nicky and I have known each other forever. Jews and Italians lived in different countries in Chicago back when we were coming up. One day when I was twelve or thirteen, me and my buddies Izzy Abramowitz and Jacob Rubenstein were feeling full of ourselves and we decided to do a little trespass over the border where these two countries met on Roosevelt Road. We've left Jewland and gotten maybe fifty feet into Italianland when we're jumped by four dagos who are older and bigger and stronger than us. We're down on the ground in a flash, getting stomped bloody.

"Then Nicky happens to walk by. He's about our age and fresh off the boat and living in the Grand Crossing area where Calabrian people dominated until the colored started crowding in. I guess he still has a sense of old-world justice that tells him four big against three little isn't copacetic, so he starts pulling his fellow guineas off me and Izzy and Jack, talking a kind of Italian to them they pretend not to capish. One of them in particular, the leader of this group, is offended at being told not to kick the shit out of Jews who have strayed into his territory, and he pulls a knife. Nicky pulls one too and slices this guy right across the chest. The last we saw this guy is dribbling blood and the other dagos are carrying him off. Then Jacob and Izzy and Nicky and me head back to Jewland for a sausage roll.

"Nicky makes us his team right away. He takes a look at Jacob and renames him 'Sparky' because he's built like a spark plug. He calls Izzy 'Nano'—that's Italian for midget—because Izzy is about five feet tall and has this squeaky voice. Me he calls 'Mone' with an accent on the 'e' because they say my name *Salmone* where he comes from."

Geist turned to point at one of the photos on the wall. It was a sepia shot of four teenagers in floppy newsboy caps with cigarettes dangling out of their lips as they lounged in various attitudes of defiance against a wall. Two were strangers, but a third boy, hawk-faced and louring, was obviously an early version of Fortunato and another was Geist himself thirty or so years and as many pounds earlier, with that Buddha smile and a body like a projectile.

"The Dead End Kids," Jack said.

"No, the Alley L Boys, named for the first stop on the Chicago elevated. We put a thumbprint on our neighborhood."

"You all still friends?" It was another way for Jack to ask about Fortunato.

"Not like in the old days, but yes. I saw Izzy a few times during the war when he was in the Air Corps working as a mechanic at March Field. He was the one of us that was really smart, secretly playing the piano and getting good grades to honor his parents and then hitting the streets with us at night to honor Nicky. Knows everything about planes now and just got hired by Grumman Aircraft to work in the international operation they're setting up in Europe.

"Sparky, not so bright but loyal. I lost track of him for a few years, then he recently came out here for a little while when he was bumming around after getting discharged from the Army. He and Nano have always been closer to Nicky than to me. They idolize the guy."

"What do you make of him going to war?" Jack's interest in Fortunato was winning out over his distaste for Geist.

"What can I say? All that commando stuff surprised the shit out of me."

"Why did he do it?"

Geist gave it some thought and then said, "Listen, Nicky is one of those guys who don't do things just for one reason, okay? Sure, he loves America. Who doesn't? Land of the free, a great fucking place. But come on, he's *Niccolo Fortunato!* He still thinks like an Italian and talks Italian half the time. Someone pisses him off and he doesn't say, 'Hey you, I'm mad as hell.' He says, *'Non capisci una fava'*—'You're stupid as a bean.' I halfway learned Italian myself just by running with him all those years.

"Anyhow, Nicky wasn't too crazy about all those Brown Shirt cocksuckers running the old country down and then allowing Hitler to call the shots from his rathole in Berlin. Probably had some other reasons for going over there too."

"The girl?" Jack asked. "Where does she factor in?"

"Valentina?" Geist seemed surprised to be asked about her. "She had a hard time of it in the old country. Nicky thinks she has talent and brought her over here to make her a star. He believes that stars can't be touched."

"You agree?"

His eyes grew even more hooded: "Anybody can be touched."

Then he presented his palms: "But what are you writing, a gossip column?"

"No," Jack saw an opening to use what he'd just learned from Selkirk, "but speaking of gossip, what about the rumor that the main reason Fortunato's out here is because Chicago feels you might be losing the fight with the ASE?"

"So finally we get to the subject—Hollywood's labor problems."

"According to Selkirk, you are Hollywood's labor problem."

"Write down this prediction on your little pad. Selkirk is going to get his off-button pushed pretty goddamn soon if he doesn't watch himself."

He glowered at Jack while recovering his composure and then continued: "Okay, now I'll tell you who's who and what's what. The International Brotherhood of Technicians and Actors, of which I'm an officer, is legit. It's part of the AF of L, which is a hell of a lot more than you can say for Selkirk's little branch office of the Comintern. We unionized this town. We've been here walking the walk all these years and now this Bolshevik parachutes in to fuck our thing up. There's just one question: whether the studios think they can use Selkirk to break us. They try that and there's going to be blood in the streets."

"There was blood in the streets yesterday," I interjected.

"What you saw was just basic training. Wait till the real war starts."

Seeing Jack's skepticism, Geist added, "Why don't you run all this by your old man? He can tell you who's who and what's what."

Jack scowled: "I don't check out every idea with my father before I have it."

"Of course you don't," Geist chuckled derisively.

For the next twenty minutes, Jack questioned Geist closely about what he mockingly called his "union philosophy," and Geist taunted him with minimal answers.

Finally Geist stood up, and his twin bodyguards reflexively moved in closer.

"Hope I've helped you out."

"You have," Jack replied with equal insincerity. "Very illuminating."

"I leave you with two things," Geist said. "One, Selkirk's goose is in the oven just waiting to be cooked. And two"—here he held up the index and middle fingers of his right hand tight against each other—"there's not even this much space between Nicky and me. He's out here on his own business, not on mine."

Then he walked out, with his Dragon Boys following close behind.

SIX

It took us about five minutes to get to Warners. It seemed half asleep after the pitched battle of the previous afternoon. A pair of guards indolently eyed the handful of pickets standing sullenly on the sidewalk outside the entry; a single Burbank policeman sat in a cruiser parked across the street reading a book and eating a banana. I noticed how different the vehicle was from our beat-up East Coast cop cars—brightly waxed and riding on fat whitewalls.

We were heading to Harry Warner's office when I heard Jack's sharp intake of breath. I looked up and saw what he did: the girl from yesterday's party coming toward us.

She appeared to be in her film costume—black peep-toe heels and a sleeveless white dress with a full skirt—and walked in a kind of trance, her lips moving slightly as she worried a spot on her left forearm where the raw skin had been disguised by thick makeup. Close up, she was thinner and more delicate than I'd realized in the sighting the previous day, and although her body was frank and supple her beauty weighed on her like a birth defect. When she saw that we were staring she winced slightly and averted her eyes.

Jack stepped forward. "Is this the face that launched a thousand ships and burnt the topless towers of Ilium?"

She was startled.

"I've seen you in your slip," he blushed as an even more sophomoric pickup line slipped out.

At first I thought she was going to run, but instead she crossed her arms protectively over her breasts and faced us head on.

"I mean that I saw your screen test," Jack continued lamely. "Mr. Warner showed it to us yesterday. It was wonderful. I'm Jack Kennedy, by the way, and this is my chauffeur, Billings."

I tipped the bill of an imaginary cap when she looked my way.

"I must go now." She took a couple of steps, but Jack impeded without actually blocking her.

"Don't leave yet, Delphine."

Again she looked surprised. "Delphine is what they named me. It is not my name," she said coolly. The words carried just enough accent—"name-*ed*"—that I thought if she actually made it in the movies, she'd probably spend her career playing not only French, but Hungarians, Tunisians, Gypsies, white Russians and other exotics.

"What is your name then?" Jack pretended not to know it.

"Valentina," she said reluctantly, like someone who considers it an obligation to honestly answer questions asked of her.

"Valentina," Jack mouthed the word like a gumdrop, then crooned softly, *"My funny Valentine, sweet comic Valentine. You make me smile with my heart ..."*

She looked at him as if he were deranged, but I could tell that she was fighting against the undertow of that brilliant Kennedy smile.

"You have a hard day at the office today?" he asked.

"I have been here since before six o'clock." When she was less guarded, her voice became husky. "Since before there was sun. During that time I am before the camera for maybe five minutes only."

"I'm sure you were wonderful," Jack worked to deepen his conversational foothold.

She scratched at her arm and seemed about to become lost in thought again.

"Can I call you Val?" he asked.

"I don't think so," she frowned. "I don't think it necessary that you call me anything at all."

He ignored the rebuff: "Are you finished dazzling the camera for today?"

She gave a minimalist nod.

Jack pointed back at the Zephyr in the distant parking area: "I have a very nice car. Why don't I have Billings drive you home?"

She shook her head: "No, I must meet someone."

"This someone you have to meet—is it a friend or more than a friend?"

"You ask very many personal questions." Her cheeks reddened with annoyance as she stepped onto the lawn to get around us, wobbling slightly as her sharp heels sank into the grass, then returned to the pavement and briskly walked away.

"Jesus!" Jack said as he watched her go.

He was generally averse to making a play for other men's women—partly because of his own embarrassment of riches, but even more because he believed, as he liked to say, that "none of them, however beautiful, is worth a confrontation with some raging cuckold." But he watched this woman with such longing as she disappeared around a corner that I could tell that if he had a chance with her—Niccolo Fortunato or not—all such compunctions would be out the window.

* * *

When we got to Harry Warner's office his secretary handed Jack a note. He read it aloud: "I had to take a meeting. If I don't keep an eye on my brother, he goes berserk. Anyway, why should my name be in the same newspaper article with those two *shtarkers*? Do it without me, okay?"

"Okay." Jack spoke to the paper as he tossed it in a wastebasket.

Walking back to the parking lot, he kept talking about the girl, asking me, in that obsessive way he had when he was actually querying himself, what it was about her that was so distinctive.

"I don't know," I finally replied. "Not enough protein?"

"Come on, dammit, Lemmer, I'm serious."

Then we saw her sitting in the back seat of the Zephyr.

Most of my life I have just allowed myself to be borne unresisting on the tide of the present moment, taking for granted extraordinary experiences that I should have realized at the time were mysterious and possibly filled with deep portent. A few times, however, I have understood that what I was witnessing was of such consequence that it would alter profoundly everything that came after. One such experience, as I have said, was that first meeting with Jack when we were boys. Another was seeing Valentina Moretti in the back seat of Jack's 1941 Zephyr at Warners on that postwar September afternoon.

I have never forgotten the forlorn way she was sitting—like an unclaimed human parcel someone had left for us. I've never forgotten the thousand-yard stare and the melancholy Mona Lisa smile as she absentmindedly worried her arm. Most of all, I have never forgotten the look on Jack's face when he saw her—pure anticipation slightly shadowed by doubt, as if he suspected that he might soon discover the truth of the observation by Oscar Wilde he quoted so glibly about there being two types of tragedy in this world: not getting what you want, and getting it.

I got into the front seat and was hit by her scent, Coty's L'Aimant, whose notes of bergamot and geranium filled the car with latent drama. I saw Jack hesitate a second after opening the back door, giving himself one last chance to reconsider before sliding into the seat beside her.

We all sat there in silence, jointly considering the gravity of what would come next. Then Jack said, "Drive, Billings."

"Where to, sir?" I played out the charade.

"Wherever."

* * *

Seeing a street sign pointing to North Hollywood, which I mistakenly assumed was a part of Hollywood itself, I headed in that direction. As we left the tidy neighborhoods of Toluca Lake, I glanced at the rearview mirror and saw that the girl was looking at the back of my head as if trying to identify me by the whorls of my cowlick.

I heard her whisper to Jack, "He is truly a chauffeur, this Billings?" In all the time I knew her, she would never call me by any other name.

If he had known her better, Jack would likely have replied, "No, this Billings is actually a distant member of the Jukes family my father is trying to rehabilitate," or, "No, Billings is a defrocked priest who drives for me during the week and says Mass for deviants in a secret grotto near Sunset Boulevard on Sundays."

Instead he looked at her pensively and said simply, "Billings has been around forever."

As I continued west on Riverside Drive, Jack and Val stared out of their respective windows to keep from having to look at each other.

Neither of them made a sound until I sneezed and she murmured, *"Salve."*

Then Jack directed me to Ventura Boulevard.

It seemed like a long time passed before Jack asked her, "Where in Italy are you from?"

"Naples and then Rome."

"Naples got knocked around pretty badly in the fall of '43."

"Knocked around?" She was indignant. "Almost totally destroyed by the Americans, you mean. People live in caves because of your bombers."

Jack waited an interval and then tried again: "How is it that you speak English so well?"

She didn't say anything for a while, and I thought that maybe she was done talking for the day. When she finally spoke, her voice seemed to be coming over a long distance line.

"My mother is a seamstress and when I am a girl, she became friends with an old English lady living in Naples and trades her embroidery for giving my brother Franco and me English lessons that taught us to say things like 'with all due respect' even if we disagree strongly with someone, and 'sorry, you're sitting in my chair' when it is the person who is sitting there who should be sorry. Later when we move to Rome so my mother can work in a factory sewing uniforms for the soldiers Mussolini sends to Abyssinia, she saved her money to send me and Franco to a small American school where English is taught. I keep studying English later on at university."

"Whatever your mother did worked very well," Jack said. "You will never be criticized for mispronouncing words as I sometimes am."

She gave him a confounded look, and then, allowing some time for a transition, she said, "Wherever we're going, it is taking forever."

"As the Irish writer James Joyce says," he replied, "the longest way round is the shortest way home."

He had a ragbag of such quotes that he deployed strategically to show people that he had erudition as well as dazzle. But Val's only reaction was to lean her head against the window and close her eyes. When I glanced in the mirror again a little while later, the tic of a sleeping newborn's involuntary smile was playing with the corners of her mouth, and Jack was staring at her, transfixed.

After perhaps fifteen minutes, as we ventured deeper into the Valley, she jerked awake and looked around self-consciously. Jack leaned forward and said to me, "If you keep going this way, Billings, we'll be in Arizona pretty soon," then pointed at a sign for Topanga Canyon and told me to turn.

We crested the hill and threaded down through a heavily wooded gorge, then suddenly hit the Pacific Coast Highway and were eye level with the infinity of water gleaming cerulean in the late afternoon. When I looked at Jack in the mirror, he gestured with his head to turn right toward Malibu.

I assumed that he was heading us to the beach house, but when we were still several miles away he pointed at a ramshackle restaurant on the left side of the highway: "Pull into the parking lot here and we'll watch the sunset."

The girl, who hadn't said a word for half an hour, looked at the restaurant's name, A Taste of the Sea, and listlessly mouthed the Italian translation: *"Sapore del Mare."* The moment I stopped the car, she got out, kicked off her shoes and headed toward the water. Jack and I followed, the waves blowing a thin mist in our faces after smacking down on the sand.

When we caught up to her, Jack pointed at the bloody sun whose slow-motion fall into the ocean was now perceptible to the naked eye.

"Think it might hiss when it hits the water?" he nodded at it.

She ignored him, still stuck in her own thoughts. "Did you know that today is my mother's birthday?"

"I had no idea." Jack shot me a concerned look.

Saying nothing more, Val picked up the hem of her dress and walked into the surf.

I thought she might squeal coquettishly and let the waves play tag with her feet. But she walked straight out, slogging through the tide as if hypnotized.

Soon she was in up to her waist and heading further out to where the water hit her chest. She began bobbing up and down, her face dipping into the water, her dress blossoming around her like a white sea-flower.

Jack charged into the surf and I followed. The riptide cut me down and the water on my glasses distorted Jack as he high-stepped through the waves like a running back. He was wet up to his armpits when he reached the girl and grabbed her by the shoulder to keep her upright. She was coughing up seawater. Her wet hair curled on her neck and she had the look of someone in the clutches of petit mal.

Jack used the surge of the waves to help him swim-walk her back to shore. When he got her up on the sand, she collapsed and lay there for a minute like a beached mermaid. Her face looked moon-blanched; her lips were a cyanotic purple.

"Damn it, Lem, she's freezing." Jack snapped at me. "Go get my jacket."

When I returned with it from the car, she was back on her feet, shivering violently with one arm on Jack's shoulder to keep from falling. He pulled the jacket over her. In drawing the lapels together he inadvertently brushed his fingers over one of her breasts.

"Sorry," he mumbled, drawing his hand back quickly.

Although still a little woozy, she looked at him squarely, enjoying his discomfort. She made a cup of one hand and rotated it back and forth slowly in the air.

"American boys feel the breast as if they are squeezing a citrus."

"It was an accident," Jack stammered.

Then she seemed to sag: "Perhaps if I ate something..."

I pulled a fresh pack of Beeman's out of my pocket. She crammed four sticks into her mouth and chewed rapidly, gulping in the sugar. Then she spit out the wad just as a man and a woman holding hands walked by.

"They will think I hock a loogie."

"Where did you hear that?" Jack couldn't help laughing.

"From the American GIs in Emilia. They teach me about hock a loogie. At first I think it is 'hawk' like the bird." She pulled at the front of her wet dress to keep its cling from saying too much about her contours. "But what is a loogie and why would a hawk have anything to do with it?"

"Good quesions." Jack sent me another look of concern and started leading her toward the restaurant. "If we eat something maybe we'll figure out some answers."

When we entered, the handful of early diners stared at us as if we were shipwreck survivors. We slid into a banquette, our wet clothes making squealing sounds on the Naugahyde. Val immediately grabbed rounds of melba toast from the cracker caddy, ripped open the wrappers, and crammed them into her mouth until her cheeks were puffed like a gerbil's. She chewed methodically, not speaking until she had swallowed several mouthfuls.

"My mother would be forty-five years of age today. She was born the year of the new century. She had me when she was just twenty and my brother Franco two years later."

She was speaking too loudly, causing Jack to look around nervously. He searched for a subject that would bring her down a notch.

"Judging from 'hock a loogie,' you seem to speak American very well."

She wasn't sure what he meant: "I tell you already I learned English in an American school when I am a girl. I also study the language and the history and customs of the U.S. when I am at Sapienza University in Rome."

She stood abruptly and went to the table next to us and asked a middle-aged man who was smoking between courses for a cigarette. He looked at her apprehensively, handed over his nearly full pack of Chesterfields and said to keep it.

Sitting back down, she put the cigarette between her lips and peeked up almost flirtatiously, inviting Jack to light it. Next came the orgasmic gasp as she drew the smoke into her lungs, expelled it through her mouth, French-inhaled it again into her nose and exhaled once more, then held the cigarette at arm's length while picking languidly at a speck of tobacco on the tip of her tongue with her other hand.

"I'm surprised you are a smoker," Jack said after this kabuki had ended.

"Why is that?"

"It just doesn't seem like you."

"But you have no idea at all of what is like me."

Her froideur caused him to excuse himself and head for the restroom. She watched him go, took another drag, and crushed the half-smoked Chesterfield, imprinted by her bloody kiss, in the ashtray.

She saw me staring at the angry spot on her left forearm and covered it with her right hand.

"If I had dressed myself I would have long sleeves. But the costume people at the studio says no sleeves for the role I play and then covers with makeup."

After Jack returned, she made the decision to take her hand away from the spot.

"It's where my number would have been."

"Number for what?" Jack looked at her forearm.

"For dying."

"Dying?"

"Yes. They made you register before they made you die. That is why I keep trying to rub the number off even though it was never put on."

Val now had her elbows on the table and was staring down at the

Formica, aimlessly finger-curling the damp strands of hair that partly hid her face.

"They were going to send me to the Polish camp where they sent my mother. The number on my mother's arm was B12294. If I had been there when the numbers go on, mine probably would have been B12295 because I am always right next to her. Who knows? The tattoo is not usually thought of as a mortal wound—a few punctures with a needle that bleed a little before they're washed with green ink. But the one they placed on my mother's arm caused her death."

"You're Jewish?" Jack said the word with the careful formality of someone who assumed that "Jew" was an epithet.

"Yes." She looked combative for a moment before continuing evenly, "Part of me is—through my mother. But a part was enough."

We were in uncharted territory. Anne Frank was still years away; Auschwitz was an unknown place not yet established as a synonym for unfathomable evil; and the night-and-fog films showing the matchstick bodies in hasty piles alongside the parchment skeletons of the living dead had not yet made the newsreels.

Of course, there had been rumors the past few years that the Office of War Information was suppressing intelligence about what the Nazis were doing to the Jews, for fear that it would affect the war effort. But although the GIs who had liberated the death camps were now returning with firsthand accounts, few of us yet had any idea of the magnitude of what had happened. While waiting for Jack at Union Station the previous morning, I'd been shocked by an *LA Times* story on the Nazis' killing of the Jews of Europe that speculated "as many as 500,000 may have died."

When the waitress brought our food, Val moved hers around on her plate with a fork as if it were a construction project. After a long silence, she looked up at Jack and abruptly asked, "Do you believe in God?"

This caught him off-guard and he blurted out in reply, "Do you?"

"I believe it is not considered polite to answer a question with another question," she said sternly.

He gave a nervous laugh. "True, it's just that nobody has asked me that since I was ten years old."

"Well, do you?"

"Yes, of course I believe in God," he blustered.

And he did, in the same way he believed in the Democratic Party: as a given, not to be questioned or even really thought about.

"My brother Joe and I were altar boys."

"You have a brother?" She was suddenly alert.

"Had. He died in the war."

"Oh, no." She looked at Jack as if seeing him for the first time. "I have a brother too. He also died."

Then there was a flash flood of tears she tried to stop by waving a hand up and down in front of her face as if cooling hot food.

"Franco had shiny black hair and a large nose. At our school the girls chase after him. He was always—what do you call it—a joke man? He is talking with my mother and me in the kitchen sometimes and then suddenly makes himself fall down. For no reason. Then he gets up and a few minutes later suddenly fall down again. Or he pretend a bee is chasing and runs around the room knocking everything over trying to get away. There is much laughter. But he is also a very good violinist and when he wasn't making us laugh could make us cry by playing from the concertos of Antonio Vivaldi."

"What happened?" Jack asked.

She looked at him closely before answering, trying to make sure he was genuinely interested.

"Even though he hates Duce, when war comes Franco joins the army because his friends from the orchestra he plays in have joined and he doesn't want to disappoint. The last time my mother and I see him is on the day the 18th Bersaglieris stand at attention in Piazza del Popolo for a ceremony before they leave for Russia. Franco looks very handsome in his uniform and after the speaking and the band music finish he makes faces for our camera wearing one of the Bersaglieris' big hats with the black grouse feathers. Then they march away. What could be worse for an Italian than to die in the freezing cold of that horrible place Stalingrad, fighting for one horrible man against another horrible man? My only defense is always to imagine that when the bullet or the bomb came for Franco he was thinking of a funny joke or humming a passage from *L'estro armonico.*"

Watching as she wiped her cheeks with her wrists, Jack said, "So what about you? Do you believe in God?"

"Yes." She didn't hesitate, although what had just been said gave the question a different weight than the same one when she had asked it.

"But your mother and brother and all the others..."

"Yes, I know," she interrupted. "Hitler. Always Hitler. In doing the things he did, Hitler was trying to kill God, but for me he did not succeed. In spite of what happened, I always believe. I abide by the Latin phrase, *Credo quia absurdum*. Believing is not meant to be easy. I think that God watches. He is interested in us and the way we sometimes do things that even he cannot predict. Some of what we do must make God weep for shame. Other things must make him smile with delight."

"I'm with Pascal," Jack was trying to impress her again. "I read about his wager when I was in college. Believe in God because you have everything to gain if you're right and nothing to lose if you're wrong."

"Only a coward makes a bet he can't lose," she said curtly. "We must put something at risk in the things that are important to us."

I tried to help dig Jack out: "It wasn't as bad in Italy as in other places?"

"As bad?" She gave me a scalding look before relenting: "No, you are correct, I suppose. Killing people efficiently in large numbers is not in the nature of the Italian. It requires too much effort.

"We have Jews in Rome since before Jesus Christ. In our time there seems to be not many only because most are married to Gentile people so no one really knows who are the Jews. Many of the Jews do not know themselves. I didn't—even though people would sometimes say to me when I was growing up, 'Moretti, this is a Jewish name, no?'"

"Is it?" Jack asked.

"Yes. I am always Catholic and my mother does not tell me about being part Jew—from her parents—until I am sixteen. It was not a moment of large drama. Finding this out merely seemed a little strange—like being *mancina*, a person of the left hand—but nothing more than that."

She lit another Chesterfield and gave Jack a grim look through a veil of smoke as if blaming him for the fact that she was revealing so much. "Every person is a mystery, no?"

He nodded amiably.

"Then why is it that you should try to solve the mystery of me within an hour of our first meeting?"

She saw that he was wounded by the comment and immediately softened. "I told you that today was my mother's birthday. This is why my heart is sad and I cannot be pleasant. You can understand this?"

"Yes."

"Perhaps you understand too that I cherish the pain I feel because it is the only thing I have left of her."

He nodded again, and after a minute he looked at his watch: "It's getting late. We should go."

The banquette was damp with seawater when Val stood up and Jack led her out of the restaurant, leaving me behind to pay the bill, as usual.

A half moon hung in the night sky like a lemon wedge. Val studied it for a long while before climbing into the Zephyr.

"Where now?" I started the engine.

"I will direct you." She spoke before Jack could say anything. "I'm expected somewhere. I should have been there long ago."

She told me to turn off the Coast Highway onto Sunset and was silent until we had passed through Beverly Hills into the center of Hollywood. There she directed me to go left on Gower and from there head up into Beachwood Canyon.

When we got to the top of the hill and began to wind around to the Overlook, the Hollywoodland sign emerged on our right, a ghost of itself because the four thousand light bulbs that once made its fifty-foot letters visible for twenty miles had been stolen during the war. We looked at the downtown to our left, the lights glittering in the distance as we continued on to Arrowhead Drive, where Val told me to turn left.

Midway down the cul-de-sac, she pointed at a ranch-style home at the top of a sloping lawn defined by three palm trees and said "There."

Fortunato was standing under a yellow porch light with a cloud of bugs circling his head while he stared out implacably at the night.

I happened to glance in the rearview mirror just as Val slid toward Jack, put one hand on the back of his neck and nuzzled her face against his chest. He tried to grab hold of her, but she quickly retreated to the door, got out and ran toward the house.

She stepped up onto the porch, said something to Fortunato, then tried to go around him, but he blocked her. She was still wearing Jack's coat, and he picked up a lapel and then dropped it in a flamboyant gesture of disgust. She said something more emphatic, and he slapped her. Still defiant, she lowered a shoulder, forced her way past him and disappeared inside.

Jack was reaching for his door handle, but I gunned the Zephyr, throwing him back against the seat as we peeled out.

* * *

When we got back to the beach house, both of us were still caught up in the viscous aftermath of what had just happened. Jack went directly inside and sat at the kitchen table typing his notes of the interviews with Selkirk and Geist for an hour or so, while I worked at a week-old *New York Times* crossword. After he finished, he put "How Are Things in Glocca Morra" on the record player and stood at the bay window watching the whitecaps. Then he limped to the bathroom and began running a bath. As he stripped and lowered himself into the tub to soak his back, more painful than usual because of his exertions in the surf, I knew he was trying to figure out his next move with Valentina.

Like all the Kennedys, he never hesitated to cast stones into the pond, and also like them, he never reckoned on how the waves they created might eventually lap on his own shores.

Suddenly a glaring light swept around the walls of the living room; it came from the headlamps of a car turning around out front. I went to the window and saw a cab—the first of many that would come and go over the next few weeks—pull away as Val came up the walkway with Jack's coat folded over her arm.

"I brought it back, Billings." She handed it to me when I opened the door. "I know the place to come from the envelope in the pocket."

She was vivid. Her cheeks had a hectic flush; the pigment of her dark eyes seemed to have ripened since we last saw her.

I pointed down the hall where the door was cracked open enough to show a slice of Jack's back in the tub. She looked at me, then shook her head slightly as if disagreeing with a caution I hadn't given, and headed toward the bathroom, shedding her clothes as she went. Jack turned slightly when he heard her, and a look of wonder came over his face.

"It is Val," she said to him. "I have come to be with you."

Unable to force myself to look away, I saw the profile of an audacious breast as she removed her bra and then the tight rump when she slithered out of her panties, grabbed his shoulders to steady herself and stepped into the tub behind him. I could almost feel on my own skin the kiss of her pubic hair and then of the raspberry nipples traveling down his spine as she slowly lowered herself into the water, wrapped her arms around him, and rested her cheek on his back.

SEVEN

The next morning I woke at 6:15, just in time to see Val close the front door behind her. After hearing a cab pull away, I drifted back to sleep and didn't get up until Jack did, around nine.

I assumed he'd be happy that she was gone. Glad as he always was to be into a woman, he was always gladder yet to be out of her, free from the potential entanglements she signified and able to reunite with his male pack. But this morning he was filled with discontent and immediately began interrogating me.

"What time did she leave?"

"At dawn."

"Why didn't you stop her?"

"You mean physically restrain her?"

"No," he was petulant. "But you could have told her to wait for a minute and woke me up, or convinced her to stay and have breakfast or something."

"I assumed that she had an early morning call at the studio. Or that she wanted to get back to Fortunato before he called out the carabinieri."

He shot me a dirty look and stalked into the kitchen. After jamming a piece of bread into the toaster and loudly rattling the pages of the *LA Times* for a few minutes, he got Harry Warner's secretary on the phone and, calling her "Toots," sweet-talked her into giving us a pass to get on the set of *Tomorrow Is Too Late*. When he hung up, he snapped at me, "Come on, let's get this show on the road!"

Tomorrow was one of those low-budget noir films that were about to become Hollywood's genre of the moment, as doubts about what lay ahead in the postwar world quickly undermined the euphoria of victory. It was based on a short story in the pulp magazine *Black Mask* by James M. Cain, whose work provided an endless supply of noir plots in the next few years, and was directed by Frank Talbert, a reliable second-stringer who was in high demand because he always brought his films in on time and under budget.

The lead was John Payne, on loan from Fox and in the middle of his slow-motion transition from song-and-dance man to outcast hero. As Val later grudgingly summarized the klunky plot—"bad bolognese," she called it—Payne played Glen Dobbs, a former LAPD detective who joins the Marines after Pearl Harbor and is badly wounded at Iwo Jima after fighting his way through the Pacific. He comes home to find that his old job has been given to someone else and that his fiancée, who works at the British consulate in Los Angeles, has not only become the mistress of the consul general, played by a wintry Adolph Menjou, but has joined his conspiracy to smuggle Japanese war criminals into Southern California, give them new identities in return for gold bullion, and help them emerge as genuine U.S. citizens by hiding them in plain sight for a time at Manzanar and other relocation centers where Japanese Americans had been interned since the beginning of the war.

Dobbs's cheating former lover was played by Veronica Lake, who seemed to appear in all of Talbert's films, although Val told us that he sometimes rolled his eyes during her scenes and referred to her under his breath as "Moronica."

"Naturally because I am now Delphine, I play a French woman, Lily Fontaine," Val added belligerently.

Trapped in French Indochina when the attack on Pearl Harbor occurs, Lily makes her way to the Pacific Coast and gets a job at the British consulate. She accidentally discovers what the consul general and Lake's character are doing, and is fired and threatened with death if she talks. Shunned and penniless, with nowhere to turn, she enters a social freefall and lands as a call girl. After Dobbs comes to her for information, Lily agrees to help his private investigations into the consul general's scheme. Along the way, they begin a brief and doomy love affair, which ends when Lily takes a bullet intended for Dobbs.

As Jack and I tiptoed onto the set, we were shushed histrionically by a young female production assistant. We saw Val standing in chiaroscuro lighting next to Payne at a street-corner façade. She was wearing a smart lavender suit and her lustrous black hair had been styled to look wild from exertion.

Stage hands were dropping dry ice into huge vats to make the fog that will envelop the two characters when they try to escape the villains on their trail. It seemed to take a long time for the vapor to gain critical mass. When two giant fans started blowing it toward Val and Payne, the force made his tie flap around. Talbert yelled "Cut!" and ordered the fans turned down. But then the fog disappeared except for a few wisps scuttling over the floor.

Val stood there in a zen of boredom, while Payne raged at the stage hands: "Come on, guys! We're not trying to alter the nation's weather patterns here!"

Then he yelled at Talbert: "Why do we need fog anyhow? There isn't any fog in LA. All we have is fucking smog! If you wanted fog you should have set the movie in San Francisco!"

In the disruption that followed, Val saw Jack and her face came alive. She ran over to us and whispered, "Today I was forced to say the same thing nine times: 'I don't know about tomorrow. But I know that I love you today and that today is forever.' To say this one time is an insult to the mind. To say it over and over because Mr. Payne can't remember what he is supposed to say in return is *idiota*."

The stage hands were now yelling back at Payne, who continued to inflame them. Talbert finally slammed his copy of the script down on the floor, yelled "That's it!" and stalked off the set.

"Thanks be to the gods!" said Val. "This film does not have one true thing in it." She headed for the exit and we followed.

The sun hit like a death ray. With my hand as a visor, I saw that Val was once again trapped in her haughty loneliness. She and Jack looked past each other, neither of them sure if what had happened the previous night still had consequence.

"Well, we might as well go home," he said tentatively.

"Home?" Val repeated the word as if she had never heard it before. She didn't say no, but plodding to the car she was so remote that I wondered if each new encounter would feel like meeting her for the first time.

She was silent as we retraced the previous day's route, but smiled automatically at Jack whenever she saw that he was looking at her.

"You smile, but you're not happy," he said.

"People in this country believe that someone who is not always happy is not normal."

Her brooding formality terminated the discussion. I noticed that they were again sitting as far apart as possible and both were staring out their respective windows.

After twenty minutes or so, as we were heading down through Topanga Canyon, Jack spoke. "I just thought of something."

Val didn't respond, so I stepped up to the straight-man role: "What's that?"

"It makes absolutely no sense that sex organs should be in the middle of the body. It's awkward and inconvenient."

It seemed out of character for people who didn't know him well, but Jack sometimes said and did screwball ad-lib things—sending someone a telegram out of the blue that read, "Please disregard previous telegram," for instance, or issuing a goofy non sequitur like this one. Close friends recognized these actions as signs that he was nervous or, more likely, bored.

But his words caused Val to shrink deeper into her corner of the back seat. When I glanced at her face again a moment later, however, I saw a hint of sly intelligence poking up through her melancholy.

"But where should the sex organs go, then?" she asked tentatively.

"Hmm. Good question." Jack pretended to ponder it. "Okay, I have it. Our sex organs should be in our feet. That's the perfect place for them. Think of how easy it would make things. No pulling and tugging at the clothes. Just take off your shoes and socks and there you are. And think how wonderful it would be if you were wearing sandals or going barefoot."

"The feet." Val looked down seriously at her own. "Perhaps this is a good thing if one is a dancer. But you can imagine the problem for a clumsy person whose feet do not perform gladly. Also, we could not help but look down at them as they were doing their work and that would cause red faces. Sex may be inconvenient now, but at least we don't have to watch while it happens. Also, the feet become very sweaty from being inside shoes and often don't smell good and the toenails are sometimes sharp. No, the feet cannot be the right place."

"Well, where do you think the sex organs should be?" Jack was grinning now, knowing he'd struck gold.

Val pressed her index finger against her temple to indicate deep thought and then held it up as if struck by a revelation.

"I have the answer. Our sex organs should be in our backs. Yes, our backs. There is no doubt."

"Now that's an interesting idea," Jack made a show of pondering it. "But why exactly the back?"

Val surprised me by starting to giggle: "The back because then we would not have to put false looks of passion on our faces. We could allow the eyes to roll around in dismay while strange things were taking place in the back without worrying about offending the other person. We would also not see the looks that pass over each other's face because of all the many little inconvenient things that happen in moments of sex—the strange sounds that are made and organs that refuse to obey commands and act as if they have their own minds. Because we were not looking at each other we would not have to ask—how to say in English?—*Come stato per te*? and other questions whose answers we don't really want to hear. And if sex organs are on the back, then while they are doing their work we could also be doing other things like reading a book or having a cigarette or painting the fingernails. Or making a photo, or looking at birds. Or best of all, eating."

"Eating while having sex," Jack tried to keep a straight face. "I have to admit that's a very strong argument."

The two of them continued to riff on this and other subjects all the way back to Malibu, suddenly as much in synch as Abbott and Costello.

When we arrived at the beach house, they raced for the front door like teenagers. I stayed behind, leaning back against the Zephyr's hood to absorb its warmth for a minute before heading to the beach to watch the afternoon body surfers shooting toward the shore like torpedoes.

When I returned an hour later, the house was filled with the meaty smell of sex. And they were not yet finished. Sitting on the couch, I could hear the squeaking mattress and the yum-yum murmurings through the walls of the bedroom. It seemed to take as long as Ravel's *Bolero*, but eventually they found a culmination that left Jack audibly grinding his teeth and Val purring, *"Arrivo, Gianni. Arrivo."*

And then, after a short silence, she added thoughtfully, *"E buono, Gianni. E buono."*

* * *

They came out of the bedroom awhile later, so sated that they seemed comatose. Jack got out the bulky portable record player and put on Yip Harburg's song for Val. She listened with a puzzled look as he sang along.

"I have never heard such words as these before," she said when it was over. "What is this Glocca Morra? What is Kilkerry? What actually is this woman singing about?"

Jack explained that it was about Ireland's neverland of dreams, which tugged especially hard at the heart because of the country's reality of poverty and violence and blighted hope. She thought about this for a minute and then took his hand, "Yes, I understand now. A place where love can happen even when the world is against it."

"Something like that," Jack said, holding her eyes with his.

I made scrambled eggs and raisin toast. As we ate, Jack kept replaying the song, turning the volume down so that its romance could subliminally collaborate with him while he interrogated Val to keep her from leaving.

He asked about her schooling, the neighborhoods where she'd lived in Naples and then Rome, and how she became an actress.

"This all has to do with Jews," she said, chewing a small forkful of egg for so long that it seemed stuck in her mouth.

"Doesn't everything?" Jack took a chance.

She looked at him as if he were a naughty boy. "At first nothing happens to Jews in Italy. You know, don't you, that Jews from all over Europe come here because it is one place Jews are not certain to be killed. For a while Mussolini ignores Hitler when he says get your Jews, just as many Italians ignore Mussolini when he makes his Manifesto on Race that says Jews cannot hire a non-Jew as a domestic, Jews cannot work in banks or put the death notice of a Jew in the newspaper. But then Mussolini falls and the Germans take over and things change.

"Even though we know the end is coming, many of us at university do something very strange. We do not flee or take up weapons to protect ourselves, as you might expect. We stay where we are and form groups to do such things as read the novels of Marcel Proust or cook the food of Mexico or make Cubist painting or do the dances of Bali. I had already been doing plays with my brother since we were children and so I form with seven of my English-speaking friends an acting company that will perform classical drama in English.

"Some people cannot believe it, how obsessed all of us become with these private pursuits, and they criticize us. You hide your head inside the sand like the ostrich, they say. But the reason we did this should have been clear to them—allowing these subjects to consume us also allows us to forget for a time that we cannot prevent the worst that is soon to happen."

She talked awhile more, then began to collect her things.

"You aren't leaving, are you?" Jack moped.

"I must."

"Please stay," he begged. "I won't be able to go to sleep without you."

"I think you will sleep because I know you are very tired." She gave him a significant look. "I must go. I am expected."

I had never really seen Jack jealous before. Normally he was pleased to have someone else pay the emotional upkeep on his conquests and in fact relieved not to have responsibility for filling up the long nonsexual hours. But while he had only known this girl for a little more than a day, he seemed shaken by the idea that she might have someone else. While she waited for the cab, he was agitated, giving petulant responses to her attempts at conversation.

When the driver sounded his horn and she headed toward the door, he suddenly said, "You'll have to choose, you know."

"Choose?" She looked at him uncomprehendingly.

"Between him and me." Jack spoke the words as if they had been physically extracted from him.

"It is a little soon for the ultimatum, no?" she said. "And who is this him that you're talking about?"

"Fortunato."

She teased him with a sneaky little laugh: "I could never choose against him."

Jack's face fell as she let him dangle for a moment.

"I could never choose against him because he's my father."

Then she was gone.

EIGHT

Later on, when he had become blasé and venereal, and when sex, while even more an addiction, had also become something of a chore for Jack, a note of dolor and finally of ennui entered his amours. I remember in particular a somewhat forlorn call from the White House in the spring of 1962 when Jackie was off on her Pakistan tour.

"The Leader of the Free World here," he said when the operator put him through. "In the presidential bed with a white girl and a Negro girl. If I only had an Indian girl too they could make me a Neapolitan sandwich. Tasty! And what am I doing, you may wonder, as these two girls give evidence of being interested in knowing each other carnally? I am reading the *Wall Street Journal* and wondering what my administration can do to improve its standing with the Rockefellers and others of their ilk. Should I be worried?"

By then he had become JFK, that familiar stranger whose cheeks were slightly puffed from steroids and whose sham hardiness came from the methamphetamines handed out by Max Jacobson, the ghoul of his administration known as Dr. Feelgood. Jack's former droll facetiousness had fermented into negligent sarcasm, and his once fierce desires had dwindled into rote satisfaction.

But during our brief interlude in Southern California when he was still Jack, a romantic at heart, although an irregular and deeply wary one, he stepped out of the armor of irony that had been so crucial to his survival and would be so instrumental to his future success, and allowed himself to fall in love.

It was immediate and intense, literally overnight, a direct hit by that sudden strike of emotion the French call *coup de foudre*. It electrified him over the next few weeks as the three of us moved into a heightened zone of fast-forward.

It was all the more dramatic because love was not something Jack ever wanted to happen to him. He had always regarded love as self-delusion and weakness, which was why he had tried so hard to scour a need for it out of his psyche. He had been scarred by his parents' parched marriage, which he once described to me as a "wasteland with children," and would sometimes grumble, when we were younger and I was speaking effusively of my feelings for Kick, "You just don't get it, do you? Love is for suckers."

But Val instantly erased all the doubts about deep emotional connections that Jack had accumulated and caused him to dive head first into waters whose depth he didn't bother calculating.

It was partly about sex, of course. "It's like going all the way for the first time every time with her," he later said to me, acknowledging the jejune clumsiness of the words by a self-critical blush.

She was the first woman he'd had after all those girls. But she was also the first and only one for whom the act involved feeling as well as friction; the first to make him feel the need for something more than a spasm of release and the sense of self-possession it brought; the first whose own fervor quickened him. And the first and perhaps only one he really *touched*—so much so that once early in their days together I saw her knees buckle slightly and her eyes go blank after he had been rubbing her back during a long hug and realized that she had just had a fleeting orgasm.

Jack's problem was not whether to be in love—that was no longer a matter of choice—but how exactly to go about it. Because he had convinced himself that love was not in the cards for him, he seemed clueless how to comport himself now that the lightning had struck. He was like someone on a crash program to learn a foreign language for an emergency trip abroad.

Generally he succeeded with women by giving them a brief look at the rich complexity of his temperament and leaving it up to them whether there was to be a next step. But with Val he was frontal and direct; an arrow of desire always nocked into a tautly drawn bowstring. He did things I had never seen him do before and would never see him do again, things that would have convulsed him in condescending laughter if someone else had done them. Pacing nervously around the living room if she was even a little late and then rushing up to her the minute she came through the door to center her face with both hands and tenderly pull it to his for a lingering kiss; always surreptitiously searching for her fingers and entwining them with his when they were sitting next to each other; allowing, even inviting her to massage his neck and shoulders and run her hand through his hair, a deep act of faith for someone who was by nature so deeply ambivalent about touch; and always following her hungrily with his eyes as she moved around the room unaware that he was watching.

When a romantic song he liked came on the radio, he would raise Val up and begin to dance. It was not the energetic foxtrotting of our youth that he would make into a sort of demolition derby when we were at a school mixer, bumping shoulders with male friends also on the floor, mugging at them as he twirled by and in effect dancing with them rather than his female partner. Here he snuggled into Val, his eyes closed tight as his body merged with hers into a oneness that shuffled so slowly in a square of such diminishing size that after a minute or two they seemed to be dancing on the pinpoint of eternity.

And sometimes when he did these things he would shoot me a look of dismay as if to say, "Who is this fool and why is he doing this crazy shit?"

Val's love was more somber, more considered and aware of contingencies, and because of this it appeared to me even deeper than Jack's. Like everyone else, she was swept up in his venturous élan. But she also understood that at this point he was still making himself up as he went and had as yet not taken on the burden of moral seriousness. Her feelings for him were based in part on what I always thought of as a Christian hope.

Once after returning from a walk on the beach the two of them sat on the sofa leafing through magazines, their feet and fingers touching. When Jack nodded off after a while, Val rested her copy of *Time* on her chest and studied his features as they dropped their guard in sleep, then looked over at me and whispered, "I think Gianni will be a good man someday, don't you?"

* * *

Within days he was pressing her to move into the beach house. She kept telling him it was too soon, but her resistance quickly crumbled under his reckless onslaught.

On the morning we arranged to pick up her belongings, we assumed we'd be driving to her father's house, which caused me, at least, some anxiety. But she told us that while she sometimes stayed at Fortunato's place in the Hollywood Hills, her belongings were at a Toluca Lake apartment a couple of blocks from the studio that Warners had rented for her at the beginning of shooting to make early morning calls easier.

It was a smart little place with a single bedroom and a galley kitchen, a sofa covered in a print of crocuses and a large fiddle-leaf fig in a sunny corner of the living room. The only problem was the deafening all-day construction noise six days a week at the large apartment complex going up a few doors down.

When we arrived to pick her up, she was waiting at her front door with a battered European-style leather valise secured by wide belts. Leaning against it was a small oil painting of a lovely dark-haired woman.

"It captures you perfectly," Jack said.

"It is not me," Val smiled sadly. "It is my mother when she was about the age I am now."

"Well, she is almost as beautiful as you are," he tried to bail himself out.

"More so," she corrected him. "Much more. And beautiful from the inside out."

When we got back to the beach house a few hours later, she promptly mounted the painting in the living room. Surprisingly, it not only seemed compatible with all the nautical objects, but organized them into an odd unity.

Jack stood beside her to admire it. "So you're here for good, then."

"You mean forever?"

"Yes," he became earnest. "Why not?"

Looking thoughtful, she said, "Forever is a place very far away from here. You know that. We might get to there one day, but many things can happen along the way. What is important is that I'm here now."

NINE

The next month and a half was an eyeblink in time, but as it was transpiring, it sometimes actually did seem like they stood at the gateway to forever. They moved through a forcefield in which they communicated by the flick of an eyelid, mind-read each other from twenty feet away, and constantly rehabilitated their neural connection by brushing against each other as if accidentally while passing in a room.

There were times when Val was still powerless to keep herself from retreating into a grim solitary confinement, physically present but emotionally inaccessible—assailed by dark moods whose time of arrival and intensity couldn't be predicted. But she seemed to spend a larger part of each passing day in the light, and her high spirits had less trouble escaping her overcast. The abrasion on her arm was healing, and that elemental *tristesse* which neither sympathy nor argument could dispel when we first met her at last began to yield.

The vehemence of their feeling brought both of them forward. After all these years, I can still see them sitting in facing sofas in their bathrobes, tousled from a quick shower, lazily postcoital after just gorging on each other. Jack is looking at her expectantly, wondering if she will take the lead; Val rests an elbow on the arm of the sofa and props her chin on her palm, effortlessly beautiful as she eyes him from within the still-damp hair, thickened by toweling, that has caused a partial eclipse of her face. They chat desultorily like runners warming up until some subject arises that has potential and then they are off.

Often it was just extemporized sexual afterplay, but sometimes they headed toward serious subjects. Before and after Val, Jack was deeply allergic to women he saw as "intellectual," always coming to me or another of his friends when he had accidentally become involved with one of them and saying in a panic: "Jesus, this one has *ideas*. You've got to get me out of this!"

Val was all heart and intuition, but oddly, she did not have what in those days was considered a feminine sensibility. On issues of importance, she did not defer and was not tactical or demure in her talk, instead challenging Jack as a matter of course with her shrewd intelligence and solid grasp of the world situation. They fired arguments at each other like tracer rounds about subjects ranging from whether the Czechs could resist Soviet domination to the possibility of justice being served in the Nuremberg trials that were about to begin, and I think Jack always learned something from these encounters.

In the pattern they established, he sometimes ribbed her for her moral absolutism while she mocked his provincialism.

Sometimes it was a small matter, as in his refusal to eat any food not smothered with white sauce. But occasionally it was something more meaningful. When he casually referred to one of the set decorators on her film as a "fag," for instance, she raised her hand like a traffic cop to signal a pause in the conversation, put on an expression of deep thought, and then said, "I have a proposal I think you might like. You should use our Italian insult *finocchio* instead of that word you just used, which is not so nice a word. *Finocchio* is much more pretty. It came about because once upon a time they burn homosexuals at a stake in my country, but being Italian they also throw fennel seeds on the fire so it will smell good. If you were to begin using this word *finocchio* instead of the one you use, people will admire you for being so *cosmopolita*."

The only subject she tried to rule out of bounds was her father, which of course made Jack even more obsessive in his pursuit. He wanted to meet Fortunato and kept nagging her to introduce him. She kept refusing. He asked why, and she tried to deflect him: "Why would you want him to enter this Glocca Morra of ours? He does not belong here. You can understand why he is a painful subject for me, because of what he does for a living."

This just made Jack more inquisitorial, and Val finally tried to take the subject off the table once and for all: "If you must know, I already did ask him to meet with you and he said no."

"Why?"

"His exact words to me were that he didn't want to know you until he was absolutely certain he wouldn't have to hurt you."

Jack's thoughtless laugh alarmed her.

"You think this may be a joke?" she scowled. "If so, I assure you that you have no idea of the kind of man my father is."

One afternoon when Jack brought the subject up yet again, she gave a fatalistic look, lit a cigarette and, trying to hide in its smoke, began to talk in the factual monotone of someone who'd just been injected with sodium pentothal.

"My mother said she knew only two stories of my father's life in the business of crime. Just two. One he told himself. It was about the Sicilian criminals of New York who despised him for his birthplace and always called him 'the dirty Calabrian.' They once capture him when he travels from Chicago one time for business. They put him in a storage room with no windows for two days. He tells my mother he thought he might never get out. He had nothing to defend himself with, no weapon or heavy object. But he still wore a large silver crucifix that he brought from the old country—'big as a bishop's,' he told my mother. He took it off and began sharpening the top of the cross against the stone floor during the long hours, and one day when his jailer came to bring him food and water he stabbed him in the chest several times and then escaped. At the end of this story, my mother said, he smiled in that romantic way of his that wrinkles the corners of his eyes and says, 'Since then, I have always been a religious man.'

"The other story comes from a sister of my father who came from Reggio for a visit. She told how he was once in deep conflict with another Chicago criminal who was his sworn enemy. This man had many bodyguards and lived in a house with the fortifications of a castle. My father got three of his own men to wear uniforms of service workers and go to his opponent's house saying they had come to repair a dangerous gas leak. When they were inside, they pulled guns out of their tool bags and killed everyone there."

But then she tried to close off this narrow opening: "I'm sure you must know more than I do about the life of this man you Americans call Nicky Fortune, so there's no point in going further."

"I only know a few facts," Jack complained.

"Even for a daughter there are only a few facts," she said with exasperation.

"Tell me."

"Well, okay," she sighed. "He met my mother in Naples when he is there to do business. His people in Calabria are 'Ndranghetisti and cousins to the Camorra he comes to deal with. He met my mother walking on the Lungomare one day and was with her for a few weeks and I was the result. He was good to her until the time came to return to America, and then he became very cold.

"He comes back to Italy two years later to do more business with the same people in Naples and was back together with my mother for a few more weeks before leaving her just as before. This time Franco was the result.

"He returns only once after that. It was Christmas when I am four and Franco just learns to talk. He arrives from America like a god falling from the sky, giving presents and U.S. dollars and handing out to children chewing gum that makes bubbles. He was from a poor family but now he dresses like the owner of a bank. His shoes are so polished that they looked like they are made from black glass. When he takes us out to dinner in Naples all the other families in the neighborhood where we live follow a few feet behind us on the way to the restaurant as if he is a cardinal and he throws coins to the children. Every Christmas for many years I hope he will suddenly appear like that again. But he never did.

"It is to his shame that one of the reasons he did not come back was what he called my mother's 'bad blood.' My mother took revenge by calling us by her father's Jewish name. That is why I am Valentina Moretti and not Valentina Fortunato."

She stopped to glare fiercely at Jack, as if he were responsible for her inability to stop talking.

He tried to josh her out of it: "Is this the Italian evil eye we hear so much about?"

"If I were to give you *malocchio*," she answered sharply, "you will feel it and you will be cursed until you do this to break the spell"—here she bent slightly and held out a hand in which her index and pinkie fingers were extended and her middle and ring fingers curled into her palm under her thumb.

She abruptly went outside and walked down to the water.

"Get ready in case she decides to swim out to God again," Jack said to me as we watched. But after standing at the ocean's edge for a couple of minutes Val returned to the house.

"These are my very last words about him." She lit another cigarette and slumped back down on the sofa. "In October, about two years before today, the Germans and their criminal Italian friends are ready to begin the collection of Jews, starting in Trastevere and then across the river. Many go to churches so friendly priests can convert them. This is not for me. I never before felt like a Jew but at this moment I want to shout it in the streets and refuse absolutely to un-Jew myself. In any case, the Germans are not stopped by this stratagem of conversion for long. Men and boys who say they are Catholic must lower their pants for proof by foreskin. The Church saves some who come for sanctuary but gives up others.

"At this time, my acting troupe at university produces our one performance of *Agamemnon* that we have been practicing with the certain knowledge that they will soon come for us too. And they do. My mother and I hide with Roman friends who live in Suburra for almost a month. We are finally picked up when a neighbor sells us to a group of *squadristi* for six thousand lire.

"We are sent north to a place called Fossoli di Carpe that was a prison for English soldiers captured by the Italian army in North Africa but is now a place to gather Italian Jews until the trains are ready to take them to Poland.

"The day we arrive we have to stand at attention before the German commandant. His name is Rilke. He comes to stare at me particularly when we assemble. After a long watching, he shakes his head and says, 'Another Jew, such a nuisance,' and walks away.

"The commandant became fixed with me..."

"Fixated?" Jack asked.

"Yes, he became fixated with me. Most of the German officers simply take the women at the camp they wanted and rape them, carefully washing themselves afterward to remove all scent of the parasitic vermin. But this Commandant Rilke was too vain for that. He thinks I should fall to him without being forced because of his great sexual charm. What I decided was to allow him to caress my breasts and kiss my shoulders but nothing more. His touch was like swallowing arsenic, but I felt rewarded at the end of our encounters to see him bent over with thwarted desire and to know that he knew he had been brought to this state by a Jew.

"As I have already said to you, my mother was sent to Poland in a cattle car that pulled up on our railroad track just after the beginning of 1944. I would have to invent in my imagination what then happens to her if not for a woman called Francesca Lazzarini who comes to find me after liberation. Francesca and my mother become friends in the camp and sleep together in one bunk where the lice attack like Hitler's Wehrmacht. The two of them make a dough from sawdust and leaves and tiny pieces of sugar beets they find buried in the ground and bake it into little loaves that make them starve more slower. They promise each other that if only one survives she will find the other's family and tell them everything. My mother did not survive but Francesca does. She finds me and tells what number was tattooed on my mother's arm and these other things."

"You were lucky to make it," Jack said with genuine relief when she paused to light another cigarette.

"Lucky?" She gave a wan smile. "Perhaps. But not just lucky. At Fossoli, the *Ebrei misti* are taken last—the ones of mixed parentage like me. There is also the fixation of Commandant Rilke, who refuses to abandon his plan of seduction. And because I have studied at university, I was given the job of organizing records. This was so the people who opened the cattle cars could write in their book who it was they were giving a tattoo and then soon giving the shower. I would have been put in a cattle car too when no more records were needed, but I was rescued before this happened."

"By U.S. soldiers?" I asked.

"No, by the Italian fighters of the *Resistenza*. Early one morning in February of last year, I am getting water from the well and suddenly guns are firing everywhere."

She leaned forward to look closely at Jack. "This is what I believe you have been particularly wanting to hear.

"As I look at the *partigiani* pulling down the barbed wire, I see my father. It was an older face now than the one in the photographs in our parlor, but I would know it anywhere. I am shocked. Why has this man come from the safety of America to this dangerous place?

"He was not the leader of the group and not as young as the others. They have berets but he wears a hat with a feather like the Alpini. Guns are exploding. I fall down and cover my head. When I look up, he is shooting a German guard near me with his rifle. The bullets tear little holes in the back of the guard's uniform when they come out."

"I knew about what he did after Sicily," Jack said, "but not about this. He was a hero."

Val gave him a pitying look. "I would ask you not to praise him too highly. My father is a person who may surprise you by his bravery but surprise also by his cruelty. He admits that many of the things he has done in his life were evil, although he tries to apologize by saying that they don't represent him as he really is. When he tells me this, I reply to him that we are not who we say we are; we are what we do.

"I know little about his actions as a person of crime but what I do know makes me ashamed. Yet I cannot deny him. He gave me life twice—once through his seed and then again as this man who came to Fossoli to save me."

By this time she was so pale she appeared to need a transfusion. A concerned look came across Jack's face, and he stood up, ready for the story to be over. But she wanted to finish.

"When the Germans are all dead or run away, he tries to put his arms around me, but by then I am thinking: Where are you when Franco is made to march into the snows of Stalingrad? Where are you when my mother and I are hiding from the Germans in Rome? Where are you when they put her on the train?

"There are no more guards so I just walk out the gate. I did not ask permission. He starts to follow, but I turn around and shake my finger to him. Oh no you don't!

"I walked for two days. As I reach a place with umbrella pines on both sides of the road, I see things on the ground beside the paving. At first I think they are melons. But as I come closer, I realize they are the heads of dead Italian collaborators who have been buried alive. Dogs have chewed on them.

"I am given a ride by American soldiers in a jeep—the first one I have ever seen—all the way to Rome. These are the GIs who teach me about hock a loogie. They take me to an officer in the U.S. Army who gives me work as a translator, which I am glad for because it brings money and makes my English better. I am living by myself now in our old apartment. That is where Francesca Lazzarini manages to find me many months later."

"You were hiding from your father?" Jack asked.

"Yes, from him and other things. But he finds me in Rome just as he finds me in Fossoli. By then he has discovered that I was an actor at university. He tells me that he will bring me to America to be in the moving pictures and we will live here happily ever after, as the children's books say.

"On the ship taking us to New York he is charming and reassuring. I try to ask him seriously about the evil he has done, but he only tells me that he has been a 'tool of necessity' all his life. I ask myself, what can these words even mean? He is a stranger, but I have no one else left in this world so I make the decision to allow him to love me."

At this point, she crushed her half-smoked Chesterfield in the ashtray, crumpled the half-full pack and threw it in a wastebasket, saying with distaste, "I will stop smoking now forever."

TEN

Jack had flirted irregularly with the idea of being a writer since his final year at Harvard, when his senior thesis about the gathering storm in Europe was published as *Why England Slept* and became a low-level bestseller in 1940. But while he was glad to see his legend inflated and to one-up his brother Joe, he also knew his father had made the book a success, getting Arthur Krock, his lackey at the *New York Times*, to act as Jack's rewrite man, agent and publicist.

His nebulous literary ambitions had gone dormant during the war, and he had initially taken the job with Hearst only to keep his father off his back. But now that he was dimly visualizing a future with Val, he began to think seriously about actually trying to make it as a journalist.

For the first time since I had known him, he forced himself to get up before eight. He established a routine in which he did his reporting in the mornings, came home in the early afternoon to write for a couple of hours, then dictated his copy over the phone to New York so he could spend the evening with Val.

A lot of his work resulted in three-column-inch filler pieces that didn't deserve more space than that. But some of his writing was lively, insightful and clear-headed.

As he burrowed deeper into the issue of Hollywood's labor warfare, he saw the studios' dilemma. However unsavory and costly the bribes they had been paying Geist, the status quo this larceny purchased at least kept their trains running on time. If they recognized Selkirk's Association of Studio Employees they would lose these advantages, but the widespread innuendos about the producers being in bed with the Mob would end and perhaps they could hold off state legislative watchdogs who had been salivating at the prospect of a big investigation of Hollywood for years.

Jack was secretly rooting for Selkirk because he was the underdog and the bold persona he had created made him good copy, and more practically because Jack didn't think he could win. He had two or three more interviews with him in the weeks after the "War at Warners," as the conflict we had driven into on Labor Day was now being called. One of his pieces—written after he joined Selkirk in the cockpit of a light plane he flew over an ASE picket line at Fox so he could lash out at the studios' collusion with Geist's "criminal enterprise" over loudspeakers tied to the wings—made the front page of the *San Francisco Examiner*, flagship of the Hearst news empire, and was syndicated in all the Hearst papers. Jack was proud enough of the lede to have it framed and sent back to Hyannis: "It was a Piper Cub, not a P-51 Mustang, and we were dropping leaflets, not bombs. But the payload was still incendiary and it made a direct hit in the newest front in the war being fought on the West Coast for control of the entertainment industry...."

One afternoon in late September, Selkirk stopped by the beach house with some documents concerning the IBTA's financial corruption that Jack had asked him about.

Jack invited him in along with his two longshoremen bodyguards, but Selkirk said, "No, they aren't housebroken yet," and made them wait on the porch.

He looked around appreciatively at the living room and its ocean view. "Wonder how the poor people are doing."

"Earned by the sweat of my brow," Jack pretended to be insulted.

Selkirk came close and made a show of examining his forehead: "I don't think so."

I pulled a beer out of the refrigerator and offered it to him.

Selkirk shook his head, "Better not. I've got to meet one of Zanuck's guys at Fox today—behind the scenes, of course—so I need to keep my wits about me."

Jack took the beer, opened it with a church key and forced it on him. Selkirk said, "Up the revolution!" then drained it in a single long guzzle. He toyed with the can while we sat at the kitchen table talking about subjects ranging from the upcoming World Series between the Tigers and the

Cubs, to Selkirk's growing up in Australia, which he described as "a cowboy movie with horses and guns and wide-open spaces just like yours, but without the one crucial element—the guys in white hats and black hats."

"No cowboys and Indians in the Soviet Union either," Jack needled him.

"No," Selkirk chuckled. "There it's Cossacks and serfs."

He was totally at ease with himself, virile and amiable—Jack's kind of guy.

After half an hour of chitchat, he stood and stretched, and did one jumping jack as a pun. "That one's for you," he said to Jack, then headed out the door

Jack followed him out and yelled, *"Dasvidaniya!"*

"See you in the funny papers," Selkirk replied as he drove off with his bodyguards stoically crammed into the back seat of his little Chevy convertible.

But as much as Jack enjoyed their badinage and admired Selkirk's talent for agitprop, he was under no illusions about his politics. While he wasn't as heavy-breathing an anticommunist as the Old Man, who had blandished J. Edgar Hoover so constantly about "the red menace" that the FBI chief appointed him a special agent for Massachusetts, Jack was also under no illusions about the USSR. I remember one prewar family discussion when the Old Man and Young Joe were having a slightly nonsensical argument over what was the worst thing Lenin had done—wiping out the kulaks or killing the Tsar and his family—and Jack spoke up with a certainty that silenced them both: "No, the worst thing Lenin ever did was Stalin."

He felt that the Party had played a particularly rancid role in the film world during the time of the Popular Front and was now trying to protect the gains it had made then. One of the pieces he wrote during this time was a profile of John Howard Lawson, onetime head of the Screen Writers Guild and still the CP's point man in Hollywood. In their interview, Jack got Lawson to acknowledge that some of "his" writers did an entire script just to be able to insert a few seconds of "progressive thinking" into a film, usually aiming for the most expensive scene so it wouldn't be cut. The piece quoted a comment that Lawson had carelessly made to Jack: "We tell our people that even if you've got a non-speaking role as a bystander wearing white flannels on a country club veranda, try to look decadent and to convey attitudes about the evils of the class system."

* * *

One morning when Jack finally got a go-ahead for an interview he'd been trying to set up for a couple of weeks with Paramount's legendary Adolph Zukor, I decided to go watch Val film a scene on location in Bunker Hill. During the war, the government had required the studios to shoot over half of each film outdoors to save on building materials for sets. That order had recently been rescinded and most movies were headed back inside, but Frank Talbert wanted some exteriors in the decaying area to help establish *Tomorrow's* dark mood.

The estates built in Bunker Hill forty years before by some of LA's early entrepreneurs had once been the crown jewels of the city's architecture—Queen Anne Victorians with gingerbread bric-a-brac and scrolled porches—but when the realities of city life got too close for comfort in the mid-Twenties, these men of wealth and power had moved on to Beverly Hills and other more protected venues. Their old mansions were remodeled into a warren of bleak one-room residency hotels and taxi-dance halls populated mainly by single men who congregated on the sidewalks like a surrendered army.

Bunker Hill's deterioration was the perfect metaphor for *Tomorrow's* themes of venality and betrayal. The voice-over of another noir shot there around the same time called it "once a choice place to live but now a place for people with no other choice."

Since rubbernecking at location shoots was a spectator sport in Southern California, Talbert had stationed a "director" with a megaphone and a cameraman and a dozen milling extras at an intersection a half mile away. While a crowd gathered there, he was free to set up his scene in which Glen Dobbs and Lily Fontaine are walking down Third Street and then, realizing that they are being followed by a pair of thugs, try to get away by running down a steep stone staircase to Hill Street below.

Because he was shooting their escape close up, Talbert asked Val and Payne to do the scene without stunt doubles. She immediately said yes. Payne seemed to have doubts; he joined her only to keep from looking like a weakling.

He was right to be concerned. Even though they started by taking it easy, the momentum built as they headed down the stairs made them lose control. At one point Payne stumbled and probably would have bounced his face on the stone if Val hadn't grabbed his arm and managed to keep him upright. Their out-of-control descent gave the scene exactly the authenticity Talbert had been hoping for, and by the time they reached the bottom of the stairs and the cameras stopped rolling he was smiling broadly. The crew cheered as Val flexed her biceps like a bodybuilder while Payne sulked on the sidelines.

When I left the shoot, she was still in high spirits and gave me a big smack on the cheek. But she showed up at the beach house a couple of hours later in a black mood. Jack wasn't home yet, and she paced around the living room for several minutes before dropping into one of the sofas.

I started to speak, but she gave me a fierce look that chiseled her face even more finely: "I am not talking about it, Billings. Don't ask me. It is too embarrassing."

So I kept silent, and after a moment she said, "Okay, I will tell you. After you left, Mr. Talbert takes me aside and says that he liked my bravery in going down stairs but there is a problem. I say what. He says that people who see this film will not accept that I am a person who can sell sex for money. He tells me that I appear too much the good Catholic girl for this to be believed and we must do something."

"What did you say?"

"I say I once was Catholic but now am a Jew."

"Then what?"

"He says that the Jew does not come through. I tell him that while it is true that I have no intimate knowledge of the life of the prostitute, this is because I don't need such knowledge. I say to him, 'That is why it's called *acting*.' But he shakes his head and says, 'You are acting but you do not convince.'"

"So what will you do?"

"Mr. Talbert says the studio has arranged for me to see a madame named Temple Rose and get some instruction. Can you believe it?"

As it happened, I'd seen a slightly facetious but very readable feature story in the *Los Angeles Examiner* a few days earlier about a woman named Ginger Adams, formerly one of Temple Rose's "pleasure girls," in the writer's inventive phrase, who had filed a lawsuit against her for wrongful termination. There was a large photo of Adams, a big-featured blonde with a beauty mark on her cheek, taken at the court proceeding, with a smaller inset shot of Rose herself, an attractive woman in her mid-thirties with large brown eyes, a retroussé nose and a sly vulpine smile.

According to the story's rambling background, Temple Rose's claim to fame was having noticed that prostitutes had been central figures in movies almost from the beginning—actresses such as Garbo and Janet Gaynor having gotten Oscar nominations for portraying them—so there might be a place for a high-class operation in which sex for hire had some of the chic and sizzle that it does on the big screen.

She recruited her team from among the hundreds of girls who came to Hollywood from small American towns every year, paid for a screen test, and then became sales clerks or waitresses while waiting for the call that never came. They could be presented as almost-starlets to Rose's customers, many of whom were associated with the film industry. Rose made telephone appointments for them with men whose backgrounds she checked before allowing them to have a "date" with a member of what the *Examiner* story called her "harem."

She didn't worry much about the LA cops because she paid them well and was herself, according to innuendoes in the *Examiner* piece, the long-time girlfriend of a locally famous vice sergeant she had gotten to know when he raided her office a couple of years earlier.

I offered Val some of these details on the way to the meeting with Rose, but she was not interested in having her slow burn extinguished.

The office was on the second floor of a tidy three-story office building on Melrose. It had a small reception area that led to a sitting room whose tufted oxblood leather sofas and dark oak had the look of a London gentlemen's club. As we entered, Rose was sitting at her desk waiting for us with a droll smile, her animated face framed by auburn hair done up in victory rolls. The desk was littered with found objects from the war—a tiny brass model of a P-38, a live .50 caliber shell, a folded fan with Japanese characters inked onto the wooden ribs. There was also a photo of an open-faced young man in Marine dress blues.

Rose took one look at Val and shook her head in wonder: "They said you were unbelievable, but oh my God, honey, you and I could make millions. Arab sheiks would come here on their chartered airplanes and get down on their hands and knees just to see you up close."

Val answered with a look so fierce that it caused Temple to laugh.

"Just saying, honey. Just saying. I know you've already got a job."

Val stayed silent with her eyes averted, so Temple kept talking: "They told me you need a little tutorial about the world's oldest profession. That's why you're here, no? To get a little better at creating the illusion?

"Okay, the first thing to know is that all my girls whistle while they work. You might have read about Ginger, but she was just mad at me because I found out she was a dope fiend and fired her. My girls don't do drugs. Anyway, they threw that suit of hers right out of court, so that's that."

Still trying to thaw Val, she continued her patter: "By the way, that name they gave you, Delphine LaReve, isn't going to win any awards for originality. But no matter. Once people get a look at you they won't care what your name is. That's the great thing about Hollywood anyway. You can change all the things you carry with you when you get here—your history, your face, and also the name your parents saddled you with. Just toss that stodgy old name in the wastebasket and pick another one that sounds better."

She pulled a book out of the case above her desk. "This is *Sanctuary* by Billy Faulkner." She flashed its dust jacket and extracted an autographed five-by-seven photo showing the author sitting in a poolside chaise wearing a swimsuit, a sleeveless undershirt and his Mississippi clodhoppers, pounding on a portable typewriter balanced on his knees.

"When I first got out here in 1939, I was Rosalie Kazak from Omaha. I came because I loved movies. Billy came because he bounced a check for three dollars at an Oxford liquor store and didn't want that to happen again. When I met him, he had just done his first script for Howard Hawks—*Today We Live*. Sometimes he'd come over to my place, all very platonic, with a flask of bourbon and his pipe and sit around griping about Hollywood, which he still to this day calls 'the plastic asshole of the world,' though he's done well enough for himself that he now has a place over at the Garden of Allah.

"One day not long after we first met, he looks at me and drawls, 'Kazak… now that's awfully Central European, don't you think? Calls up a picture of people standing around on street corners wondering who's going to hand out the bread and when the secret police will arrive. And while I suppose there's some virtue in having a palindrome for a name, if I was you I'd try for something a little more euphonious and easier on the imagination.'

"So he gave me a copy of this book and told me that the girl in it is named Temple and that this is a good name even though she's not a good girl, and that I might be more successful if my name was Temple Rose, say, instead of Rosalie Kazak. I made the change the next day and it worked. Voila! A new me!"

She must have seen a dubiousness on my face I didn't realize it was conveying. "You think that someone like me couldn't possibly know a great writer like Billy? If so, that's because you don't know Hollywood. This is a small town inside a big city. Everyone is connected. The big-timers to the minor-leaguers; the makers to the takers; the evil ones to the good—what few of them there are. Hollywood has its kings and queens, but it also catches all kinds of common people in its spider web."

She then turned to Val: "You're not going to find any stuffy little back rooms with daybeds here, honey. Just me and my desk and a couple of filing cabinets and a telephone. Here's how it works. A customer—let's call him John—rings me and says, 'You have any recommendation about what I should read tonight?' I say, 'Oh yes, John, several good ones. But I know from your reading history that there's one in particular you might like. It has an interesting heroine who engages in some surprising plot twists. She's about five foot six, a statuesque brunette with a creative personality.'"

I couldn't help laughing, causing Val to stare daggers at me.

Temple continued, "John will ask where he can get a copy and I'll say, 'There's a bookstore at the corner of Sunset and Vine and you can find it there right in the window. You'll recognize it by the cover showing the heroine looking very alluring in a lavender dress and a mink stole. You should be there by 9:30 because that's when the store closes.'"

Val had her question ready before Temple finished: "Why do they do it, these girls?"

"No ladies of the night in Italy?"

"There is war there," Val replied. "War makes people very desperate."

"Desperation is always the fall guy," Temple swiveled her chair back and forth in semicircles. "People like to think that girls like mine have this job because of the father who died in an industrial accident and left the family penniless; or because of the uncle who shows up for dinner and a piece every night; or the beloved boyfriend who turns out to be a fancy man in disguise.

"Such things happen. Tragedy is in the air we breathe. But it's also just a fact of life that some girls like to file index cards for a living and some girls would rather fuck."

Seeing Val flinch, she pulled an oversized scrapbook from a drawer and set it on the desk, riffling the pages to show closeups of her girls. The photos were hand-colored and looked like high school graduation portraits—blondes, redheads, brunettes—a wholesome fantasy world of possibilities. Associated with each was a ledger page filled with columns of numbers.

"All the girls get a Wasserman every month, and we keep them right here on file for customer viewing. They're all clean as chrome and doing pretty well for themselves. Here are the financial records for 'Amber,' for instance. You can see how much she has made over the last year and see too that she has kept a good chunk of it. She has a nice little Plymouth coupe, a one-bedroom apartment just off La Brea, and $800 in a savings account. And she's taking some night classes. Might even have read one of Billy's books, who knows?"

A man wearing a wide-shouldered suit and a fedora whose snap brim shadowed his face entered the office without waiting for a response to his brief knock.

Temple walked over to him and took off his hat, holding it with her fingertips while giving him what began as a chaste peck and ended with her darting a saurian tongue over his top lip.

"This is Jimmy," she presented him to us. "Does he have cop written all over him or what?"

"Jim Adcock," he shook my hand and gave a little bow to Val.

Then he looked at Temple Rose: "I had a minute and I thought you might be free for a quick coffee. I can come back later."

"I'll just be a little bit longer." She took Val's hand and led her toward the sitting room. "Why don't you boys stay here and spit and shuffle your feet and tell lies about your sex lives while we ladies finish our conversation in private?"

When the women had taken seats in the adjoining room, Adcock perched on the corner of the desk. "Temple's really something, isn't she? And I've got to say your girl is an absolute sweet potato."

"She's not mine. I'm just the escort. Warners sent her over to get some advice on preparing for a part."

"Nobody better than Temple to help if it involves the man-woman thing," the cop said as a doting smile pacified his craggy face: "We met when Vice got an order to come over here to try and bust her. But look around you: it's clean as a stationery store in here. We came up with nothing. I was ready to leave. But one of my guys figures he'd at least get a little feel for his trouble so he tells her he's sorry, but he's got to pat her down. As he knelt to do her legs he started running his hand up the inside of one of her thighs. She gave him this cutting look and said, 'I'd be careful up there if I were you. It bites.' That cinched the deal for me."

We had chatted for about twenty minutes when the women emerged from the sitting room, their arms hooked, Temple continuing their conversation: "... so while we have what you might call 'tricks of the trade,' the basic fact to understand about this job—a fact all my girls understand very well—is that men simply can't help themselves. Utterly incapable of restraint. I've always wondered if the male black widow thinks it was worth it when the female is biting his head off after they finish."

Temple noticed that the photo on her desk had caught Val's eye. "My little brother Kenny." She gnawed at her bottom lip. "He was killed at Okinawa."

Tears began spilling out of Val's eyes.

"You too?" Temple asked.

Val nodded, unable to speak.

"A brother?"

Val nodded again, her chin quivering.

Temple reached for her and held her in a tight hug before pushing her back at arm's length to look deeply into her face. "I'd like to see you again. We wouldn't talk about business. We could just talk about life. Life with a capital L. Would that be all right with you?"

Still teary, Val nodded. Temple kissed the tips of her index and middle fingers and brushed them over Val's cheek as we headed out.

On the way home, Val was chatty and at ease. She wasn't ready to try to get inside a high-class call girl's skin, at least not the way the method actors who arrived in Hollywood a few years later probably would have done. But she was more confident about playing the part, and gave a sultry smile when we turned onto our driveway.

"Mr. Talbert will be very surprised by the terrible things of sex Lily Fontaine will now do."

ELEVEN

For a week or so, when Hollywood's labor war seemed to be drowsing, Jack and I made the long drive to Warners every day to pick Val up at the end of shooting. Several times I thought I saw the same black Buick Roadmaster dodging in and out of traffic behind us.

"We're being tailed." I twisted around to look out the back window when I saw it again one afternoon. "I'm sure of it. That Roadmaster is back there again."

"I don't see anything." Jack gave a blasé look in his side mirror. "It's probably just your imagination, which might be more hyperactive than usual because of excessive seminal retention. There are a lot of Buicks on the road."

"Maybe it's Fortunato."

"Even if it is, which I doubt, Val and I are both free and white and twenty-one." He was exasperated now. "We're on a pretty good run and I'd appreciate it if you didn't fuck things up with your dire imaginings."

He must have felt bad because a few minutes later he told me that he'd rented a cabin in the San Bernardino Mountains for the weekend and I was invited.

"Myself, I'd prefer a twosome, but Val wants you to come with us. She's worried that if we leave you alone again, you might decide to drop the electric heater in the bathtub. You can reprise your immortal role of Billings the chauffeur."

"At your service, Sir."

They had already taken off for a couple of weekends in Palm Springs, just the two of them, staying at the Hotel Del Tahquitz, which was run by Fritzi Ridgeway, an old-timer who had starred in silent horse operas with William S. Hart and had a bit role in *Tomorrow.*

Jack liked it there, particularly after he ran into Bob Hope one morning while buying a donut. Val liked it too, but wanted to experience something more "primitive."

"She's all fired up because she thinks this cabin will be like the Alaskan shack where Charlie Chaplin eats his shoes in *The Gold Rush*," Jack said. "She says that all Italians love that movie."

On the drive up into the mountains he congratulated himself that the place had cost him only seven dollars for the weekend, but when we got our first look at the cabin at the end of a rough dirt road, I heard him mutter, "I paid too much."

It had one large room with two iron-frame beds and one naked light bulb dangling from the ceiling. The kitchen consisted of a sink with a pump handle and a small stove running off a propane tank standing near a gamy outhouse in the back yard.

Val bounced on one of the beds as Jack inspected the corners of the room for scorpions. By the time we had unpacked, I noticed that the two of them were locking eyes.

"There are lots of great hiking trails," Jack said to me.

"You mean here's-your-hat-what's-your-hurry?"

"Something like that."

I put an apple in my pocket, filled my thermos with what we had been told was pristine spring water and took off.

Indian summer was on the warpath in early October, even at three thousand feet. Hiking up a steep path, I noticed that the forest floor was littered with deadfall and mentally audited the area for fire trails.

After about half a mile I crossed over the ridgeline and followed the trail down the other side of the mountain. Eventually I came to a shaded spot where a large pine had been felled sometime in the past and now lay in a decomposing column with tumors of amber resin beading up on the bark. Its stump served me as a resting place. A lizard skittered in the leaves near my feet. I heard a shrill piping overhead and looked up to see a hawk balancing on the thermals like a tightrope walker.

I had brought a letter from Kick that arrived a couple of days earlier to read again. She had taken a flat in London after feeling like "a ghost" for the last few months at Chatsworth, the ancestral Cavendish estate, where the wife of her late husband's younger brother had now succeeded her as the Duchess-in-waiting of Devonshire and would someday be in charge of the manor's 126 rooms.

"Today was wonderfully warm for a change," she wrote in her back-handed scrawl. "I felt like a butterfly coming out of the chrysalis and decided to flutter off for some shopping. I bought the most cunning yellow sleeveless dress and put it on right there in the shop and then wore it all around Kensington for the next couple of hours. I felt like I was thawing after being frozen for the past year. Billy wouldn't mind, would he, Lemmy?"

I sensed that she had begun the next leg of her journey, although I couldn't have imagined that over the next couple of years she would become a leading member of the London smart set, featured in a picture spread in *Life* magazine that showed her heavily made up in a shimmering blue cocktail dress, drinking a sidecar and smoking a Gauloise in a holder as long as the one Audrey Hepburn later waved around in *Breakfast at Tiffany's.*

Nor that she would embark on an affair with Lord Peter Fitzwilliam, Catholic but divorced, who, at a net worth of some 45 million pounds, was one of the richest men in England, although for Kick his attraction was his person, not his money. Shortly after they began seeing each other, she called me over the quavering transcontinental line and talked for a long time in a jaded, slightly drunken voice I'd never heard from her before about how she had been such a fumbling sexual naïf with Billy that when he asked her for a blowjob on their wedding night she had actually held his cock in her hand and blown on it. But now, she said, she had learned what love was: "repeated doses of Peter." The pun on Freud was a sign of how far she had come.

But all that, and her troubling death with her priapic lord, was still in the future, and I sat there in the San Bernardino Mountains imagining her incandescent innocence as she walked past the Victoria and Albert in her new yellow dress.

I sensed rather than heard someone behind me and turned to see Niccolo Fortunato leaning against a tree about fifteen feet from where I was sitting.

This close he was an artifact: the blank eyes and long nose pointing down at a strong chin dimpled at its center came from Roman portrait sculpture; the features couldn't have been more immobile if the face had been injected with curare. He was younger than I had assumed from the glimpse we'd gotten at the Warners party and later on his front porch—perhaps late forties; of middle height but seeming taller because of his lean dancer's body. He was dressed in corduroy pants and a shooting jacket, despite the heat, and projected a languid *bella figura* as well as a coiled menace.

Watching me intently with raptor's eyes, he picked a needle off a pine tree, stuck it in his mouth like a toothpick, and let the silence press down. Jack's father got leverage by doing the same thing, and the fugitive thought flitted through my mind that the two men might be similar in other ways as well.

"Do you have a black Buick?" I blurted out.

"Yes." His smile looked like dental pain. "You have seen me following you?"

I nodded.

"I haven't been hiding."

I couldn't figure out anything to say, and sat there dreading what was next.

"I am concerned for my daughter. She is not a little girl any longer and I can't tell her what to do, but she doesn't know much about this country. In spite of her experiences, she believes that people are good and life is fair. But I know that evil is an active principle in the world and would have made sure she understood this too if things had been better between us."

There was a rough candor in how he spoke as well as what he said. He struck me as a man who prided himself on not using emollients when he talked about himself.

"I'm not very trusting, which is why I keep an eye on your friend and you too, since you seem to be his Siamese."

He took the pine needle out of his mouth and studied it. "Even if you don't see me, I'm probably nearby, looking for one sign of insincerity, even one small indication that Valentina might suffer as a result of the attention your friend gives her."

"Jack would never hurt her," I stammered. "He loves her."

"Love," he mouthed the word as if tasting for an expiration date. "We'll see. Anything's possible, but I know something of his family. These are careless people. They use others and allow them to get hurt in the damage they create as they try to attain their objectives."

I looked away, but he saw what I was thinking.

"Even those of us who don't always live inside the lines of the law have principles in our private lives. You shouldn't think of this as a contradiction."

In the silence that followed, I heard the hawk again.

Finally he asked, "What do you know about Valentina's past?"

"Just the little she told us."

"Did she tell you about being taken by the Germans?"

"Yes."

"And about how she got out of her prison camp?"

"She said you came in shooting."

"I ask only because I want to make sure that you and your friend know what she has experienced and how far I will go for her."

"She hadn't heard from you in twenty years," I frightened myself by saying this.

He blinked rapidly. "I'm not in the habit of explaining myself, especially to strangers, but it is true that perhaps I was not the kind of father I should have been. But I'm also not the kind of man who makes the same mistake twice. Know for certain that I watch over her now."

I thought he had finished, but he didn't move.

"My friend Jack would like to get to know you," I finally said.

"*Know* me." His look was like one I'd seen on Val's face when she was secretly amused. "Yes, my daughter has told me he mentioned this. I said to her I would meet him only when I was sure that the two of us would not find ourselves at odds."

"She put it differently to me—that you didn't want to meet him before you were sure that you wouldn't have to hurt him."

"I did say that," he admitted. "Like I told you, I do not have a good feeling about this friendship between them."

"But why?"

"Given all the factors, it seems unlikely that he can benefit her. Leave it at that."

It was quiet for too long. I knew he was playing a game of chicken with me, but I couldn't keep from breaking the silence first: "Jack greatly admires what you did in the war."

When he replied, the words were as devoid of emotion as his facial features. "I don't ask to be seen as a patriot. I made contact with the people in Washington for one reason only: I needed a way to get into Italy and connect with the right people there so I could do what was necessary for my daughter. I am very far from what you'd call an idealist."

He glanced down at the ground. "Being able to kill people without wondering if they deserve it: that's the only good thing about war. Those I've killed ignore me during the day. It is only at night that they appear. This does not especially bother me. I almost look forward to seeing them."

Then he came up so close to me that I could see the enlarged pores on his nose and smell the wintergreen tang of his breath. "Did Valentina tell you that I promised her she would be safe in America?"

I nodded as sweat slid down my sides.

"Even people who are not my friends say I keep my promises."

His eyes released me and he stood back. "You don't say much. Maybe you're better at listening than talking. I hope so because I want you to tell your friend what has been said just now. This is serious business."

He never raised his voice. He had a blemished dignity, even a certain finish, I thought, until he abruptly rattled off a burst of Italian: *"E che non si cazzeggia piu!"* He translated as if for himself, "We're not fucking around here!"

He brushed off the front of his jacket, and just before walking away he slowly raised his right hand, made the fingers into a gun, smiled at me, cocked the hammer of his thumb and let it fall as he mouthed the word *Bang.*

* * *

When I arrived back at the cabin in a flop sweat, Jack was sitting at the kitchen table with a surfeited look. Val was on her side facing away in one of the beds, the sensuous curve of her rump edified by a flimsy après-sex negligee. She sat up and pulled a comforter over herself, and said she would cook dinner if we got bread and lettuce for a salad.

I wanted to drive to the little store we'd seen on the way in, but Jack said he preferred to take in the good mountain air. For the first quarter mile down the dirt road, both of us were quiet, for different reasons.

Finally I told him, "I saw Fortunato."

That stopped him in his tracks. "You're shitting me."

"No, it's true. He followed me on my hike. I was as close to him as I am to you right now."

"Jesus!"

"He admitted he's the one who's been following us all this time. The dark Buick we've been seeing is his."

"How long did you talk to him?"

"Several minutes."

"What about?"

"About Val."

"And…"

"And about you and your situation with her. He said to tell you that he's got his eye on you and he's ready to go to the mat if anything goes wrong. He even talked about how he's not bothered when the ghosts of the people he's killed come to visit him."

Jack blanched, and then started forward again. "Like I told you, I'm happy, Val's happy. There's no problem here. If I could meet him, I'd take care of all the doubts."

"He also said that he's not fucking around. When someone like Fortunato says that, you need to listen."

"Just gangster melodrama."

"I think he meant exactly what he said."

But Jack had already put my caution behind him.

Trekking back up the road with our supplies, he was sweating heavily and I could tell that he regretted his decision to walk instead of drive.

Val came to the cabin door to receive the groceries with her hair gathered in an up-do and a fey look on her face. She appeared to be wearing nothing but an apron and high heels. "My gift to you for walking all the way up from the market," she pointed down at herself. "Now we have some fun."

She turned and walked across the room to the tiny stove, naked in the back except for the apron's thin drawstring around her waist. Her perfect ass cheeks jiggled as she shook a pan on the fire while prancing to silent music.

We were both mesmerized by the spectacle. Finally she turned to present a steaming pan with a magician's flourish: *"Ecco! Pasta all'amatriciana!"*

She put it on the table and then looked at Jack and began singing "How Are Things in Glocca Morra" in a quavering soprano, with stylized hand movements and drawn-out syllables that made the song into a sort of homemade Neapolitan bel canto.

When she had finished a verse, she sensed that something was bothering me. "Why are you sad, Billings?"

"Don't mind him," Jack said before I could reply. "It's that time of month."

I smelled Val's distinctive bouquet when she came over to ruffle my hair: "No matter what it is, Billings, good food cures all of our maladies."

Then she pointed at the pasta and commanded, *"Mangia!"*

* * *

After dinner I drove the Zephyr home, leaving the two of them to spend the night at the cabin and return the next morning in a car that Warners had agreed to send. I replayed the encounter with Fortunato over and over during the nearly three hours it took to get to Malibu in heavy Sunday evening traffic.

By the time I arrived, a sudden squall had come up off the ocean and the wind was howling like a Greek chorus. Inside the beach house it smacked the bay window every few seconds like a fist. I secured all the doors and windows and then cowered on the sofa as I had done after seeing Mischa Auer in *The Monster Walks* when I was a kid. And like then, I suddenly panicked at the thought that I had not locked the monster out, but inside with me.

I slept badly, and the next morning I was wakened by the sound of the front doorknob being turned aggressively, followed by a loud pounding on the door. Rehearsing the hell I was going to give Jack about forgetting his key again, I got up and unlocked the door. Standing there, impatient as always to put his thumbprint on reality, was Joseph P. Kennedy himself!

New York

*

March 30, 1981

TWELVE

When we were at Choate, I sometimes tried to tell Jack about my dreams as I was just waking up. He always interrupted me with a huge histrionic yawn that concluded with a loud smacking of his mouth. Pulling the covers up over his head, he'd say in a muffled voice, "What could be more boring than someone else's dreams? Spare me. I'd rather hear about your bowel movements."

Maybe he would feel differently now if I could tell him about the dreams I've had lately—one blending into another; all labyrinthine and all drawing their jumbled dreamwork from the high points of our lives together.

Last night, the main feature was about the Cotton Club. The first time we actually went there, Jack and I were college freshmen; Kick was still at Sacred Heart but we snuck her there too. We all got dressed up in evening wear and had a hell of a time. Later on, the Old Man found out about it and ripped Jack and me royally. But it was worth his wrath. Kick was at the apex of her bloom, wearing her first off-the-shoulder dress. She had her hair in an updo showing the nape of her neck, a spot every man in the place, including the wary Negroes, would have given his life to nuzzle. She was laughing and tossing her head in that effulgent way of hers that added so much wattage to a room.

On that actual visit, Cab Calloway, wearing his vanilla tails and high-stepping like a drum major, strutted over to our front-row table in the middle of "St. James Infirmary," bringing the spotlight with him, and jabbed a long finger down at Kick while he chanted, "Hydee-Hdyee-Hydee-Ho..."

My dream, of course, mangled this and other facts and recombined them into a menacing dada. Calloway was dressed like Chiquita Banana. Val joined Jack and Kick in a conga line behind him while I stood apart, nervous because I realized something they didn't: that the people at the Cotton Club were not the unduly polite conked-hair Negroes we actually encountered back then, but the resentful militants of a later time, wearing shades and dark watch caps over their Afros and shooting hard looks at all the whites.

One of them, a Mister T lookalike with a heavy noose of gold chains around his neck, loomed up in front of me to stab a big index finger in my face: "Whatchu lookin at, boy?"

As I cowered, Jack congaed by and saw my predicament. "Don't worry about these jitterbugs, Lemuel," he called out in a lighthearted way. "They won't hurt you. They know that Bobby and I are going to set them free."

The dream ended abruptly as Kick, with one foot bare and a red dancing pump on the other, stepped up portable stairs in a shimmering blue cocktail dress with sequins like fish scales and entered a gleaming twin-engine airplane that had taxied up to the club's entrance on 142nd Street. I screamed to her that she was in danger, but she ignored me. The plane took off with a midget pilot at the controls and got smaller and smaller until it was a tiny aluminum coffin in the sky.

I woke with a jackhammering headache and knew immediately that I would spend another day feeling that my charge was off; another day dealing with the revolution of inanimate objects, as forks and pencils seemed to jump out of my hands by their own volition and skate over tabletops just beyond my reach; another day of uncertainty about whether the relationship between cause and effect still held; another day of being pathetically grateful when I found my keys and wallet right where I had left them.

I could imagine what Jack would say if he were still here: "You need to take a Midol and get control of your emotions."

In fact, I emitted blood sometime during the tangled night, from my nose. When I saw a copper-smelling Rorschach on the pillowcase, I felt once again that death is in my vicinity—hanging around more than stalking—although I know that when we finally make contact it will not be the operatic finale that it was for all the others, but something far more mundane, like barking your shin on an unseen piece of furniture when you get up to pee in the middle of the night.

I went to the bathroom and cleaned myself up, then came back to the bed and sank into a hospital sleep for an hour or so while the volume gradually increased on the street sounds of the Upper East Side—the sirens and horns and the construction noise blending in the dissonant chamber music of urban life. Still carried along by the deep currents of the dream, I thought about all of them, my people, all gone in their violent moments but all still alive for me.

* * *

I hold Daniel Goldman partly responsible for the dreams as well as this penny-ante existential dread I've been feeling. About ten days ago, I received a manila envelope from him with some Xeroxed pages and a note saying they had been culled from what he grandly called the "Joseph P. Kennedy Papers." Not knowing how ruthlessly this hoard was scoured and sanitized by the family, he probably doesn't realize that this will always be the greatest story never told.

"I thought the enclosed might interest you," Goldman wrote, "and perhaps jog your memory and even encourage you to tell stories into the tape machine I left with you." Then came the threat: "I'll be calling soon so we can discuss all this."

The Xeroxes have been on my nightstand since then. The first one—a Cartier-Bressonesque photo of Jack, Val and me completing a ride on the Griffith Park Merry-Go-Round—causes total recall. We had scrambled for our favorite mounts as the previous ride was gliding to a stop. Jack climbed onto a valiant black stallion with flaring red nostrils. Val chose a more feminine palomino in front of him. I trailed behind both of them as their Sancho Panza on a small, squat horse with a drab hide.

"Let's catch her," Jack turned to yell to me as the calliope music started up and the platform began to move. He whipped his horse across the withers with the reins.

"You'll never," Val said over her shoulder. Posted elegantly in her steed's stationary stirrups, she looked like a model advertising the equestrian life.

The merry-go-round reached cruising speed, and at each revolution I focused momentarily on the spectators in the sitting area. On a couple of turns, I saw a figure standing on a bench with a camera pointed at us, largely concealing a disconcerting face. The image he snapped that ended up in the so-called Joseph P. Kennedy Papers captures our dismount, and the essence of our position in the universe just then.

In the photograph, Val is stepping off the platform, suspended in midair with one hand grasping at empty space, appearing uncertain where or how she will land. I've just dropped the bridle of my horse and I'm moving forward on the apron of the carousel as if to stabilize her. Jack is standing next to his steed, smiling the smile of someone who has not yet heard the bad news.

Goldman had copied the back side of the photo too, showing the block-printed words, "Here she is." And below that, "Beaufort 10/6/45."

The next Xerox was of a letter dated October 13, 1945, on the official letterhead of the FBI. The typed "Dear Mr. Kennedy" had been struck out with "Dear Joseph" handwritten over it in ink:

> Receipt is acknowledged of your air mail of October 9.
>
> Thank you for your views on the labor situation in Hollywood and thank you too for the actions you have already taken during your brief time in Southern California to convince the men who count there to do everything in their power to oppose the advance of communism in the entertainment industry.
>
> I am confident that the American people would be as appreciative as I am if they knew of the good work you were doing behind the scenes in getting the studios to act with one patriotic voice.
>
> If fellow-traveling unions are to be allowed to pull the strings in Hollywood, it is inevitable that moving pictures, which appeal so intimately to so many millions, will speak to these millions in the secret code of the Politburo. This is not something we can allow to happen.
>
> On the other matter you mention, I certainly understand your concern about how actions your son John has undertaken there might affect his future. I agree with you that this man Fortunato is thoroughly unsavory and that connections with him would have a negative effect on a young man's ambition to participate in public life. Such a man debases our society and is not worthy of U.S. citizenship, which in any case is not his by right of birth. I also agree with you that if Fortunato continues his criminal activities it should be in the country from which he came rather than in our own great nation.

As you may know, I do not enjoy the same intimate relationship with the current administration that I did with FDR. Nonetheless, I have approached presidential aide Gen. Harry Vaughan, and he has agreed to bring up the question of Fortunato's deportation with President Truman at an appropriate time. I will keep you advised of what develops.

In the meantime I wish you continued good luck in your work, whose success is vital to every American.

—Sincerely yours,

The signature "Edgar" cut through the typed "John Edgar Hoover."

Thinking it would put pressure on me, I guess, Goldman had highlighted "Fortunato" and "your son John," the yellow marker pen connecting these words and making them into questions. But of course he didn't understand the only real epiphany of this sordid letter: that the Old Man was moving against Fortunato at the exact moment he was making the vile bargain with Val that she thought would protect her father. She believed the Old Man when he told her that he could have Fortunato sent back to Calabria with the snap of his finger. She was almost right.

The third Xerox, different from the other two in time, place and substance, was of an antique snapshot with serrated edges, taken with a Brownie, that showed Jack and me standing on the bank of the Spree River crossing our streams of urination in a perfect X during the 1937 trip we took to Europe. We were smiling broadly, not only from the bladder relief, but also because we'd escaped getting arrested at a stop in Berlin less than an hour earlier for yelling "Hell, Hitler" at a Nazi Youth rally where everyone else was robotically chanting "Heil."

This photo had been taken by a hearty burgher who'd stopped his bicycle on a spillway above us when he saw what we were doing. Its distorted perspective made it look like our penises were touching. The bicyclist would probably have turned the roll of film over to the Gestapo as evidence of our degenerate antisocial activities if Jack hadn't offered him a five-dollar bill for it. That this photo should eventually have come into the Old Man's possession is a mystery but not a surprise.

At first I thought that Goldman had included it with the other two as a little gift of nostalgia for me. But then I read the scrawled P.S. at the bottom of his note: "I must tell you that I find it genuinely moving, this love of yours for the President," and understood that *love* had invisible italics that made it a shot across my bow. This Xeroxed page might actually have been the real reason he had made contact—a little graymail to make me more willing to "just tell stories."

I hope it will not disappoint him to know that he is hardly the first to launch such innuendoes and that I am very far removed from giving a shit. As early as our first year at Choate, Headmaster St. John had become concerned enough about my relationship with Jack to peremptorily order me one afternoon to the infirmary, where the school doctor performed what at the time was the gold-standard test by inserting a tongue depressor deep in my throat. He had to report back to the headmaster that I gagged, unlike certifiable queers.

Others lobbed insults over the years—among them, Ethel's psychopathic brother George Skakel, who once screamed at me unprovoked in the middle of an extended family dinner to stay away from his sons, and the ever-awful Gore Vidal, who at a 1976 cultural event in D.C. introduced me to a couple of congressmen as "the aging Queen of Camelot."

But strangely, the Kennedys themselves never wondered—not about me and not about me and Jack, which suggests that for all their power and glory they always remained at heart peasants from County Wexford, who, having reluctantly acknowledged that the world is round, refused to believe that it also has peaks and valleys.

They were almost right. The love of my life was a platonic love except for once. Toward the end of spring term of our first year as roommates, after I had established myself as sidekick everlasting, Jack had another bout of his chronic illness, this one coming on so fast and violently that I thought he would die. Joe and Rose, who had been through countless of these crises, didn't take this one seriously until I called them a third time in a full panic and said that they'd better come quick because his fever had spiked to 104 and the Choate doctor had no idea what to do.

Jack had already gone past his usual giddy defiance of death, past the fast talking of high fever, past the deep full-body ache and joint freeze that made him keen with pain. This time it seemed that he had surrendered to his sickness and was allowing it to carry him away.

Barely aware that I was keeping watch, he was looking straight up at the ceiling, holding up his quivering hands like a baby fearful of being rolled over.

"I'm going away from here," he whispered as his eyes flipped white.

Then: "Please, God; please, God; please, God," the words straddling the line between prayer and blasphemy.

And then, dimly sensing I was with him: "Oh, Lemmy. Please. Help. Me."

But how? I'd already given him alcohol rubs to keep him from burning up and forced him to drink several cups of hot water laced with minced garlic, my mother's no-fail remedy.

Desperate to keep him from passing into the next world, I pulled back the sheet and was hit by heat from the blast furnace of his body. His sternum poked up pathetically through his parchment skin. He was panting like a dog. I began to cry. And then, not knowing what else to do, I took his silky boyhood in my hand and raised him from the dead.

Did I save him? Or exploit him? Or both? Did this act, so much more consequential in its implications then than now, even matter?

These are questions of fifty years' duration that have never been answered. But this much I know: After the shivering spasm and involuntary bucking of his body, his tremulousness abated and he seemed to cool a bit and finally fell into a sleep that was troubled but not the coma I had feared. He was able to speak semicoherently to his parents when they arrived two hours later with a specialist from Boston University's School of Medicine.

This fugitive moment was incinerated in his fever; Jack never talked about it afterward and neither did I. There was never any need. As long as he was around, the role of accomplice kept me well sublimated. It wasn't until the years after Dallas, when I was so alone and trapped in the past tense and so consumed by fantasies of Niccolo Fortunato's possible involvement in Jack's death and even Kick's, that I sometimes found myself in the stalls of public restrooms looking down at two sets of pants and underwear puddled on the floor while making what Jack himself no doubt would have called the beast with four feet.

The Kennedys were oblivious to this new self of mine. I continued to be a fixture at their ceremonial occasions and functioned as their institutional memory in matters particularly involving Jack's early years. Only Jackie seemed to notice. She once approached me, post-Onassis, at some social function and initiated a conversation that ended with her saying elliptically in that breathy voice of hers, "It isn't what you do that's important, but what people see you as doing. So be careful, dear Lem, and be discreet."

We both knew what she was talking about.

“Discreet,” I said to her with a reassuring smile, “is my middle name.”

And so it has been until now.

Hollywood

✳

October/November 1945

THIRTEEN

When the Old Man turned up at the door of the Malibu beach house while Jack and Val were still away at the mountain cabin, he pushed his way right into the living room, not bothering with a salutation. He wore an overcoat despite the early promise of heat, and the brim of his hat was jammed low on his head, bending his ears downward like Elmer Fudd's. Behind him was his henchman Molly Maguire, with the look on his face of someone listening to music no one else could hear.

Arriving a few seconds later was a thin, slightly stooped man wearing an ice cream suit with black and white spectator shoes. Even in his natty attire, this man seemed an animated aberration. His gait was so loose-jointed that he appeared to ooze rather than walk. His face looked like it had been assembled from a box of spare parts: large doggy ears; a liver-colored birthmark splattered expressionistically on his jaw and neck; discolored front teeth resting on his lower lip. Frog eyes provided the finishing touch, the right one looking piercingly ahead while the left one wandered lazily to the side.

"This is Beaufort." The Old Man saw me staring at him. "He used to work for Edgar and now he works for me. He's got a little bit of wall-eye, but we don't care..."

At this point, the strange-looking man sidled up and issued a correction, his words arriving on a thick cloud of juniper: "Divergent strabismus, actually. Wall-eye is a misnomer."

"...because we don't judge a book by its cover," the Old Man ignored him. "Beaufort knows his stuff. He has a good attitude—can-do; one of those guys who believe that the glass is always half full."

"Right, because he drank the rest of it," I heard Molly Maguire mutter.

The Old Man shot him a warning look before addressing me: "Where the hell is Jack?"

"He'll be back soon," I replied.

"I asked you where he is, not for his schedule." He turned away irritably and went into the bedroom to begin scrabbling ratlike through Jack's personal belongings.

"Howya?" Molly elbowed me in the ribs as he moved to station himself at the doorway with his arms folded over his chest, like one of those Secret Service men in the Kennedy future.

"Working away," I repeated a phrase I'd heard him use dozens of times himself.

"Working away." He nodded agreeably. "Aren't we all."

Molly was brawny but balanced, looking like he could throw a hard right cross while doing a soft-shoe. A ringer for the character actor Victor McLaglen, he was bald on top but had a healthy fringe above the ear; a jaw that looked like it could break a fist; and a tuneful Irish voice. The skin on his hands was rough as stucco.

"How's Bridget?" I asked.

"Fierce, as always," he chuckled.

Bridget was the name Molly had given the straight razor that nested like a viper in the side pocket of his jacket. Jack and his brothers liked to tell about the time he turned her loose on some petty criminal who'd made the mistake of threatening the Old Man on a Boston street corner. Striking in a blur, they said, Bridget left this man with a hand clapped over the blood spurting from the side of his head as he searched for his severed ear, which lay like a dead frog on the sidewalk.

Molly's given name was Francis Aloysius Maguire. According to his legend, he had been brought to Boston from Ireland as a child sometime before the turn of the century by his widowed mother, who died soon after their arrival. He was fifteen and living with distant relatives and sometimes on his own when the Old Man happened to be walking through Roxbury one day and saw him hitting ferocious line drives in a sandlot baseball game.

Big Joe had just entered Harvard and was desperate to make the team as first baseman, so he hired this raw-boned boy to help him with his swing, in return giving him food and space for a bedroll on the floor of his dorm room and soon after paying him a few dollars a month to provide what he called "beef on the hoof." Because of Francis Maguire's anarchic fearlessness, Mr. Kennedy had at some point early in their lifetime relationship rechristened him "Molly" after the Molly Maguires, the secret society of Irish immigrant workers that had launched a terror campaign against the predatory mine owners in the Pennsylvania coal fields during the nineteenth century.

It was a challenge for Molly to sign his name; he first had to inscribe small circles over the paper like someone warming up. But he had a keen intelligence and was a determined collector of arcane facts and phrases, including some in French and Latin. He could bring Big Joe to tears with his sentimental blarney and send him into knee-slapping, gasping paroxysms of laughter with his corny jokes. (A shady-looking guy comes up to a businessman in Times Square, opens his jacket, flashes some photos and says, "You want to buy some pornography?" The businessman says no. "Why not?" asks the shady-looking guy. The businessman says, "Because I don't own a pornograph.")

I'd first met Molly at Palm Beach when I came down from Princeton one spring break to be with Jack. The afternoon I arrived, he and the Old Man were in the "bullpen," a private males-only enclosure off the family pool. Their noses were white with zinc oxide, their chest hairs swirled with cocoa butter, and their naked groins draped carelessly with white gym towels.

Jack and I stood there in the shadows watching them for a minute. Then he got that glint in his eye and whispered, "I'll give you a fin if you take off your clothes and walk in there and do 'I'm No Angel.'"

Five dollars was real money for a scholarship boy during the Depression, so I got my nerve up, stripped down to my birthday suit and pranced into the bullpen crooning in my best Mae West imitation, "Aw, come on, let me cling to you like a vine. Make that low-down music trickle up your spine. Baby I can warm you with this love of mine. I'm no a-a-angel!"

Big Joe never looked up from the paper he was reading, but Molly gave me a sideways slitty-eyed smile. "Whatever Jack is paying you to expose that little fella of yours to this infernal sunshine is not enough." He shooed me away: "So go along now, cover yourself up, make an act of contrition and leave poor Mr. Kennedy to read about the world's financial catastrophes in peace."

Now, standing at semi-attention outside Jack's beach-house bedroom, Molly joined me in watching the oddity of Beaufort slowly moving around the living room, running his fingers along its crevices and recesses, picking up objects and caressing them before setting them down again.

"I know your thoughts, Lemoyne," Molly said in a stage whisper. "That this is an abnormal being, more like a newt than a person. And you're right. The Giver of Life must have been asleep at the loom the day this brute was made."

Beaufort sensed that we were talking about him and came toward us. His good eye gave me an incisive look while the roving one seemed to be checking the room for something more interesting.

"Let me introduce myself properly. I'm Emile Beaufort. Of the Baton Rouge Beauforts."

"I'm Lemoyne Billings of the Baltimore Billingses."

Beaufort nodded and moved away after giving me a handshake that was limp, damp and brief.

"Fuckwit!" Molly whispered. "Supposed to have been one of Hoover's best snoops at the FBI before becoming a lick-arse to Mr. Kennedy. They say he can fit a tiny Kodak into a Kotex box and get a photo of cupid's warehouse without the lady even knowing; and record a voice from a hidey-hole fifty feet away and make it sound like a fly in the ear; and use his little moving picture camera the size of a potato to capture a naked couple jagging all unawares in their parlor, although from the looks of him I don't imagine he's got very much going on in the trouser department himself. But having a face like a wheelbarrow full of rectums is a terrible price to pay for all these talents."

"I can hear, you know," Beaufort said, his wandering eye giving us a morose look from the other side of the room.

Molly ignored him: "The Boss calls him 'a sharp tool.' I guess that's part of the reason he's here—to help cut the red menace out of the motion picture world."

"And who better?" Beaufort spoke to our conversation.

"Pride is the fool's ambrosia," Molly replied caustically.

Both of them shut up the instant the Old Man reappeared.

Beaufort sidled up to Big Joe and said unctuously, "I've seen enough. My cab is still waiting, so I think I'd better go. I've set up shop at the Hotel Highpoint on Western Boulevard and I'll be there if you need me."

"I know the Highpoint. It's a goddamn fleabag."

"I have a suite."

"What did that run you, all of three bucks a night?" the Old Man jeered.

"It's quite nice," Beaufort was wounded. "It will do well enough for my purposes."

The Old Man watched him leave, then grabbed the phone off the kitchen counter, gave the operator a number and promptly began muttering, "Come on, I don't have all day."

He gave a few terse instructions to whoever finally answered, ending by saying, "...and I want you to get the Schencks, the Warners, and the others in a room as soon as possible. But leave that limp dick Louie Mayer off the list. And start prepping them to face the fact that these cheese dicks in the Association of Studio Employees actually represent a threat to our way of life."

Hanging up, he gave me the once-over and I got the same queasy feeling I did the first time I met him.

"Jack didn't think I would find him," he exulted.

I gave a noncommittal look.

"So what the hell's going on with him anyway?"

"Well, he's writing his column for Mr. Hearst."

"Don't bullshit me, Lemoyne." He came several inches closer. "You know what I mean. What's with this girl he's shacked up with? Her knickers are all over his bedroom."

"She's in the movies," I said weakly.

"Tell me something I don't already know."

"She's Italian and she got caught up in the war."

He shot me a withering look.

"She's a very nice person." I was babbling now.

"I'm sure I'll love her to death." He was disgusted. "But I'm not sure I'll love her criminal father."

"Jack says he's a war hero."

"For a minute or two, maybe," the Old Man snorted. "But now he's back to who he was in the first place and will always be—a piece-of-shit mobster. Lesson Number One: Step on people like that and you'll get them on your shoes and track them all over your life."

Like the Kennedy kids themselves, I was reduced to speechlessness in his presence.

"Do not encourage Jack in this," he ordered. "He has things to accomplish. It's not the time for him to get sidetracked in some infantile romantic pash. This thing won't last."

He delivered this last sentence as a fact, not a prediction, then glanced at his watch. "I've got an early lunch. Tell Jack I'm at the Biltmore and need to hear from him soonest."

He nodded brusquely at Molly: "Come on, let's get busy."

Watching them trudge up the sandy driveway to their waiting cab, I was weighed down by the heavy sense of portent the Old Man always left behind as his calling card.

* * *

When Jack returned a couple of hours later and I told him that his father had paid a visit, he gave a look of incredulity that quickly deteriorated into resignation.

"How the hell did he find me? The guy is unbelievable. He ought to work for the Missing Persons Bureau."

Psyching himself up to call his father took half an hour. The conversation was one-sided and brief, and he hung up looking like he'd been beaten in the kidneys with a hoe handle.

"He give you the business?" I asked.

"And how."

"What did he say?"

"Among other things, for me to get my ass over there right away. You drive so I can put my thoughts in order and maybe hold him off for a minute or two when he starts in on me."

The Biltmore was a grand hotel, even by eastern standards, and while Jack was upstairs taking his medicine, a short middle-aged bellboy who looked like he'd just stepped out of a Philip Morris ad saw me gawking and offered a little guided tour.

We started at the impressive vaulted reception area with a fret-worked trompe l'oeil plaster ceiling that looked like wood, and then passed through spacious sitting rooms with frescoed ceilings and wall murals, some painted with 24 carat gold accents, including a large scene of the Roman goddess Ceres greeting the Spanish conquistador Vasco de Balboa as he first set foot in the New World.

We stopped at a banquet room that had been a speakeasy during Prohibition, the bellhop said. He opened a secret doorway leading to a low tunnel that exited onto the parking lot: "Here's your getaway when the cops stage a raid."

Then we walked through the Music Room, which the Kennedy campaign would use as its headquarters during the 1960 Democratic convention, and through the exquisite ballrooms, to the Palm Room. I was looking at one of the small "Biltmore angels" carved on the ornate pilasters, her furled wings setting off pert breasts as she knelt invitingly with her naked nether parts disappearing provocatively into a reptilian tail, when Jack caught up with us. He was clearly rattled.

I waited until we were back in the Zephyr to debrief him: "So what did he say?"

"That I was spitting in the face of my destiny."

"He used those exact words?"

"Yeah. He must have asked Molly for an elegant way of saying that he's sick and tired of having his grand plan for me to be his political stooge constantly fucked up."

"Did he rip you about Val?"

"Of course. He's got a file on her already. He said foreign women are trouble. Foreign Jewesses doubly so. I have no idea where he dug up that detail. He wants me to be a big boy and write her a Dear Jane letter."

"What did you say?"

"No dice."

"Those words?"

"Yeah."

"And what did he say?"

"'We'll see about that.'" He paused to submit to a forceful yawn before continuing: "There may be a little bit of silver lining. He's got one of his sinister intrigues going on with the studios and their labor problems and that could take the heat off me for a while."

But we both knew that our time in Hollywood had just been divided in half: before Joseph P. Kennedy and after.

FOURTEEN

Two days later I still felt trapped in the Old Man's forcefield. After catching myself standing at the kitchen sink for several minutes vacantly watching the morning sun climb up the side of the beach house next door, I decided to get out and about.

Jack had the car, so I walked out to the highway to thumb a ride into Santa Monica. Wartime camaraderie was over, and it was fifteen minutes before an old pickup that looked like it had been traded in by the Joads stopped for me. The long-faced driver didn't speak a word until he dropped me near the arched blue neon sign of the Santa Monica Yacht Harbor.

Then he said, "My brother didn't even make it onto Omaha Beach, he died in the water," and drove off.

I went out on the pier and watched the daytime fishermen staring at their bobbers for a while before going into the arcade to play some of the games—the gripper machine, the mutoscope punching bag, the alley-cat shooting gallery. I spent ten minutes feeding coins into the Love Meter, but no matter how hard I squeezed the handle, I couldn't do any better than Naughty But Nice. The machine's message seemed to be confirmed when the guy waiting behind me took over and immediately hit Hot Stuff.

I stopped in a sandwich shop that had Game 2 of the World Series on the radio and ordered a tuna melt. Virgil Trucks, my favorite because of his nickname "Fire," was on the hill for the Tigers, down 1-0 to the Cubs in the fifth. I thought it might be another heartbreaker for him, but in the bottom of the inning his teammate Hank Greenberg came up with two men on. Just home from four years of active duty, the "Hammering Hebrew," as the announcer called him, hit a three-run homer. That was all Fire Trucks needed, and he closed out the game.

It was late in the afternoon when I got back to the bungalow. Still excited for the Tigers and a little woozy from the noise and lights of the arcade, I saw that our front door was slightly ajar. I entered cautiously and heard sounds coming from Jack's bedroom. I grabbed a paring knife off the drain board as I passed through the kitchen.

The bedroom doorway smelled like it had been doused with gin. I yelled, "Come out of there!"

After a moment, Beaufort emerged, the adverse claims of his face trying to cooperate in an ingratiating smile.

"Emile, Emile Beaufort," he grabbed at my hand.

I drew it back. "I know who you are."

"Mr. Kennedy said it would be okay for me to look around."

"This isn't Mr. Kennedy's house."

"He wanted me to check and make sure that his son's security is not being compromised."

"We both know that's horseshit."

Beaufort shrugged as if to say that he'd given it the old college try before drawling, "Well, you probably know better than I that Mr. Kennedy worries about his children and wants what's best for them."

Worry wasn't the right word. From the time they were teenagers, the Old Man had conducted surveillance on his kids, steaming open their letters, suborning their friends to find out about their current doings, and sometimes having them followed—all part of his eternal quest to turn knowledge into power.

"So what?"

"Well..." He seemed to want me to finish his thought.

"Are you spying on us? Are there microphones and hidden cameras in this house?"

"I do not spy." His good eye looked away when he said this. "My work involves nothing more than the acquisition of information."

"Just like the guy who takes pictures of people in flagrante over the transom with his Graflex Speed Graphic."

"Very tacky," Beaufort said with hauteur, "and primitive too. Something I would never do."

"If you want to acquire information about people you should have stayed with the FBI."

He was affronted: "I remained at the bureau all during the war for patriotic reasons. But now it's peacetime and there's no longer any need to sacrifice for the good of the country. Mr. Kennedy offered me an opportunity to enter private enterprise. Mr. Hoover said he was sorry to see me go but he told me he certainly understood the desire for a nest egg."

He was warming to the subject. "I am quite proud of what I achieved. I began my government work countering Nazi agents and ended it countering Soviet agents. I'm the one who proved that the spy Elizabeth Zarubina had infiltrated our atomic bomb project through a cell she set up at Los Alamos."

"Congratulations. Never heard of her."

"Trust me. It was big. Very big."

Seeing that I didn't care, he frowned. "You don't want to live under Communist domination, do you?"

"Right now, I mainly don't want to live under your snooping."

He shook his head sadly, gave me a smile that was tailored for the simple-minded, and ambled toward the front door, bizarrely whispering "Farewell" over his shoulder as he evaporated into the afternoon light.

I was still fuming when Jack and Val arrived an hour later. I pulled him aside as soon as she was occupied and told him about the encounter with Beaufort.

He shrugged stoically: "So what's new? At the beginning of the war when I was having a thing with that Danish girl, Inga, Dad bugged my phone constantly, maybe with this guy's help, who knows? I only found out about it because the recording system went haywire and one day I picked up my phone and heard the replay of a conversation I'd had the previous evening."

Val waited until there was a lull in our conversation to come over and put a hand on my sleeve: "Today is October 4."

When I gave a blank look, she was slightly affronted: "Our one-month anniversary, don't you know? A very big moment and tonight we celebrate."

"Yeah, we've got a table for three at Ciro's," Jack added. "We need to leave in forty-five minutes. That gives you time to spruce yourself up so people won't think we're tripling with Lon Chaney Jr."

I tried to beg off, pleading a headache, but Val seized my hand and held it to her cheek: "We are a triangle, Billings. If we will lose one of our sides we will collapse."

* * *

We drove to Sunset Strip, which still felt like something of an open city, the identity it had acquired in the late Twenties when it was the place to go for bootleg liquor and other forbidden things, and when local criminals were so blatant in their activities that a group of concerned citizens once put up a billboard reading "Keep Chicago out of Los Angeles!"

Now it was more subdued, but still a place apart—an unincorporated area outside the LA city limits, under the jurisdiction of the county sheriffs rather than the heavier hand of the LAPD—where the rules still knew how to bend. Bugsy Siegel and Mickey Cohen and their crews still treated it like their clubhouse, while Zanuck, Sam Goldwyn and other moguls won or lost a few thousand dollars in their standing poker game every Thursday night upstairs at the Melody Room. Girls a step down from Temple Rose's worked the sex industry with the hicks who showed up on the weekends hoping to take a little walk on the wild side.

Ciro's was at the center of things on the Strip, having inherited pride of place from the Trocadero, which had reigned supreme during the Thirties before closing its doors. When we arrived at half past seven there was already a long line. Jack flashed his ID at a security guard, who checked his list and let us cut in front of the plebs who had no chance of getting in before midnight.

The interior was spiffy as a foxtrot, with a red ceiling, plush gathered curtains on the walls, and statuettes of chubby putti smugly cupping baskets of flowers in their hands. I was able to make out the signatures of Mary Pickford and Cary Grant among the dozens on Ciro's Scroll of Fame in the lobby before Jack yanked on my sleeve. The maître d' charted a serpentine route to our table, passing within a few feet of Xavier Cugat, who was standing in front of the bandstand holding his beloved chihuahua in one arm and languidly waving his baton with his free hand as his musicians went through a rote version of his signature song, "Perfidia."

We ordered the house specialties—Caesar salad, half turtle and half cream of pea soup with sherry and whipped cream on top, and a chateaubriand for three—and then searched the crowd for celebrities whose names would appear in the columns of Luella Parsons and Hedda Hopper the next morning.

"There's Rita Hayworth," Jack inclined his head so he wouldn't appear to be staring at the star along with everyone else in the restaurant. "The 'Love Goddess.'"

"Born Margarita Carmen Cansino, as Temple Rose would probably tell you if she were here," I said to Val.

"Such beautiful red hair," she examined Hayworth closely, "but she appears to be here alone. And she pretends she doesn't know that everyone looks at her."

"If we come back here this time next year after the movie's out, people will be looking at you," I told her.

"They already are," Jack said proudly.

"Don't be foolish, Gianni," she tucked in her chin and gave him a saucy sideways Lauren Bacall look. "Mr. Talbert's film will disappear like a ship that has been struck by an exploding mine, and by next year it will require a large expedition of deep-sea divers to bring my career up from the bottom of the ocean."

Our food had just arrived when the maître d' suddenly reappeared, fastidiously directing two busboys carrying extra chairs and place settings. Then we saw the Old Man pulling Gloria Swanson toward us. He sat her between Jack and me and squeezed his own chair in next to Val, relishing the awkwardness.

Swanson gave us a haughty look, bearing herself like the Screen Queen she had been twenty years earlier in what was now already being seen as Old Hollywood, when her sultry kohl-eyed portrayal of Sadie Thompson helped make the case for censorship in the film industry. She had been left behind by the transition to talkies and her own middle age, but while she had virtually disappeared from the screen over the past decade, she still knew how to make news—most recently by accusing her fifth husband at their divorce trial of having had black-market butter on his crêpes Suzette every morning throughout the war—and how to retain her mystique.

Especially with the Old Man. Even though their rut was long since over, she would always be his greatest trophy—his Marilyn—acquired during his rapid and improbable climb as a Hollywood producer. He had eventually grown as brazen in the possession of her as he had been groveling in the pursuit—fucking her over at the same time he was actually fucking her as producer of the catastrophic *Queen Kelly*, her last big silent, which according to lip readers featured filthy denunciations of Big Joe as a stand-in for dialogue. Yet she unaccountably still had a soft spot for him, and whenever he was in Hollywood she let him flash her around town like an antique diamond stickpin.

She was tiny, not quite five feet tall, with size four shoes, thin penciled arches for eyebrows and a turned-down mouth conveying a grim pessimism about the human condition. Her makeup was so thick that her facial features seemed mortared in place. She was wearing her trademark beret and a fox wrap with glass eyes glaring out of the snarling head on one shoulder and claws sharp as switchblades on the other.

She unfolded her napkin and perfected the symmetry of her silverware, saturating these mundane gestures with the deep theatricality that Norma Desmond would employ in *Sunset Boulevard*, Swanson's great curtain call of a role, a few years later.

After the Old Man had ordered for both of them without asking her what she wanted, Swanson stared enviously at Val and asked, "How old are you?"

"Twenty-four."

"I was once almost as beautiful as you are."

Val gave a genuine blush and Swanson presented us with her profile.

"The fleeting grandeur of their youth makes so little impression on the young," she spoke imperiously to the room. "They have no appreciation of the transitory nature of their life course."

After letting this pronouncement settle, she turned to Jack: "I suppose you don't remember my visit to your family in 1929?"

"How could I forget?" He gave her a buttery look. "You landed at Hyannis in a seaplane and Dad went out to get you in our speedboat. It was the grandest entrance ever."

"Oh, there were others even grander, I assure you." She hoisted the corners of her mouth in a mysterious little smile before continuing: "I autographed the wall of your sister Kathleen's playhouse."

"I remember," Jack chuckled. "Dad had it bulldozed a couple of years later so we'd have more room for football, but at the last minute Mother ran out and saved the board that had your signature."

Swanson's eyes narrowed at the mention of Rose, the rival she had vanquished so easily.

"Does she still have it?"

"On the mantle in her bedroom."

"Her bedroom," Swanson scoffed as she inserted a cigarette into an ivory holder. She pointed it at the Old Man for him to light, then swung it upright and smoked grandiosely.

While Jack and I were watching her act, the Old Man was moving in on Val. Smiling so broadly that you could see his molars, he scraped his chair ever closer to hers. At first she was welcoming, trying to make a good impression as he analyzed the angles of her face and gave advice on how to tilt it to take advantage of studio lighting, how to hold her upper body when sitting on a sofa, how to steal scenes without being accused of trying.

"He's swarming her," Jack whispered. "If I'd known he was going to show up I would have warned her what to expect."

That's what he had done with the debs he invited to Hyannis for house parties during his college years. At the end of those evenings, when everyone was retiring, Jack always cautioned the girls to lock their doors because, as he said euphemistically, "Dad tends to get a little frisky at night."

Jack and I worked through the meal as if it were a military campaign, while Swanson posed for the nearby tables and the Old Man bore down on Val. By the time Ciro's special baked Alaska had been eaten, the coffee finished and the complimentary cognac refused, he had his face so close to hers that they could have rubbed noses. He had lowered his voice so I couldn't hear what he was saying, but I saw that Val was listening in the way that children do—totally intent, frowning as she tried to decipher the import of his words.

"The cobra hypnotizes the rabbit," Jack whispered to me, but he couldn't bring himself to object.

Swanson saw what was happening and rose majestically: "Joseph, we really must be going. I might be reading for a part early in the morning and I want to look refreshed."

The Old Man got up reluctantly, said a perfunctory goodnight to the three of us and put a hand on Swanson's shoulder, guiding her out of the restaurant in a way that made it seem he was pushing.

Val watched them go with a stricken look on her face.

Jack asked her what his father had talked about.

"He said he didn't think Warners was the place for me," she answered evasively. "He wants to take me to other studios."

"What did you say?"

"That I have a contract."

"And then?" Jack pressed her.

"He said that contracts can be broken."

"And then?"

"I said we would speak more about it."

Now he was concerned. "Why would you do that?"

She looked away. "He is your father."

FIFTEEN

In early October, Selkirk's Association of Studio Employees, trying to recapture the momentum it had achieved during the previous month's "War at Warners," grabbed headlines again by staging another big demonstration at MGM. The highlight of the festivities came when, in the middle of the violence between cops and the ASE, a handful of the strikers wearing their military uniforms and battle ribbons formed a column and marched through the fray carrying a giant American flag. Whenever the flag approached them, the cops would snap to attention and salute, then resume their hand-to-hand combat with the strikers as soon as the honor guard had moved on past.

But this battle had the feel of a last hurrah even as it was happening. A few days later, Selkirk was hit with a restraining order to stay away from all the studios, and of course he ignored it. The same afternoon, he showed up at Paramount's gates with Helen Keller, Judy Holiday and a handful of other stars, including Burl Ives, who sang several exuberant choruses of "Blue Tail Fly," which the crowd unaccountably interpreted as a protest song.

Selkirk was arrested and sentenced to a couple of nights in jail. The *LA Times* buried the story on page five and ran a photo of his arraignment that made him look old and adrift. Clearly the air was going out of his movement.

"A steep fall in a short time," I said to Jack as we discussed the article over breakfast.

He shrugged. "Selkirk's facing what the Soviets call 'the correlation of forces.' The newspapers are bored and ready to move on to the next story. And the studios are deciding that Geist is the lesser of two evils." He paused, then added mordantly: "Dad strikes again."

"You really think he's playing that big a role? He's only been here a little more than a week."

"Are you kidding? His fingerprints are all over this thing."

He was referring to the producers' reaction to a three-judge federal panel that had just delivered a ruling that the issues between the two unions and the studios should be fully negotiated during a thirty-day cooling-off period, and that the ASE strikers in the meantime should be able to return to work immediately. The studios didn't argue against it, but said it would be unfair to fire the newly hired replacements, so the reinstated ASE workers, many of them construction supervisors who hadn't swung a hammer in years if ever, would be reassigned as journeymen carpenters on hot sets. When a large majority of them refused this humiliating demotion, the studios handed them severance checks prepared in advance and fired them for good, all consistent with the court order.

I thought I might find an indirect way to ask the Old Man if he had really helped design this strategy. But when he showed up in our driveway a couple of days later, Solomon Geist was sitting next to him in the back seat of a gaudy aqua-colored Cadillac, with the scarred Draco driving and his twin brother riding shotgun. I went out to greet Big Joe, but he waved me off, peevishly mouthing through the window, "Not now."

I retreated into the house and watched out the kitchen window, expecting that he'd eventually come in and Geist would drive off. That may have been the initial plan, but after twenty minutes of animated conversation between the two, accompanied by chopping hand gestures that spoke a language of their own, the Cadillac turned around and headed back out to the highway.

A harsh wind rushing in from the Pacific the next day bruised the sky. Jack was "on assignment," a phrase of trade he had taken to using, and I was vacuuming the living room and hoping for an afternoon burn-off when I heard the *LA Examiner* thunk against the front door. The headline story detailed why Ike had just fired Patton from his post as military governor of Bavaria, laying out in detail the general's casual attitude toward denazification and his desire to make confrontation with the Soviets a priority.

Just below the fold, in the local news slot, was a story about four longshoremen who had been gunned down "gangland style" in MacArthur Park the previous evening. Looking at the headshots of the murdered men, I recognized two of them as the bodyguards that Jack and I had met several weeks earlier when we first visited Selkirk's office.

* * *

The Old Man was in the middle of our lives now. The three of us never knew when he would show up, but it was always without asking and usually when we thought he was occupied elsewhere. We made detailed escape plans, but he used his secret resources to figure out where we were and then appeared with a little smile of triumph on his face in the middle of our getaway. On the rare occasions when we managed to evade him, it felt as though we'd just tunneled out of prison.

"Same old thing," Jack said when I asked him about it. "He's calling the music and we're doing the dance. It's been like that my whole life. Whenever I start to feel that I'm really on my own, he reels me in and I realize that the sense of freedom I've had was an illusion because he's had me on the line all along."

Once, we didn't see him for three days. Then he and Molly suddenly walked into the beach house just when we were sitting down to the dinner Val had cooked, and he began brusquely interrogating us about what we'd done during his absence. After we finished eating, I took Molly aside to ask where they'd been.

"To the little desert town in Nevada called Las Vegas. It's a scorched scab of a place, but the Boss thinks it will be something big because wagering is permitted there and the working poor of Southern California might someday come in great numbers, especially if Mr. Ford ever figures out a way to cool the inside of his cars. We were at a building site with little pink flamingoes stuck in the ground to mark the layout of what they say will be a luxe hotel offering the ability to sit in a chair and watch prancing showgirls while playing the ponies wherever they happen to be running anywhere in the country, and to do other things legally that a person shouldn't do at all. Workers were crawling over this site, and a couple of pistoleros were keeping watch from the battlements. More than this, I cannot tell you."

On some of his unannounced visits, the Old Man left Molly behind and brought some anonymous chorine with him, different women with the same ironed platinum hair and blank look of hearing loss. He introduced and then ignored them, focusing instead on Val—sizing her up, monopolizing her conversation, and emotionally manhandling her with his attention.

When they were standing together, the Old Man would step in a little closer to her, and she would back away. He would then advance into the space she had vacated, prompting her to retreat again. Before long, they would have moved in lockstep from one side of the living room to the other.

Sometimes when the Old Man dogged her, she would catch Jack's eye and give him an imploring look. After a particularly grating encounter he would say, "I've got to do something." But his father was too much for him and he couldn't bring himself to do anything.

Val seemed to be sinking back into that self we had first met: often moody and withdrawn, gnawing at her fingernails, moving from lassitude to hyperkinesis with no transition, shadowed by mortality. And I noticed that she had begun worrying at the ghost tattoo on her arm again.

SIXTEEN

In mid-October, Talbert set aside several days to film backstory scenes with John Payne and Veronica Lake in La Jolla. Jack was busy trying to document the story of the annual payoffs the studios made to Geist, so Val spent most of her days at the beach house, usually silent and remote, until she suddenly had to leave for some engagement she didn't talk about when she returned a few hours later on.

Up to this time, the only women I'd ever really seen close up were the Kennedy girls when Jack and I were kids. But that was sisterly asexuality, even with Kick, although I had desperately wished it could be something more. Watching Val now, as she padded around the house like a jungle cat, had the feel of a first experience.

Her mundane acts were erotic epiphanies. Hiking the hem of her dress above the triangle of a bare upraised knee to paint her toenails; making a moue in the bathroom mirror when slowly applying lipstick and then finishing the job with a half-sucked fingertip of Vaseline for high gloss; brushing her lavish hair until it crackled with electricity, then gathering it into a snood that looked like an oriole's nest; working her arms with the slow purpose of a contortionist to reach back and unlatch her bra.

Once I saw a slice of her nakedness visible in the half-closed door of the bathroom as she stripped to her panties, and then, after shimmying her hips to drop them to her ankles, kicked them up with a toe to catch them in midair.

She was silent for long periods. When she did talk, it often seemed to be meditative, an attempt to weld together the disparate strands of her life. Once while walking past the painting of her mother that now hung on the living room wall amidst all the nautical objects, she stopped and said abruptly, as if we were in the middle of a conversation, "She didn't take lover until more than ten years after it was clear that my father would never return. He was a printer named Tomasso Croce. He was a gentle man who loved Charlie Chaplin and would sometimes go hunting with his *lupara* and bring home rabbits for our Sunday dinner. He cared deeply for my mother. Tomasso's heart gave up one day while he was waiting for the trolley in Piazza Venezia. My mother never had another man beside her in bed again. It was like she was a virgin once more when the Nazis took her to her death."

She slumped down on the sofa, leaned her head back on the neck rest and continued speaking to the ceiling.

"She made Franco and me costumes so we could do plays in our bedroom when we were little. We both wanted to be other people who might be interesting enough that our father would someday want to be with us. But at university, I act for a different reason as well—to try on other people the way women used to try on the dresses in my mother's shop. I find that I love especially the heroines in Greek plays we perform because these women know so deeply who they are and that they must follow their heart no matter what the outcome."

"I think you were playing one of these women in the film your father made of you."

"I forgot that you saw that."

"Harry Warner showed it to us because Jack couldn't stop talking about you after he saw you that first time at the studio's birthday party."

"It was not good, that film. I did not like the photographer my father paid to make it. He was a rude man who was angry that I was speaking English. He wanted me to wear less clothes even than I did."

"Jack was transfixed from the moment you came on the screen. We didn't know what character you were playing, but we couldn't take our eyes off you, even though the sound was bad and we couldn't hear what you were saying."

"I was saying the last speech of Cassandra in *Agamemnon.* This is the role I played in the one performance our acting group did two days before the Nazis began the gathering of Jews in Rome. Many students come to see us."

"Cassandra is the one who saw the future but wasn't believed."

"Yes, a woman others think is a raving crazy person when she tells the truth. This is Apollo's curse on her for withholding from him the opportunity of her body. But it is just seeing and not being believed that is her tragedy. It is also having to live day after day with what she knows must necessarily happen to her and never being able to put that knowledge aside even for an instant.

"In the play, Cassandra has been brought home by Agamemnon as his concubine after watching the Greeks kill her family every one of them at Troy. Life is very bad for her in the kingdom of Mycenae. Because of her special sight, she knows she is to be killed by Clytemnestra along with Agamemnon himself. Imagine knowing you will meet your end alongside a man so evil that he sacrificed his own daughter just to ensure fair winds to the battlefield. But in her last speech Cassandra accepts her unfair fate as the will of the gods. That's the speech I was giving in the film you saw."

Here Val stood up and seemed to grow taller and more regal, as poised as a ballerina. Her face became transcendent as she held out her hands in supplication.

"Never a bride, never a mother," she recited, "unfriended, condemned alive to solitary death. What law of heaven have I transgressed? What god can save me now? What help or hope have I, in whom devotion is deemed sacrilege? If this is God's will, I shall learn my lesson in death; but if my enemies are wrong, I wish them no worse punishment than mine."

She remained standing there for a long time, caught up in the moment she had created.

Then she turned and gave me a penetrating look. "I am sad for you, Billings," she came closer, "that you will not have a woman's love."

I started to reply, but she put a finger on my lips and then brought my face close for a kiss that lasted just long enough for the tip of her tongue to dart into my mouth like an inquisitive minnow.

Over in a second and inviting nothing further, it was the kiss of a lifetime.

SEVENTEEN

Late the next afternoon, Val telephoned and told Jack that she had an early morning call and would be staying at her Toluca Lake apartment that night. He said he would drive over and stay with her, but she told him it would be hard enough to get up before dawn without having him beside her.

It was the first time in over a month and a half that they had been apart, and it obviously set him back. He hauled out his portable Underwood and tried to write a story he owed the *Examiner*. After staring into deep space for a half hour, he put it away and picked up his worn copy of *Pilgrim's Way*. But he couldn't concentrate on that either, and spent the rest of the evening sulking like a rainy-day child.

The next morning he arranged to pick Val up later that afternoon, which made him optimistic again. He said he'd been doing overtime all week and had a right to skip work, so after breakfast the two of us sat on the deck in our bathrobes playing gin rummy and listening to Artie Shaw records. Jack floated along on a stream of consciousness that meandered from Shaw's superiority to Shaw, to how Shaw could possibly have managed to get both Lana Turner and Ava Gardner to marry him, to the fact that Val vaguely resembled Gardner but was five times better looking for reasons he was explaining in detail when there was a loud knock at the door.

"You get it," he told me. "Probably someone selling encyclopedias. It will give you an opportunity to tell him you don't need one because you went to Princeton."

I opened the door and saw a somber young man dressed in a suit and tie, with a nametag bearing the Paramount Studios logo.

"Are you John Kennedy?"

"In my dreams." I pointed at Jack, who by then had come inside to see what was up.

The kid spoke rapidly, shifting his feet nervously and struggling to look Jack in the eye: "Your father sent me to tell you that when he was leaving Paramount this morning after a meeting someone fired on his car as it was going through Bronson Gate. He's totally okay and unhurt, he wanted me to tell you, but he's being checked out at Hollywood Presbyterian Hospital as a precaution. The bullet hit the windshield but didn't touch your father or his driver, who made it out onto Melrose and kept going until he sideswiped another car and hit a fire hydrant. That's all I know.

"Your father asked me to come out here and tell you about it in person before you hear it on the radio. He said to tell you to stay put until he gets here. I'm supposed to say these words are underlined, quote, 'There's nothing to worry about and do not leave the house,' end quote. He was emphatic about it. So that's the message. G'bye."

The kid headed back to the company car idling in the driveway, and Jack bolted for his room. He soon came out again still buttoning his clothes and sliding on the floor trying to cram his heels into his loafers.

"Where are you going?" I asked as he looked for the Zephyr's keys, sending a pile of papers flying around.

"To be with Dad. Where do you think?"

"Didn't you hear what the kid said? The Old Man wants you to wait here until the smoke clears."

"You think I'm going to sit around when my father's out there getting his ass shot off?" he snapped at me, slamming the door behind him.

About half an hour later a cab drove tenuously down our driveway and I watched the Old Man step out, look carefully in all directions, ask the cabbie to wait, and hurry into the house with his shoulders slightly hunched as if fearing sniper fire. A white gauze patch with an impressionistic brushstroke of blood was taped to his forehead.

"I sent a kid out here from Paramount," he said brusquely, looking around for Jack. "Did he tell you what happened?"

"Yes." I looked at his bandage. "Are you all right?"

He fingered the gauze reflectively: "There was only one shot. It hit the windshield and I got whacked by a piece of glass. Believe it or not, they pulled it out with needle-nose pliers. It was *bang bang* and over in two seconds. No big deal. Already in the rearview mirror."

"Was Molly driving?"

He gave a distracted nod.

"Was he hurt?"

"He smacked his shoulder a little when we ran into a fire hydrant. They took him to the hospital with me. He's probably still there, but nothing's broken and he's okay too. Don't worry about Molly. He's strong as an ox."

Then he asked where Jack was.

"Looking for you."

"Goddamn it! I told the kid to tell him to stay put."

"He was worried about you."

The Old Man's anger softened. "None of my kids ever do what I tell them."

The response was so mild I wondered if he might have expected that Jack wouldn't be here and had another reason for coming. I thought he'd get to the point immediately, as he usually did, but instead he sat down heavily on the sofa and stared down at the floor between his splayed legs.

"Who did it?" I asked.

He looked away. "Who knows? It was one guy standing there by the gate waiting for us, not a firing squad. Maybe one of those lunatics from Selkirk's union."

"Why them?"

"Because they know I've been helping the studios figure out a way to deal with them," he said irascibly. "And because they're fucking Communists. Anyway, whoever it was will be dealt with, don't you worry about that. In the meantime, let's talk about something else."

"What?"

He studied his fingernails for a moment to mark a transition. "This girl of Jack's..."

"Val." It irked me that he didn't say her name after having oppressed her with his attention all this time.

"Yes, Val. She's nice enough, but you know she's a little unstable. All those Europeans are. There's something wrong with all of them because of the war, but she's also a Jewish person and what they went through leaves a particular mark, you know. You can see how experiencing all that might make someone go off the deep end. I know Jack is all tangled up with her emotionally and probably isn't rational where she's concerned, so I count on you to make sure he has perspective about things."

"Things?"

"Yeah, things. You know, things she might say or do. Things that cause trouble. Things that might absolutely need to be taken with a grain of salt. Things."

He sat there for a while looking at me—not one of his usual X-ray stares intended to make you confess or submit, but a pensive, almost vulnerable expression.

"You may think of it as my 'tomorrow the world' thinking," he finally said, "but I know Jack has a future. I know it in my bones. He's not like his brother. I can't think of Joseph Jr. without hurting. That boy would have walked through fire for me. Jack is different. He has always marched to his own drumbeat and always looked for ways to operate outside my authority. We're very different. I know that. But I also know he has great abilities and the sky's the limit for him if we play our cards right. But if he makes a mistake right now at the beginning of things, it will follow him forever. You and I are the ones who care about him most. We've got to keep things on the right track. Can I count on you, Lemoyne? Can I count on you look to past appearances and focus on what's important?"

I nodded hesitantly.

"Fine. I thought so." He got up to leave, but paused at the door. "By the way, you haven't seen Beaufort, have you?"

"No."

"I know he came over here awhile back," he said with no hint of apology, "and I thought you might have run into him again."

I shook my head.

"Doesn't matter." His voice had an unpleasant undertone. "When Molly is on the job again he'll find him."

* * *

Jack returned a couple of hours later. He had spent half the day looking for his father, first at the hospital and then at the police station, before running him down at the Biltmore.

"He was out here looking for you," I told him. "It's like musical cars today."

"He told me he talked to you, then gave me hell for ten minutes for not staying put as he ordered." Jack was still agitated. "I spend hours trying to figure out if he's okay, and when I finally find him the first thing he does is rip me. And then he won't even tell me anything about what happened. I told him that one of the detectives I talked to at the station said he thought it might have been a warning shot rather than a genuine assassination attempt, because the shooter was so close he shouldn't have missed. Dad wasn't interested. He just sloughs it off with one of his what's-done-is-done looks and starts interrogating me for the five-hundredth time about what I'm going to do with my life."

He paced back and forth in the living room for a long time before I got him to start up our gin rummy game again. The cards flew out of his hands like startled birds when he tried to riffle them after shuffling. "Son of a bitch," he shook his head.

He had calmed down by the time Val phoned to say she had another early call the next morning and had to stay at her apartment again that night. Again, he offered to drive over and be with her, but she put him off, claiming that Talbert was shooting her death scene the following morning and she needed solitude to prepare for it.

"What the hell's going on here?" he gave me a disoriented look after hanging up the receiver. "First they're shooting at the Old Man and now Val is pulling this Garbo act again."

He had been sidestepping the efforts of Len Thom, his ensign on P-109, to meet up while he was in town for a few days. But now he called Thom and set up an early dinner. He wanted me to come along, but I didn't want to listen to their recycled combat stories and complaints about what an asshole Douglas MacArthur was, so I asked him to drop me off in Hollywood. He was silent on the drive in from the beach, and the sense of foreboding washing over me was so strong that I didn't say much either.

I got out at the Pantages and walked across the street to the Hitching Post Theatre, a minor Hollywood landmark that showed only westerns, along with a new chapter of a cowboy serial every day featuring Wild Bill Elliott, Hoot Gibson, Johnny Mack Brown and other white hats. There was an actual hitching post on the sidewalk in front of the cashier's cage. The ushers dressed in cowboy gear and so did the kids who showed up at all times of the day, most of them wearing holsters with cap pistols they drew and started shooting when the bad guys appeared on the screen.

I probably would have bought a ticket, even though I was feeling blue, if the day's feature, *Pioneer Justice,* had starred someone other than Lash LaRue, who always struck me as a bogus cowboy hero—dressed in black, speaking in a bowery Bogart voice that made him more an easterner than a westerner, using a bullwhip rather than a manly six-shooter. So I continued strolling back down toward Highland.

A knot of people was forming a few doors down on Wilcox, and I allowed a large elderly woman also headed in that direction to run interference for me as I went to see what was happening.

A man with wild matted hair was down on his hands and knees on the sidewalk drawing with colored chalk. Lost somewhere in middle age, he wore a layering of ragged clothes, each stratum visible through the tears in the one on top of it. The skin under one ear was discolored and corrugated from a burn scar. He talked to himself and drooled slightly as he created labyrinthine diagrams that spilled off the curb and onto the asphalt like Dali's clock face.

The work was dime-store surrealism, but it had an alarming vehemence—elaborate cabalistic spider-web designs showing swastikas next to U.S. flags at rocket sites; the USSR bleeding into China; Africans being injected with drugs by Europeans. Small hooked-nose figures in top hats with sacks of money on their hump backs watched from their battlements at the four corners of this disjointed world. Hanging above all these details was the canopy of an atomic cloud.

"He only comes once every week or so," the elderly woman told me. "Nobody knows when he's going to show up. And nobody knows who he is."

The crowd heckled and encouraged the artist and called out questions and comments. He ignored them, working rapidly with his face close to the pavement. Then someone behind me tossed a dime onto his design. He scrambled on hands and knees to get it, angrily threw it back, stood up and did a fierce little war dance to smudge his work with the flapping soles of his overripe tennis shoes. Then he picked up his box of chalk sticks and stalked off.

This handmade vision of the apocalypse pressed down on me while I walked back up to Hollywood Boulevard, integrating itself into the metaphysical lurch I felt we'd all taken the past week and the sense we now had that we were all only characters at the mercy of the plot.

I went into the Pig 'N Whistle soda fountain, sat at the counter and ordered a chocolate malt. Above the fountain with its prancing, flute-playing pig was an ornate mirror fixed to the hand-painted tiles. The face that stared back at me from it was so unhappy and disoriented that I put down a half dollar and left before the malt arrived, and headed down to Sunset to catch a bus for the beach.

* * *

When I got back to the house, I knew Val was there by her scent even before I saw her standing spellbound in the living room scratching at her arm and looking out at the ocean through the bay window. Shadows had settled under her eyes, and rapid weight loss had sharpened the angles of her face. Afraid of startling her, I walked into the periphery of her vision instead of coming up behind.

"You're here," I said.

"Yes. This place is not easy to get to but there are very many comings and goings."

Before I could reply, she said abruptly, "I can't stay tonight either. I already told that to Gianni. But it has been too long without seeing him so I came. But he isn't here and now I will miss him."

I joined her at the window and took a chance: "I've been feeling lately that our house is being blown down."

It took her a moment to get my meaning. "Yes, blown down." She gave a heavy nod. "I do as well."

"What is the matter? Can you tell me?"

She appeared to be struggling to form a response, then shook her head and walked out onto the deck to gather herself, closing the slider behind her. Even though she seemed personally depleted, her body, outlined by the breeze flattening her clothes, was lithe and vigilant.

She came back inside a few minutes later and resumed her station at the window.

"*Dietrologia,*" she finally said.

"What's that?" I wasn't sure she was speaking to me.

"An Italian word."

"What does it mean?"

"*Dietro* means behind." She took a small step backward. "*Dietrologia* is the word some Italians use to mean the real truth, the deep truth they believe stands behind what only seems to be the truth. I think my father is one of those people. They don't accept anything they are told. They think the truth is always beneath the surface or behind the curtain, or standing at the end of that hall with all the mirrors, and you must use your intuition to discover it because those who control things will create a false truth to serve their purposes."

"How would you say it in English?"

She gave it some thought: "It's very hard to translate. Maybe it would be easier if there had been Borgias in America."

"Conspiracy theory?" It was a term I'd heard for the first time at a Hyannis get-together early in 1942 when James Forrestal, the secretary of the Navy, used it to smack down the Old Man's claim that FDR had allowed the attack on Pearl Harbor to get us into the European war.

"*Dietrologia* is not theory," Val shook her head. "For people who see the world in this way, it is fact. Very deep fact. Such people believe that the official explanation given is always manufactured and the truth is always *dietro*, behind the lies that powerful people tell and the illusions they create. It is not really a philosophy but a disposition of the mind."

After a pause, she suggested, "Maybe behindness? Is there even such a word?"

"Why do you mention this word now?" I asked.

"I never considered it seriously before, because it is not the way I think. But now that it seems our house is being blown down, as you say, it may be time for me to think differently."

I would have pursued the question further, but we heard the Zephyr pull up outside. The minute Jack stepped inside, Val grabbed him and buried her head in his chest for such a long time that he finally had to gently peel her away.

"I came here today because I wanted to see your face and touch your body," she said when he tilted her head back.

"Well, God knows I'm glad to touch yours." He was happy again as he ran his hands down her back and cupped her buttocks. "I've been talking about the war for two hours and I'm ready to get back to peace time."

She looked away: "But as I already said, I will not be able to be with you tonight."

There was something so bottom-heavy in the words that Jack didn't even contest them.

"I just needed to have my eyes on you for one moment," she said.

After that, the silence in the house was like a migraine. Jack went into the bathroom and brushed his teeth for a long time while Val sat at the kitchen table violently pushing back her cuticles with her thumbnails.

When her cab honked, she started out but then stopped suddenly. "No, I won't," she said with a wild look, as if speaking to someone not in the house. Then she went out to dismiss the driver.

The rest of the evening, Jack and I tried to act as if things were back to normal. Val played along, acting vivacious all through dinner. At one point she pulled her hair down on one side of her face in imitation of Veronica Lake and peeped out to deliver in Lake's slightly asthmatic voice some of her silliest lines in *Tomorrow,* including this gem: "I loved you before I knew you. I'll love you after I'm dead." Saying it, she laughed until tears slipped out of her eyes.

When she and Jack were in bed and I was lying on the sofa mulling the coercive illogic of behindness, I heard Val murmur, as she always did just before nodding off, "Don't go to sleep before I do, Gianni."

EIGHTEEN

At breakfast the next morning Jack said, "Let's not hang around here today waiting to see what happens…"

"Or who," Val interjected. She didn't look refreshed from her sleep, but seemed determined to outrun whatever had been dogging her.

"Exactly," he agreed. "We need a little getaway and I think we should spend the day at Hollywood Park."

"We will make a picnic in the park?"

"This is not a park for making the *pique-a-nique*," Jack lightly mocked her accent. "This is a park where they make the horsie race."

She frowned, and then clapped her hands: "Oh yes, I see. A day at the races. We will have fun like those crazy brothers."

Soon we were in the car on the Pacific Coast Highway, feeling stealthy even though no one seemed to be following us. Val was wearing a white bishop-sleeve dress and a Gainesboro gray homburg. She had found a white feather somewhere and stuck it into the hat, where it stood like a tongue of ice.

The breeze coming in off the ocean was shoving the clouds around in a way that momentarily tamed the harsh October light. The salt air had a mentholated tang and felt newly made. It seemed possible that we might get out from under the fist that had been pressing down on us and that everything might yet work out.

Val chattered happily beside Jack in the front seat. He had an arm around her shoulders and was slowly rolling strands of her hair in his fingertips.

She had been to a horse race only once, she said, before the war, when she and her mother and brother had traveled to Siena to see the Palio. "There the horse riders beat each other as they ride. It is more like war than racing. Horses fall and legs break. Their eyes become very big with pain. Riders bleed from the face and arms. It is a gang of hoodlums on horseback doing bad things to each other."

"The people we'll see today aren't violent," Jack replied. "They're religious. They think that the racetrack is heaven on earth."

Hollywood Park had been constructed in the mid-Thirties by a group of showbiz personalities, led by the Warner brothers, who wanted a track closer than Santa Anita and wanted a place that actually looked like a park. The sweeping buildings were arranged around promenades, and a series of small lakes at the center of the track had swans swimming in them. There was a "privacy driveway" for the chauffeured cars of the stars and high-rollers that Hedda Hopper had in mind when she famously wrote that someone who bought a ticket could expect to see "a celebrity in every box." The park had been closed during the war but was now reopened on a limited basis, in part to raise money for Los Angeles public schools.

The atmosphere was like a country fair: people crowding the concessions and strolling around the grounds arm in arm. Val was giddy with excitement as we took our seats in the grandstand. She studied the horses through the opera glasses she'd brought, and insisted that betting be based on which horse was the prettiest or which jockey had the most stylish silks.

The horse we all agreed to back in the first race, a magnificent roan named Greatheart, came in third from last.

When everyone began to rip up their losing tickets, Val said with alarm, "What if they are making an error and some of these tickets are winning ones? Should we pick them up and see?"

Jack laughed, "Believe me, these people know whether or not they've won."

He and I were eating hotdogs and skylarking on what a good life it would be to follow the horses from track to track around the country as part of a nomadic community of gamblers, when I sensed a commotion at the end of our row. It was the Old Man pushing his way down toward us, not excusing himself or waiting for people to sit back or draw in their feet, but grinding shoe tips and banging knees as he bulled his way through.

He was obviously in high spirits. A small red mark on his forehead was the only reminder of the shooting incident a few days earlier, which unaccountably seemed to have disappeared from history.

"You know what they say," he gave a significant look at the three of us before wedging his body between Val and Jack. "Horse sense is the thing a horse has that keeps it from betting on people."

He whispered something to Val, who looked straight ahead, sitting stoically in the lockup he created, unable to rise and see the horses forming for the next race or follow their progress around the track. She was clenching her fists so tightly that her fingernails dug divots into her palms.

After the third race, the Old Man stood up and looked around the grandstand. Something up behind us caught his eye, and he bent over Val and snatched her opera glasses off her lap. As he adjusted the focus, his features hardened. I followed his stare and saw in miniature what he saw enlarged—Solomon Geist looking right back through binoculars of his own. The Draco brothers hovered over him one row up and Emile Beaufort sat beside him with a fawning smile on his outlandish face.

The Old Man stiffened and went into battle mode, dropping the binoculars and practically running down our row and then hustling up the stairs. I asked Val for the glasses and watched as he snarled a few words to Geist and then, his face engorged with rage, stabbed an index finger repeatedly into Beaufort's chest like a stiletto. I couldn't hear what he said, but I heard his yell and saw the Sicilian twins move into the aisle to quarantine him. Geist nodded at a nearby security guard, who rushed over to take Big Joe by the elbow and escort him down the stairs and out of the grandstand.

"What the hell was that all about?" I asked Jack, who had also been watching the spectacle.

"We probably don't want to know," he replied.

Val disappeared into herself. As we left the track, she told us without elaboration that she would be staying alone at her apartment again that night.

* * *

Jack's editor in New York called the next morning and asked him to get on the train up to San Francisco and do a puff piece on the formal opening of the United Nations. He was worried about what would happen in his absence and tried to find an excuse not to go. But the editor insisted and Jack gave in, after grousing about the headline that had been decided on in advance: "October 29, 1945—A Date That Will Live in Dignity."

When I picked him up at Union Station late the following afternoon, he seemed somewhat rehabilitated after a day off from Val. He had handwritten his story on the train and told me to drive to the *Los Angeles Examiner*'s office on Broadway and Eleventh so he could go in and charm some secretary into typing the piece for him and then dictating it to New York.

A half hour later he came back to the car saying, "Mission accomplished." He told me to slide over so he could drive. "The work day is over. Let's cruise."

We were continuing down Broadway when a tentative drizzle started to smear the dirt on the windshield. The sky darkened and a sudden deluge pelted the car's hood and overwhelmed the wipers. After a couple of minutes the downpour ended just as suddenly as it began and an intense sun reappeared, causing the streets to steam.

"Jesus H!" Jack raised a middle finger when the car in front of us braked for no apparent reason and we had to swerve into the oncoming lane to avoid rear-ending it. "The idea of rain in sunny Southern California is too much for these people, even when it's quickly over."

Once we were embedded in traffic again, I noticed that he kept checking the rearview mirror every few seconds.

"Is the guy you flipped off chasing us?"

"No, not him, someone else," he answered slowly.

I turned, expecting to see Fortunato's black Buick, but it was a white Chevy ragtop. It stayed with us when Jack stepped on the gas, turned onto Eighth, flashed by the baroque revival Tower Theatre and then climbed up the hill, past clusters of down-and-outers standing in front of seedy residential hotels.

"This is where one of these deadbeats staggers drunkenly into the street and we hit him and then all the others drag us out of the car and beat us to death," Jack said grimly.

I thought he would run the red light at Wilson, but he slammed on the brakes at the last minute to keep from hitting cars entering the intersection from our right and left.

The Chevy convertible came up alongside us. Jack started to sink down into the seat, but then saw that it was Clive Selkirk.

"How's it hanging?" Selkirk asked after reaching over to roll down his passenger-side window

"To the left and at my knees," Jack gave the standard naval response.

Selkirk managed a laugh even though he looked drawn and jumpy.

"I was at the *Examiner* getting an ad I tried to put in the paper rejected. I saw you come out and tried to catch up, but you were too quick for me. So I decided to tail you so you'd see what it feels like."

"You're followed?" Jack asked.

"Constantly," Selkirk had to yell to be heard over the Zephyr's twelve idling cylinders. "You still interested in the labor war?"

"Yeah," Jack said. "Is it still going on?"

"Hot and heavy. There are some new developments."

"Is one of them that your side is losing?"

"They think they've got me surrounded," Selkirk gave a big smile that failed to convince, "but they've got another think coming."

"Who's 'they'?"

"The people who know what I'm saying before I say it and know where I'm going before I get in the car. They're on me day and night."

"Beaufort," I said, but Jack didn't hear me above the traffic noise.

"We should talk," he said, extending his hand to brush his fingertips with Selkirk's.

"I'll call you."

"Okay. Be careful."

"Don't worry about me. I've still got some cards to play. You should look out for yourself, though. They've got you in their viewfinder too."

The signal had changed and horns were honking behind us. Selkirk slid back to his steering wheel and took off ahead of us.

Jack's question—*Who's "they"?*—was left hanging in his exhaust.

NINETEEN

I woke earlier than I wanted to the next morning and lay on the sofa for a long time. Seagulls were floating on updrafts outside the bay window, folding their wings at the top of their rise, dropping like dive bombers, then floating up again. I got up to investigate, and saw seven or eight gulls down on the beach harrying the corpse of a flounder-like fish that had washed up during the night. They had drilled a ragged hole in its side and were waddling around it like curious old men. Every now and then, one of them would stop to hammer at the cavity in the fish, coming away with a smear of purple gut on its beak.

I went outside and shooed them off, toed a hole in the sand, covered the fish for a decent burial, and then took off down the beach. I was alone except for a boy with an empty newspaper delivery bag over his shoulders incongruously smoking a pipe whose pungent latakia smell hit me from fifteen feet away.

When I got back, Jack was up and bustling, in a hopeful mood because Val had agreed to a lunch date when we dropped her off in Toluca Lake after the races. He had taken a long bath and put on cream-colored slacks, a Hawaiian shirt and blue deck shoes; his hair was shiny with Brylcreem.

Just as he was about to leave, the phone rang. I watched his features wilt as he listened, said a few imploring words and then despairingly set the receiver in the cradle.

"Well?" I asked.

"She said she has to cancel because she claims Talbert decided on the spur of the moment to shoot some additional exteriors in San Pedro."

I didn't say anything.

His eyes bored into me. "You know when a woman's lying. It comes off her like a bad smell. Maybe she has someone else." Then he added, "Maybe I should find someone too."

"Wouldn't be hard."

But then he seemed to deflate: "No, this is not one of those problems you can fuck your way out of."

After pretending to read the headlines of the *Times* for a couple of minutes, he said, "It's too quiet. Let's get out of here."

We'd driven into Hollywood so often in the past few weeks that the Zephyr seemed to know the way. As we passed Westwood, we saw several zombies and werewolves, one miniature UCLA football player, and a nurse holding the hand of a fat little chef in a toque and starched apron—all of them walking along Sunset.

"It's Halloween," I said.

"Trick or treat," Jack shot the kids a grim look.

About a mile further down Sunset, I asked where we were going.

"Around," he said curtly.

"Around where?"

"Around to the places Val likes to go."

"Maybe she's actually in San Pedro today like she said."

He gave me a "Yeah, right," look.

We stopped first at the Formosa Cafe on Santa Monica Boulevard. It was next to a storage lot that Warners had bought from United Artists a few weeks earlier and Val sometimes went there because one of the counter men made her real espresso.

The cafe wasn't open yet, so we drove up to Pickwick's Bookstore. Jack knew that Val browsed there for hours at a time and had charmed the owner, Louis Epstein, into locating copies of novels in Italian by Silone and other of her favorite authors.

"Needle in a haystack time," I said when he returned shaking his head after scouring the store.

"Yeah, this is really stupid," he agreed. "We might as well go back home and start counting the grains of sand on the beach."

We headed back down Sunset, but when we got to Fairfax he turned left on a whim. "Since we're close, we might as well make a pass through Farmer's Market. She likes it there. Says it reminds her of the *mercatos* at home."

Normally he would have stopped to give the fruit a squeeze and banter with the vendors, many of them still in overalls after offloading their produce at dawn, but he walked ahead of me without paying attention. Leaving the stalls, we approached the picnic area and saw Val sitting at a table with Temple Rose.

Val was running a forefinger back and forth over her lower lip. Her mascara had melted and streaked under her eyes, making her look like a forlorn mime. She looked away apprehensively when she saw us.

Temple tried to cover for her by waving with false gaiety: "Come and have some iced tea with us. We're sharing a Waldorf salad."

Jack sat next to Val, but they seemed to be in different geographies. Temple nervously tried to fill the distance between them by launching into a comic account of how one of her girls had recently spent an evening with a very drunk Dana Andrews that ended with the actor halfway passed out at the intersection of Wilshire and La Brea.

"Shirley props him up against a lamp post to keep his face from being introduced to the sidewalk and then gets ready to leave. But Andrews suddenly comes to life and calls out to her, 'Will you wait a minute so I can tell a joke?' Shirley says okay. It takes him a second to get his mouth working and then he says, 'So what does it mean when you remember the color of a girl's eyes after the first date?' Shirley says, 'I don't know, what?' Then Andrews says, 'That she's got small tits.'"

Temple ended the story with a hopeful look, but Jack didn't even crack a smile, and I suppressed a laugh out of loyalty to him. We all fell into silence.

Jack watched Val, waiting for her to say something. Finally he stood up: "Guess we'll head home."

"Temple and I are going shopping," Val said without looking at him.

"I guess they cancelled the shoot in San Pedro."

She examined her hands as if they were foreign objects. "I guess they did."

* * *

Val showed up later that afternoon, knocking instead of just coming in, as if not sure she was still welcome. Her eyes were dilated and her skin was flushed; the rapid concussion of her heartbeat agitated the sheerness of her blouse at her neck.

"Temple tells me about Clifton's Cafeteria," she said disjointedly. "You have heard of it? She says it is a very big place and you can choose only the things you like to eat. There is a waterfall on the outside and inside it looks like many different things at once."

"Sounds like our kind of place," I said under my breath, no longer knowing what to expect from her.

"Can we go there?" She spoke hesitantly, prepared for a rejection.

"Of course," Jack said, also prepared for the worst.

She spent nearly an hour in the bedroom getting ready, but still looked improvised when she finally came out—eyes so heavily made up that they seemed to be dark pits; lipstick bleeding outside her lip lines; no earrings or other ornamentation. She was bundled bizarrely in a trench coat although the evening was not chilly.

Jack asked her if she was cold.

"I am dressed the way I feel inside," she responded enigmatically.

As I drove to downtown LA, the two of them made the uncomfortably polite conversation of strangers sitting next to each other on a bus.

"I have a surprise for you," Jack said, gesturing for me to park on Hill Street.

"What is that?" she asked.

He pointed at the boarding area for the Angels Flight funicular, built at the turn of the century to carry the elite between their mansions on the hill and the downtown level below. "They call this the world's shortest railway."

Val became animated as we took a seat in the angled cab of the bright orange car. It lurched upward and she started loudly singing "Funiculì, Funiculà."

When Jack shushed her, she was injured. "But this is a song about a funicular," she said. "When my brother Franco and I are young children and we still live in Naples we sing it when we go up the funicular to Vomero. People sometimes give us coins."

We exited on Olive Street and Val hurried ahead, going south past Pershing Square and across Sixth Street. When we caught up with her, she was staring in wonder at Clifton's façade, a three-story waterfall bordered by neon geysers and jungle foliage.

During the Depression, Clifton's had been known as "the Cafeteria of the Golden Rule" because its quixotic founder, Clifford Clinton, required diners to pay only what they could afford for the food they took. He soon opened another cafeteria on Broadway nearby, with an equally whimsical interior. Once he reluctantly started trying to turn a profit, he built a chain that would become a Southern California institution.

The inside of Clifton's was like an eccentric's warehouse. Val was entranced by the dioramas of the tropics, mountains, and deserts; the redwoods reaching up to the ceiling; the collection of statues and busts; the dried plants under bell jars, and taxidermized animals everywhere, including an entire village of prairie dogs listening intently for intruders.

We took our turkey and roast beef plates to a table near a life-sized sculpture of Christ in the Garden of Gethsemane near a mural showing Jerusalem in the middle distance. It was a testament to the extravagant eclecticism of the place that it seemed no more incongruous than anything else.

As Jack and I were eating, Val arranged the salt and pepper shakers, sugar dispenser, napkin holder and her water glass into a defensive perimeter in front of her plate. The tormented spot on her left arm now oozed bloody plasma.

She stared at the sculpture: "The best thing he said was that death comes like a thief in the night, so we must always be on guard."

Her heightened state gave her such control of the moment that it was like watching a performance.

"I believe in heaven," she said, shifting her gaze to Jack. "But I believe in what you will think is a peculiar way. I believe that we are in heaven right now—in this place and this time. Right at this moment. God created this heaven for us with all its evil and all its goodness. It is a rich and complicated place. We meet some people who are angels and others who are demons. The demons are very persistent. It is possible that God allows them too much power. They destroy the hope and joy He creates."

She kept talking in this manner, not bothering to make transitions between subjects and not expecting a response, after we'd left the restaurant and were walking back to the Angels Flight. She seemed to be relinquishing her hold on idiomatic English.

At one point, she put a hand on Jack's arm to stop him and came so close that their noses almost touched. "I am so afraid for losing you," she said, and then was off again so quickly that we had to double-step to catch up.

On the other side of Olive we saw a couple of bums yelling at each other in an escalating drunken argument. Both had watch caps pulled down over their heads and were dressed in so many layers of torn clothing that they looked like mummies. Soon they were taking slow-motion swings at each other.

"Friday night fights," Jack laughed.

Val had stopped, and he took her arm to keep her walking. But she shook him off and stood there, focused on the combat. We all became aware that the smaller of the two bums was a woman.

At first it was like a pillow fight with both of them throwing soft roundhouse punches that either didn't land or didn't hurt. But then the man finally struck the woman with a hard right cross that made a thocking sound on her jaw and sent her down so hard that she skittered along the sidewalk on her backside.

Val bolted across the street, ignoring an oncoming car that had to swerve wildly to keep from hitting her. She aimed herself at the male bum like a defensive back, knocking him down and falling on top, then slapping at his head and face impotently with both hands.

"You cannot do this! There is no justice in this!"

Jack finally got his hands around her waist and lifted her slightly so that her feet flailed in the air before he set her down again.

The male bum was silent, but the female revived and began to spit incoherent insults at us.

Taking two steps back, Val stood with feet apart and tore open her trench coat, holding its sides out with both hands like an angel unfurling its wings. She was naked underneath and cried out like a coloratura as she flashed the fullness of her glory. Both bums cowered with their arms up over their faces as if witnessing the transfiguration.

She pulled the coat back around her and recinched the belt, then took off for the funicular. Jack and I hurried after her, fearing what came next. But she entered the car of the funicular and sat there listlessly as we began to slant downward to Hill Street. Watching her, I could see that she had rubbed her basic being just as raw as the spot on her arm.

* * *

Val quickly ran inside when we got back to the house. She had thrown off the trench coat and was waiting for Jack when we entered. Her naked body locked onto him as if magnetized; her face was flushed and feral when she grabbed the back of his head and gave him such a carnivorous kiss that I half expected to see him come away bleeding from the mouth. Then she seized his hand and jerked him toward the bedroom so hard that he stumbled along the way.

The noises she made penetrated the shut door; they were so coarse and carnal that I went outside and sat on the deck.

When I came back inside an hour later, they were quiet.

I tried to go to sleep myself, but the events of the evening wouldn't let go. I was still awake at 2:15 when Val emerged from the darkness of the bedroom, now wearing underclothes. She padded to the bay window and looked out enigmatically, as she had so often in the past weeks. The full moon showed her high color and her luxurious hair, gathered into a bun that was already collapsing. Her disregard for how she looked only heightened her wild beauty.

Assuming that I was asleep, she tiptoed to the bathroom and tried to close the door without making noise. A narrow band of light escaped from beneath the jamb, and I heard a jet of urine hit the bowl. When she came out and saw that I was awake and watching, she sat down on the chair opposite me, not bothering to close her legs.

"One thing I forgot to say about heaven when we were talking tonight," she spoke in a thickened voice. "Because heaven is here and now, you understand that when we die we don't go to heaven, we leave it."

After sitting silently for a while, she stood up purposefully, picked up her trench coat and draped it around herself, grabbed the Zephyr's keys from the kitchen and walked out the door. I heard the car start and then she drove off into the darkest part of the night.

TWENTY

The next morning Jack called her apartment several times, but there was no answer.

"I can't do this anymore," he said feebly.

I stepped out onto the deck so he wouldn't see the sadness that had seized me. But the wind coming off the ocean was cold enough to shatter glass, and I came back inside after a few minutes.

By then, he was in his room extracting his dresser drawers one by one and dumping out the clothes on his bed next to his open suitcase. He had turned to the things hanging in his closet when the phone rang. Dropping everything, he ran out to get it.

"Hello? Hello?..." he pressed the receiver to his ear and listened intently. "Val?"

"Was it her?" I asked when he hung up.

"I'm not sure it was anyone," he was baffled. "It might have been just a whisper or maybe static on the line. But it could have been that construction noise outside her place in the background."

He dialed Temple Rose's number but got no answer. He managed to get ahold of a production assistant director at Warners, who told him that the major filming for *Tomorrow* had been done for over a week and they hadn't seen Val since the wrap party.

He tried her apartment again, his face falling with each unanswered ring.

He started to sag, but made an effort to rouse himself. "We've got to try to find her. She was wonderful last night but also very weird. God knows what's going on."

Because she had taken the Zephyr, we had to call a cab. I didn't move fast enough for Jack when it arrived.

"You can stay here and listen to these goddamn waves flopping in all day if you want," he snapped, "but I'm going to find Val."

On the way to Toluca Lake, he spoke only once: "Today is November 3rd, two months to the day since we first saw her at the party."

We found the Zephyr parked on the street in front of Val's apartment building, keys in the ignition, surrounded by construction vehicles and equipment. Jack knocked on her door several times and put his finger on the buzzer for a long burst. Then he tried the knob. It was unlocked and we entered.

He called out her name. The place felt so uninhabited that I half expected an echo.

"Look!" He picked up an envelope from the coffee table with *Gianni* scrawled on the front. It had been sealed and then opened and now had nothing in it.

He opened the bedroom door and started to enter but then staggered back suddenly as if hit by a powerful blast of air, almost falling into me. I held his shoulders and peeked around him and saw Val's naked body on the bed. Her face was nesting in her raven hair like an infertile egg; she was watching infinity. Looking exsanguinated, she was on her back with ankles crossed, one arm pillowing her head and the other casually grasping a wrinkle in the covers at her side: a lifeless odalisque.

Jack gripped the door jamb to steady himself while I went to check for a pulse.

Death was already staking its claim—her body heading toward room temperature; her facial muscles setting; her eyes turned to isinglass. She was a study in subtraction—the glove with the hand withdrawn—but still so perfectly sexual that I had to jam a hand into my pants pocket to quell the stirrings of an erection.

A pharmacist's vial was trapped in the shadow of her underarm, the cap off and a dozen or so tiny pills arranged almost artfully around it. I bent down to look closer and saw the prescription for phenobarbital on the label.

I tried to close her eyelids the way I had so often seen people do it in the movies, but they popped open again as if on springs, the dark pools of the irises as deep as forever. I noticed a thumbtack-sized bruise on her neck and a tiny crust of blood at the corner of her mouth.

Jack tried to come close too, but he couldn't stand the sight of her and turned to slide down the side of the bed onto the floor.

"We need to call someone."

"Your father?"

He looked at me like I was daft.

I went to the living room, got the operator on the phone and told her what had happened, then returned to look again at the still life of Val's body, awed by the magnitude of the journey she had undertaken.

Why had she come to this place to die? And why so utterly alone? And what had the note removed from the envelope said?

I found a bedspread on the shelf of the closet and covered her.

Still sitting on the floor with his back against the side of her mattress, Jack reached for one of Val's dead hands and put it on the top of his head, holding it there with both of his like a young chimp seeking grooming. And for the only time in all the years I knew him—through all the operations and pain and family tragedy—he began to cry.

I walked back into the living room to give him privacy. Looking around, I was struck by how orderly the place was, odd given that Val, like Jack, had cultivated disorganization.

We heard sirens when they were still blocks away.

The cop car beat the ambulance.

"Police," a voice called out from the doorway before a cop entered with his hand hovering over his service revolver. He was a large man with sad eyes and a big nose and a gentle pachyderm manner.

"Officer Mike William," he identified himself, "LA County Sheriff's."

"Williams?" I thought I misheard him.

"No, William singular."

I led him to the bedroom and peeled back the spread from Val's body. After putting two fingertips on her carotid, he took a pencil out of his breast pocket and used it to prod at the pills under her arm. Then he stood back, his head swaying in a slow negative that radiated genuine sadness.

"Jesus. Just look at her. Why does a beautiful woman like that want to go and do something like this for?"

Still sitting on the floor holding Val's hand, Jack spoke in a small voice: "Lem says there's a little blood on her mouth."

"And a tiny bruise on her neck," I added.

"Looks like a hickey," the cop said, giving it a cursory glance.

He saw Jack droop, and quickly knelt to pat his shoulder with guilty sympathy.

"Sorry. That was dumb of me. I guess I've seen too many of these things. After a while your ability to feel properly gets out of whack."

The cop and I stood there for a minute, unable to keep our eyes off her. The necrophilia finally became so palpable that he covered her again with the bedspread.

"Maybe you should look for fingerprints," Jack said.

The cop went down on his haunches again to be level with him. "I don't have that equipment," he said almost tenderly. "And hers would probably be the only ones anyway. But the coroner will take a look and let us know if there's anything suspicious."

By then the ambulance attendants had entered with all their apparatus and were waving us out of the room so they could begin milling around the bed and preparing to cart out the remains.

I felt like my heart had been pulled out by the roots.

TWENTY-ONE

It was dark when we got home. Jack went to his room and crawled into bed fully clothed, including his dress shoes. He didn't get up until after one o'clock the next day, when he shambled into the kitchen wearing a cardigan sweater over his crumpled clothes. He had misaligned the buttons and seemed to be tilting.

Without saying a word, he sat down at the table and began pounding on his Underwood with his face close to the keys, inserting paper and ripping it out every minute or two so forcefully that the roller whined liked a reel with a trout on the line. He wadded up the used sheets violently and threw them onto the growing mound in the corner of the room.

I asked him what he was trying to write.

"I'm just trying to get my memories of her down," he said frantically. "Everything I can think of, before it all goes away. But I can't get her words and the way her mind worked. I can't get the way she looked, the way she felt, the way she molded to me. If I had it as a writer I would be able to do this."

He hadn't eaten in twenty-four hours. He had raccoon eyes and his face was gaunt, looking like he was slightly sucking in his cheeks.

After staring hopelessly at the typewriter for a couple of minutes more, he stood up and staggered back to bed.

He was still there the next morning when the Old Man entered the house, looking around carefully before asking how Jack was.

"See for yourself." I gestured toward the bedroom.

He went in and shut the door. I could hear his voice badgering, cajoling, commanding, without any response.

Finally he emerged, shaking his head. "I got him to take off his shoes and get rid of that goddamn sweater, but that's about it. I've never seen him like this before, even when he was a sickly kid. I'm worried. He's just barely there."

By the time he left, he was issuing orders again: "Listen, you need to get him on his feet as soon as possible. Get some food into him and get him thinking straight. We need to head back to Hyannis so we can get everything back to normal and start moving ahead. I'm counting on you to do whatever is necessary."

* * *

A couple of hours after the Old Man left, Officer William showed up, his hangdog look still radiating gloom. I rousted Jack and he came into the kitchen in his underwear and house slippers.

The cop noticed his dog tags. "I tried to enlist in the Army, Marines, Navy and Coast Guard. None of them would take me, not even the Merchant Marine, because I've got a big goddamn hole in my ear drum."

At another time, Jack would have given his usual blithe response to noncombatant guilt: "Don't feel bad. You didn't miss a thing. Anyway, at heart we were all 4F—Find them, Feel them, Fuck them, Forget them."

But now his dead face just stared straight ahead.

Officer William centered himself like someone about to give a speech: "The coroner said there was penobarb in your friend's stomach, as we assumed. Apparently more than thirty pills. She wasn't fooling around. I checked with the doctor who prescribed them. He treats a bunch of people who work at Warner Brothers. He said that your friend consulted him a couple of weeks ago because she couldn't sleep. Apparently he hands these things out like Jujubes."

For a moment, Jack seemed about to cry again.

"The coroner didn't have much to say about the bruise but he did find a small amount of blood inside the mouth."

"From what?" I asked.

"You bite the inside of your mouth while you're chewing. You have a sudden muscle spasm and your teeth click. Who knows?"

Jack looked like he wanted to say something but wasn't physically able.

"I can understand why you'd want some kind of explanation," the cop tried to help him. "Nothing more natural than that. I've worked for the sheriff's office for sixteen years and I've seen enough unexplained deaths to fill a city cemetery. There's never an explanation for something like this anyway, not even when there's an explanation. After a while, you might tell yourself that some blanks just never get filled in because some situations are so random, or so much part of a pattern that we can't see. And you wouldn't be dishonoring your friend's memory by thinking that way."

Jack didn't say anything, and the cop left.

"Nice of him to come all the way out here to tell us personally," I said.

"He was just feeling guilty about the hickey comment," Jack mumbled, unable to repress his mordancy.

Officer William came back once more, about four hours later. This time he spoke from the doorway without entering.

"I got ahold of the coroner and spoke to him directly. He said that the little cut inside her mouth was not some kind of chewing thing. 'Could have been caused by anything from a fork to a fingernail,' was how he put it. Further than that he wouldn't go."

Then, seeing the raw pain on Jack's face, he added, "I'll keep poking around and let you know if anything turns up."

After he left, Jack agreed to get dressed and try to eat something. But he just stared at the egg sandwich I made for him, picking it up and setting it down a couple of times as if assaying its weight before tossing it in the trash. He agreed to go out for a drive only because I told him we could stop at the little restaurant where we'd first taken Val.

* * *

It seemed indecent that it should be one of those great Southern California beach afternoons when the sun is holding back a little but the air is fresh and formations of screeching gulls are riding the updrafts like glider pilots.

As we drove down the Pacific Coast Highway, I rattled on about things that generally got a rise from Jack—Hedda Hopper's column that morning in the *LA Times* implying with spiteful innuendo that Cary Grant and Randolph Scott were more than housemates; a radio report on how Mayor Fletcher Bowron, who had propagandized for packing off California's

Japanese Americans to relocation centers after Pearl Harbor without so much as a sayonara, was now first in line to welcome them back; a letter I'd received the previous day from Bobby, who had joined the Navy late in the war, saying that he was scheduled to get out in a week and he still felt like a "draft dodger" because he hadn't been in combat.

Only the last item got a rise out of Jack. "Ah, black Robert," he said almost inaudibly without looking my way. "Always just a bit too late and now under attack once again by his guilty Catholic self."

I pulled into the Taste of the Sea parking lot, and Jack made a beeline for the spot where Val had waded into the ocean a few weeks ago. He stood there for a long time staring at the horizon, then slowly returned and slumped down in the front seat as if he'd just finished a ten-mile hike.

Driving randomly now, I turned on the radio and tried to get him going by joining the Andrews Sisters in "Rum and Coca-Cola" in my best falsetto. But he was dead to me and everything else, so I drove home.

He plodded toward the house like he was headed to the electric chair, and was about to climb back in bed when I told him he was getting rank and ought to bathe.

"I know," he said, picking his shirt off his chest to sniff his body odor. "But right now I still have her smell on me. When I wash it off she's gone forever."

TWENTY-TWO

Temple Rose, who seemed to be plugged into everything, called the next evening to tell us that Val's funeral was scheduled for the following day, November 9, at the Wee Kirk o' the Heather at Forest Lawn.

After we got up, Jack gave in and reluctantly ran a bath. A half hour later he exited the steamy bathroom fully dressed and looking like his ghost.

His eyes were closed when we drove through the Forest Lawn gates, so he missed the brazen spectacle of the place—lawns as manicured as putting greens, splashing fountains everywhere, and bronzes of Abraham Lincoln, Teddy Roosevelt, Mark Twain and other secular figures bizarrely mixed in with statuary featuring Marcus Aurelius and Laocoön.

There were no deciduous trees whose falling leaves might generate somber thoughts. Groundskeepers and other employees wore fixed smiles. Discreet signs directed visitors to burial plots with anodyne names like Eventide, Babyland, and Dawn of Tomorrow.

Transfiguration was all around us without a sign of Death.

I knew a little about the Wee Kirk because I had followed newspaper accounts of Jean Harlow's service when it was held there a few years earlier. Louis B. Mayer himself had directed the funeral ceremony as if it were a feature film, with Nelson Eddy and Jeanette MacDonald singing "Indian Love Call" in the climactic scene. Mayer ordered the police to keep fans back until all the celebrities had made their getaway, at which point he let them release the horde of anguished female spectators to rush forward and fight over petals from the commemorative flower displays.

A platoon of cameramen had captured that spectacle, but today there was only one lonely photographer at the entry to the chapel, standing there with his press card in his hatband, checking people out before shooting to make sure they mattered enough to waste a flashbulb.

Inside and out, the Wee Kirk was an uncannily exact copy of a country church in Scotland. The sunlight streaming in through stained-glass windows illuminated scenes from a tragic Scottish courtship and cast a lucent mosaic across the pews. The organ music was mournfully upbeat; the huge wreaths of flowers at the altar gave off the smell of death with the sting removed.

Val was lying tilted slightly upward on a bed of satin in the open casket, wearing an elegant mauve silk dress. Her hands were folded over her chest, with a single white rose entwined in the fingers. A makeup artist from Warners had done her face and hair. She was perfect as Snow White in her glass coffin waiting for the wakeup kiss.

I didn't recognize most of the thirty or so people scattered like extras through the church. But Veronica Lake was there, near the back, a surprisingly petite woman whose trademark veil of platinum hair, as usual, hid one side of her face. Next to her was John Payne and a couple of other cast members of *Tomorrow Is Too Late*, along with two well-dressed men wearing matching ties and pocket squares who appeared to be low-level Warners executives. Several rows ahead of them, Temple Rose sat weeping quietly with her cheek pressed into Jimmy Adcock's shoulder.

Jack shuffled like a stroke victim as I led him into the pew behind them. Across the aisle I saw the bizarre figure of Emile Beaufort, reading a hymnal as avidly as a suspense novel, his normal eye just a few inches from the pages.

Fortunato was up front, bracketed by Geist and his twin bodyguards. Seeming to sense our presence, he stood and turned around, suddenly becoming kinetic. Geist grabbed his shoulder and whispered urgently into his ear, at the same time commanding the Sicilians to block his access to the aisle. Fortunato shot a look of unalloyed hatred at Jack and then allowed Geist to pull him back down.

After more whispering between them, Geist came back to where we were sitting.

"Why are you here?" Jack asked preemptively.

"I'm here for Nicky. And Nicky wants you to take a hike."

"Why?"

"Maybe because he doesn't think his daughter would be dead if she hadn't met you?"

"I cared more about her than he did."

"I doubt that," Geist said smoothly, "but I guarantee that you and Nicky are headed for a big falling out if you don't leave." Then he added, with oily conciliation, "I'd probably be a little more forgiving myself at a time like this, but my only begotten child didn't just kill herself."

I saw that Fortunato had stood up again. Jimmy Adcock rose too, as if in readiness, and Temple Rose put a restraining hand on his arm.

"Let's go," I took Jack's elbow. "This could get out of control. We'll say our goodbyes in our own way. This is not our show."

He pried my hand off his sleeve, but then let me usher him out of the chapel.

The sun stabbed our eyes and Jack reeled like a blind man until I pulled his dark glasses out of his breast pocket and put them on him. He resisted when I tried to head him toward the car, instead walking over to sit on a memorial bench under a tree with a sign inviting newlyweds to pose for pictures there after saying their vows in the Wee Kirk. We could hear a priest droning the Latin liturgy, an enemy language in this habitat of Scots Presbyterians, and a eulogy given by someone whose voice was unfamiliar and whose words were indistinct. Then the organ played "Over the Rainbow" and the doors opened. A youthful handler hustled Lake and Payne toward a limousine idling in the parking lot, with the solitary photographer running after them. Geist and the Draco twins smoothly handed Fortunato into another limo, which proceeded straight to the front of the queue headed to the graveside.

Beaufort was one of the last to emerge from the chapel. He headed straight toward us, but hesitated when he saw Temple Rose coming our way too, and then veered off when a police cruiser entered the parking lot.

A cop we hadn't seen before got out, hitched up his pants and centered his dark glasses with a forefinger before sauntering over to us.

"I'm Officer Decker," he spoke in a slightly adenoidal voice that accented his superciliousness. "Officer William is no longer on the case and the department asked me to come by to let you know that the coroner has determined that everything was within normal limits."

"Normal limits," Jack repeated in a monotone.

"Normal limits," the cop said again, as if closing out a litany. "The words speak for themselves."

Then, after surveying the scene, he nodded slightly and headed back to his cruiser. As he opened the door, I thought I saw Geist shoot him a look of recognition out of the rear window of his limousine.

Temple Rose watched the cop drive off: "I'm not sure you should take everything they're telling you at face value."

The way she said it caused the idea of behindness—deep meanings suppressed by official explanations—to pop into my head.

Jack looked at her blankly. She took hold of his hand with both of hers, but he withdrew it. She shook her head sadly as I guided him to the Zephyr and got him in. While I was starting the engine, she tapped on the driver's side window, and I rolled it down.

Looking across me at Jack, she said, "I know you don't want to talk about this right now and maybe I shouldn't mention it either, but if you want to know the state Val was in, you should be aware that a week ago she asked about working for me."

Jack tried to break out of his fugue state.

"I know," she nodded. "It seems unbelievable. But it's true. I already knew from the conversations we'd had that something was eating at her—taking big bites. But this threw me for a loop. At first I thought it was a joke. But she told me, 'This is the profession I deserve.' I wasn't having it, of course. I told her, 'There are many reasons to become a courtesan'—I would have used a different word with anyone else—'but a guilty conscience is sure as hell not one of them.' I tried a couple of times to get her to tell me what the problem was, but she wouldn't say any more about it."

Tears were cutting paths down through the powder on her face now: "That girl was quality. She just had too many things to deal with."

"And maybe she was a little crazy to begin with," Jack said bitterly.

"You shouldn't believe that," Temple implored. "We don't know…"

But seeing that Jack had resigned from the conversation, she shrugged and stood back from the car, releasing us. As we pulled out of the parking lot, I saw her in the rearview mirror looking down at the ground.

On the drive home, Jack stuck his hand out the passenger window with fingers flattened into a rigid wing, and angled it up and down against the wind like a child experimenting with aerodynamics. It occurred to me that everything—the bruise, the blood at the corner of her mouth, the empty envelope on the coffee table, the coroner's true opinion, the death itself—would always just be random data incapable of correlation, except in a world where all such events were presumed to have a suppressed message and meaning.

* * *

When we got to the beach house, Jack sat down on the sofa, took off his shoes, and drew a knitted throw around his shoulders, shivering slightly although it was in the high seventies.

I went into the kitchen and spent a half hour on an unnecessary clean-up and then looked in on him again. He was staring at the painting of Val's mother. The silence in the living room was coldhearted and I asked him if I could turn on the radio.

"No noise," he said, not looking back at me.

I went back in the kitchen and rustled around some more.

After a few minutes he called me back into the living room. "It's too quiet. You can go ahead with the radio."

I turned the dial until I heard Spike Jones's nutty version of "Cocktails for Two." This usually broke us up, but not today. The program was called *Make Believe Ballroom*, hosted by someone named Al Jarvis, who played one song after another with a little commentary about each and few commercial interruptions, a format we hadn't heard on the East Coast.

When the network news came on at the top of the hour, the anchor was in the middle of a detailed piece about a joint commission created by the U.S. and the U.K. to examine the question of European Jews and Palestine, when a local newscaster came on: "We interrupt this program for breaking news. Authorities have confirmed the death of a local labor leader in an incident near Pershing Square. Our reporter has just returned from the scene..."

Jack and I locked eyes when the news report played an interview with a sobbing female eyewitness.

"...and when he came out of the building I recognized him as the man who led the strikes at Warners and Paramount. He saw me looking and gave me a big smile as he got into his little Chevy. I was walking away when he started the engine, but then I heard this huge boom. I turned and saw the car suddenly expand like a paper bag with air being blown into it and then explode in a ball of fire. The guy went up through the car's convertible top like a rocket. He broke right through and came down with his head and shoulders bent and the stumps of his legs pouring blood. He screamed, 'The blankety blanks have killed me!' I can't say the word he used on radio. I went over to help but there was nothing to do. I watched his eyes go dim and he died right there in front of me."

Jack began slowly shaking his head: "Why did they have to do that to him? It was over. They'd won and he'd lost. His union was finished and he wasn't a threat anymore. He was done for. They didn't have to kill him."

He jumped up with a frantic look on his face and put on his shoes while the newscaster continued:

"... The police are still investigating, but preliminary indications are that the explosion was caused by an iron waterpipe filled with dynamite wired to the car's ignition."

Jack wasn't listening anymore. "Let's go!" he commanded.

"Where?"

"To Geist's place."

"Why?"

"He's behind all this!" Jack yelled incoherently. "We can't just keep doing nothing about all these things. I need you to drive me over to his bar right now!"

"Geist probably won't be back from the funeral yet," I tried to stall him. "Fortunato might still be with him. It could be a bad scene."

"I don't give a shit." He was forcing his arms into his windbreaker. "Let's go!"

I stayed put, gesturing for him to sit back down and pleading, "We need to think this over."

He glared sternly at me, grabbed the car keys off the kitchen table and headed toward the door. I thought he might go without me, but he stopped and stood with his back to me for a moment, then took the windbreaker off and returned to the sofa. His expression said that he was no longer trying to make sense of it all.

The next morning's early edition of the *LA Times* played the story up big, featuring faint and hypocritical praise for Selkirk by some of the studio heads, including Jack Warner, who called him "a man of strong convictions." Local labor figures were also interviewed. One of them was Geist himself, who said, when asked who might be responsible for the murder,

"Maybe another Communist. Look what happened to Trotsky. For these reds, small political disagreements are deadly things. They know how to hate. They're like tiny organisms devouring each other in a drop of water."

TWENTY-THREE

Jack got up early the next day, called the Hearst headquarters in New York and resigned. The editor he spoke with offered him a raise to get him to stay, but Jack hung up on him.

He spent the rest of the day sitting on our deck watching the waves crash on the shore and drag what little shingle there was back with them on their withdrawal. Once when I went out to check on him, he nodded mechanically at the water and said: "Sophocles heard it long ago on the Aegean..."

Rousing himself to quote from my favorite poem even when he was at the bottom of a rock slide of misery himself was Jack's oblique way of showing that he appreciated my presence. Comments like this—the right thing at the right moment—were part of what neutralized his narcissism and bonded people so strongly to him.

Tragedy was definitely not his métier. More than anyone I've ever known, he hated unhappiness. He not only didn't want to be unhappy himself, he didn't want to have anyone anywhere near him who was unhappy. All his friends knew that if they gave the slightest sign of feeling blue he would unleash cutting ridicule and then, if they didn't immediately "snap out of it," as he liked to say, he would quarantine them as ruthlessly as if they had typhoid. But now he gave himself over to an immobilizing grief, allowing it to wrap its coils around him and squeeze.

Late in the afternoon the phone rang. I waited for him to come inside and get it. When he didn't, I picked it up.

"This is Emile calling," the Bayou voice was unctuous. "Emile Beaufort. I believe this is Mr. Billings? I hope you remember me."

"Yes, the home invader."

"Amusing." He sidestepped my disdain. "I had a matter I was going to tell young Mr. Kennedy about the other day at Forest Lawn, but it didn't seem to be the right moment."

"It wasn't."

"Perhaps it is now."

"It never will be."

"Is he there?"

"He can't come to the phone."

I was about to hang up when he said, "All right, then, let me give you the information and you can pass it on to him and his father. Please tell them that I'm showing a movie. The two of them are guests of honor. The movie is being presented at the old Excalibur Theatre on Pico. Three p.m. tomorrow. It's a command performance in every respect. Tell them that they will both see familiar faces. I'm hoping to secure financing for it, so Mr. Kennedy Senior should definitely be there. And your young friend too."

"Don't expect us," I said.

"It would be a mistake not to attend," he continued, obviously enjoying himself. "Please believe me, this is something the Kennedys father and son won't want to miss. Or"—here he lowered his voice into an octave of melodrama—"have someone else see before they do."

The call was as creepy as it was corny. After hanging up, I told Jack about it. He just kept looking out at the ocean, giving no indication that he had heard me. I thought I'd better telephone the Old Man.

The line to his room at the Biltmore was busy for a long time. When I finally got through and told him about Beaufort, the only thing I heard for several seconds was the sound of two and two being put together.

"I don't know what he's cooked up, but even though he's a weird son of a bitch, he's not a man you ignore. Bring Jack over here tomorrow at 1:30 and he and I will go see what this asshole wants."

Later on, when Jack seemed to be paying attention, I told him about the plan.

"I'm not going to be part of this, whatever it is," he replied without looking at me. "I'm not interested in any of this shit anymore."

I told him that his father had been insistent.

"Up his." Jack was still staring out at the ocean.

I called the Old Man early the next morning and told him that Jack refused to come.

"Did you tell him how important this is to me?" He was ready to smash the rebellion.

"I told him."

"What was his response?"

"Up yours."

"Up *mine*?" I could hear the choler start to rise, but then he let it go. "Oh well, he's distraught. Probably just as well that he stays there anyhow. I don't know what Beaufort has up his sleeve, but it's bound to be disagreeable at bare minimum. You can come in Jack's place."

"Me?"

"Yeah. I've got Molly on something else today and I'm sure as hell not doing this by myself."

I didn't say anything right away.

"Yes?" he rammed the word into the phone.

"Yes."

There was no resisting him.

* * *

I drove to the Biltmore knowing already that I was in over my head. The Old Man had left the door to his third-floor suite open for me. He was sitting at a desk talking on the phone—not issuing orders as usual, but listening carefully and giving minimal responses. As he talked, he nervously yanked on the beaded chain of the desk lamp, turning the light on and off.

He didn't look at me until he hung up. Then he just said, "Let's go," and put on his coat and headed out the door.

While we waited for the elevator I tried to make small talk, saying that I'd read somewhere that Mickey Cohen had three double rooms with craps tables in the Biltmore.

"That's on a different floor," he said tersely. "Never seen him. Ships passing in the night."

There were three rented Chrysler Imperials waiting for us outside the hotel, each with its own burly driver.

"Our crash cars," the Old Man gestured for me to join him in the back seat of the middle one.

"Why do we need them?" I asked as the first Chrysler moved out a few yards ahead of us and the second one stayed tight on our back bumper.

"Maybe you've forgotten I've already been shot at once," he rasped. "These are armored and have bulletproofed glass. Things seem to be coming to a head. Forget about bullets, I don't want someone head-onning me or slamming into my ass."

He stared straight ahead as our convoy took off. When we passed the intersection of Grand and Third Street, I recognized it as the site of the great scene in the Harold Lloyd movie where he floods the streets with soapy water that makes cops and pedestrians slip and slide.

It took about twenty minutes to get to the Excalibur, a derelict Art Deco movie palace at San Vincente and Pico with rising ziggurat patterns cut into its stone façade. The few random letters hanging off-center on the marquee made an unbreakable code. There were no posters in the display windows at the entrance, and the thick glass on the cashier's cage had a deep fracture someone had tried to suture with a couple of layers of heavy gray tape.

We were an hour early. Apparently the Old Man had already scoped out the area because he told the drivers to park the Chryslers a block away after dropping us at a coffee shop directly across from the theatre. He demanded a table at the big front window, with a perfect view of the Excalibur's entrance.

I asked him why we were taking these precautions.

"Because Beaufort's a rat," he growled, "and you don't trust rats. And also because we don't know what he's selling yet or if someone else is backing his play."

Nobody came or went from the theatre during the time we sat silently sipping our lukewarm coffee. Finally, at a few minutes before three the Old Man told me to go in and check things out, and give him a high sign if everything looked all right.

When I hesitated, he made a shooing motion with his hand: "Go on, nothing's going to happen to you."

The theatre's double door was unlocked and when I stepped into the lobby it was dark as a cave. I half expected to be smacked with a cosh or grabbed from behind in a chokehold.

Light was leaking out from the bottom of the auditorium doors. I entered and saw Beaufort, an audience of one, rocking autistically in an aisle seat. His hair was carefully combed; the rest of him was a chapter of errors.

He waved enthusiastically as if we were old friends, while trying to hide the bottle inside a paper bag on his lap.

"I'm glad to see you but I hope you brought the Kennedys."

"Just me for now."

His wandering eye seemed to be checking out the periphery of the theatre to make sure the Old Man wasn't hiding in the shadows.

"Yes, of course. I understand. Mr. Kennedy sent you to make sure it's safe. A careful man, Mr. Kennedy. One of the things I've always liked about him. Go ahead and have a look around so you can tell him that the coast is clear."

After a quick check, I went back outside and gave the Old Man the high sign. He hurried out of the coffee shop and across the street to the theatre, leaving me behind as he practically ran to the auditorium. When I caught up, he was standing menacingly over Beaufort.

"What's going on here, you goddamn freak?"

"No need for unpleasantness." Beaufort made an effort to get his eyes in synch so he could return the Old Man's livid stare. "It's just a movie premiere. I know you like movies, Mr. Kennedy. And I believe you will want to invest in the one I'm about to show you. It's a double feature but it won't take long because they are also short subjects."

Relishing the moment, he put on a smug smile: "I think it might be better if I left so you can react to what you're about to see without my disturbing presence. But as I said to Mr. Billings, I would like to discuss the financing for this movie as soon as possible, so please contact me at the Hotel Highpoint."

He headed up the aisle in his oddly disjointed walk, pausing to turn and say with mock courtesy, "Please make yourselves comfortable, gentlemen. Sadly the popcorn machine is not working today, but the feature will begin right away."

"Son of a bitch thinks he's funny," the Old Man muttered fiercely as he flopped into a seat.

The theatre went dark and without warning Jack and Val appeared, on the bed at the beach house, all skin. There was no sound and the film looked to have been shot through a flimsy window covering, giving the print a gauzy look. But the two of them lit up the screen. She was on her side looking away, the knobs of her vertebrae curving from her neck to her waist like the keyboard of some fine fleshly instrument. Jack was behind her, one arm over her arm and chest as their bodies moved to spoon in a compatible double S. He said something that caused her to laugh into her pillow. Then he turned onto his back, his chest still slippery from sexual exertion, and looked in the general direction of the camera with the vacant face of someone who doesn't realize he's being watched.

I could imagine the rustle of the sheets as bodies shifted again and limbs lengthened and contracted. Jack smiled appreciatively as she rolled over to face him and propped her head on an elbow so she could give him a once-over. As she watched him, he pushed her opulent hair back from her forehead and then twirled an index finger indolently on one of her nipples; she responded by gnawing on his ear and picking up his lolling penis from the inside of his thigh. She was so luminously alive that I could almost smell her and feel the consequence of her nearness. But then the film ended in light flashes and a blackout and she died again.

The Old Man stood up and screamed at the projection booth, "If you think you can blackmail Jack with this, you fucking mutant, you've got another think coming!"

He started up the aisle, but the transitional flickers and test patterns of another film that immediately appeared on the screen stopped him. He sat where he was, a few rows behind me.

Also soundless, this one was shot from within the frame of some kind of opening, perhaps in the wall of an adjoining room, that gave deep perspective. Grainy and harsh, it had the feel of the contraband blue movies of the era that small groups of men watched being projected onto sheets tacked on the walls of secret locations.

A diminished version of Val appeared, sitting naked on the edge of a bed facing the hidden camera, her whole front sagging like an older woman as she looked down at the floor. The Old Man was in profile in a nearby chair beside a nightstand, leering at her. He wore only a sleeveless T-shirt.

She said something without looking at him. The Old Man smirked a reply. Then he pointed down at his groin and beckoned with his finger.

She shook her head. He gave the shrug of someone who holds the hole card and said some more undecipherable words. Val didn't move for several seconds. Then, beginning to cry, she lowered herself to her knees, crawled to him and buried her face in the pubic area just below the camera's field of vision as the film ran off its spool.

As I sat there paralyzed, the Old Man walked down to me with a look of panic on his face. His cheeks were mottled and his eyes big. I expected a brazen lie denying the empirical truth of what I'd just seen, but instead he held out his hands imploringly.

"She wasn't right for Jack. She wasn't stable and would have just held him back. Can you imagine what the press would do to us when they found out about her family tree? I had to separate them. I didn't do her any harm. Nobody was ever killed by fucking. I was just doing what was best for Jack."

"She was what was best for him, every minute of every day they were together. You know that."

The Old Man bought time by taking off his glasses, fogging the lenses with his breath and wiping them with the tail of his tie. Then, unable to stall any longer, he ratted on himself: "She went with me because I told her that if she didn't I'd get Edgar to deport her criminal father and she knew I could do it."

"You blackmailed her into betraying Jack."

He knew that this was the bottom-line truth, and for a minute he looked like he might spill everything, but then he regained control and his faced settled into a caustic smile: "I don't think the subtleties of sexual relationships are necessarily your strong suit, Lemoyne."

I ignored him: "You actually intended to hold up your end of the deal?"

The tip of his tongue explored the edges of his mouth before he replied, "Sort of an academic question now, don't you think?"

We both looked up and saw Beaufort's face briefly in the window of the projection room before it went dark.

"That son of a bitch is going to regret this," the Old Man muttered fiercely.

Then he commanded, "Don't you ever dare say a word about any of this to Jack!" and bolted out of the theatre.

I found him outside in the middle of the street, forcing traffic to stop as he looked for Beaufort, who was nowhere in sight.

* * *

Chief among Joseph Kennedy's prized mottoes—always announced as if it had just been freshly coined—was "Don't get mad, get even." But he was in an uncontrolled rage in the back seat of the Chrysler on the way back to the Biltmore, breathing noisily and working his jaw as if chewing tough meat. He looked like he might start bleeding from the ears any minute.

When we arrived at the hotel, he jumped out and headed for the lobby without a word. He probably expected me to follow, but I felt that I needed to get away and asked the valet to bring up the Zephyr.

On the drive home, I tried to put the events of the past few days into some kind of order, but it was impossible to dig a foundation strong enough to support them all.

Soon after I hit the Pacific Coast Highway, I saw a cop car about a quarter mile ahead on the soft shoulder. I was going too fast and tried to brake inconspicuously. But after I passed, the flashing red light came after me.

I pulled over and got out my license. I was fishing for the registration in the glove box when I heard a tapping sound on the window and looked up to see the rugged face of Temple Rose's plainclothes boyfriend, Jimmy Adcock. When I rolled down the window, he put his forearms on the sill and looked in.

"Is Vice giving out speeding tickets now?" I asked.

"Ah, the false indignation of the lawbreaker," he chuckled. "Actually, no, Vice is not giving out tickets. Vice just wants to have a brief word."

"How did you know I'd be coming this way?"

"Ninety percent of my job is waiting. The other ten percent is knowing where to wait."

He raised his head to squint back at the traffic, the velocity of the passing cars making his hair stand on end. Then he came down to eye level again.

"I'm here as a favor to Temple. She's tried calling your friend and says he's not all that receptive to new information right now. So this comes to you for safe keeping."

"Okay."

"Off the record."

"Okay."

"Temple asked me to drop by the coroner's and try to unravel things. He basically told me that he was encouraged from on high to put this whole thing to bed, but he also said he probably wouldn't have been able to take it anywhere anyhow. He says it's possible that there was what we public servants call foul play, but just barely possible."

"It feels like we're speaking in Braille," I said. "Where does all this lead?"

He shrugged and stood back from the window. "Not for me to say. Just filling in the picture for you so you see things the way cops do. Things rarely add up in this world, and when they do it's usually an illusion. Anyway, you seem to be the lead detective on this case so you get to follow up. Temple says the girl told her that this was very much a love story. You don't have to work for the LAPD to know that love stories are by their nature detective stories too. Good luck."

He got back into his car, pulled out around me and headed off, blending smoothly into the traffic.

TWENTY-FOUR

Jack was on his back in bed with his hands folded over his chest like a corpse when I got home. Assuming he was asleep, I began softly closing his door to keep from disturbing him when he spoke without opening his eyes.

"I'm awake. And I know what's up. So you don't have to figure out how to sugarcoat things. Temple called while you were gone. I didn't want to talk to her but I did. She couldn't stand the idea that I might really think Val was crazy, so she told me everything she knows. About Dad and everything else."

I started to speak but he raised a hand so imperatively it stopped my tongue in its tracks.

"I don't want you to say anything more about this to me, now or ever. Understand?" There was no hint of the drollery that he usually used to sweeten his serious pronouncements. "I don't want to understand the details of the sex and blackmail thing. I don't want to understand Dad's rationale. I don't want to understand why Val gave in. I don't want to understand what Dad and Geist have been doing. I don't want to understand why Selkirk had to be killed. I don't want to know where Fortunato fits in. I don't want to discover the truth of any of this, get it? I just want out."

The box springs creaked definitively as he turned toward the wall.

Early that evening the phone rang. I knew it would be the Old Man.

"What's Jack doing?" he asked abruptly.

"He's back in bed."

"Pretty soon he'll be his old self again." I heard the sound of knuckles being cracked in the background and knew he was holding the phone to his ear by his shoulder. "He's pissed off at me right now, but sooner or later he'll realize that the girl would probably have wound up in a straightjacket, given what she went through."

He knew that his words sickened me, and he didn't care.

"Anyway, time to bring this fucking farce with Beaufort to an end. I'm sending Molly over to his place tomorrow with five grand cash for the film. We pay now and get it back with interest later on. Someone from the family needs to be there. Not me, certainly. Beaufort may be a goddamn morphodite himself, but he might have some muscle lined up, who knows? And I'm sure as hell not going to subject Jack to any danger, given the state he's in. So it has to be you."

I thought of asking the Old Man how I had gone from being the wallpaper of his life to serving as his confidant and co-conspirator, the guy who caught the shit before it hit his fan, but he answered the question in advance.

"To Beaufort and whoever else is involved in all this, you're just some hanger-on. You're not someone they'll care about one way or another. So you don't have to worry. I need a clear report about what happens when that prick is paid off, so I can plan for what comes next. That's why you need to be there. Molly's good in his way, but he sometimes doesn't see the forest for the trees."

Then, with a combination of threat and supplication, he cinched the deal: "I need you to do this, Lemoyne. You're doing it for me, you're doing it for the family, but you're mainly doing it for Jack. Don't let him down."

I closed the cell door on myself: "I won't."

"Good," the Old Man said, pleased to have gotten his way as usual. "I knew we could count on you."

* * *

Late the next morning I heard the blast of a car horn and looked out to see Molly Maguire standing next to one of the idling Chrysler Imperials from the previous day. Jack's bedroom door was still closed, so I left without saying anything.

"How's that shoulder you got banged up?" I asked Molly.

He rotated it experimentally and took a batting stance, "I think I could still get around on a high hard one."

Then he said, "Tempus fugit, Lemoyne. Let's vamoose."

He filled the car with the smell of Old Spice and Pepsodent tooth-powder; his skin was taut and shiny from a close shave. He took pride in piloting the car through the heavy morning traffic, weaving in and out of lanes like a slalom skier as he timed the traffic lights. When we finally hit a red after a long series of greens, he pulled a pint bottle out of the glove compartment.

"Never too early for the little green man, is it?"

"Bushmills?" I asked.

"None of that feckin' Protestant piss," he made a face. "We would not defile our bodies with that. It's Jameson, whiskey of the one true faith."

He unscrewed the cap and offered me the bottle. When I shook my head, he shrugged and held it up to the windshield in a mock toast: "May our enemies be afflicted with itching and have no possibility of scratching."

Then he took a long swig, gave a theatrical "Ah!" and said, "Thus is the world renewed again."

He drove in silence for several minutes, but I knew that he liked to talk so I gave him an excuse to tell about his always befuddled Irish relatives by asking what was new back home. He launched right into a tale about the love life of Aileen, an eighteen-year-old second cousin living in Drogheda.

"As beautiful as polished copper, this girl; the family jewel since she was a little tiny thing and courted by many fine young fellows. But then some cabbage twice her age appears. Underneath the fancy jacket and account books he's a dirty tooth of a man. But everyone blandishes him because of his bank account and the next thing you know, he's gone and plugged the fair Aileen. If it was me that was her father, I'd be making a shambles of the villain, but because she's expecting, her father, son of my own father's brother, calls in the priest. The next thing you know, it's *omnia vincit amor*. And now Aileen, this fine lace of a girl, is harnessed to this eejit for a lifetime." He morosely contemplated the injustice of it all until we reached the Hotel Highpoint in a seedy block of La Brea.

Molly got a satchel out of the car trunk, cradled it carefully under one arm and gave it a little pat. "Beaucoup spondulicks in here." He smiled like the money was his own.

The Highpoint was a fleabag, just as the Old Man had said. The odor of fried onions hit like a rogue wave when we entered the lobby, although there was no restaurant or coffee shop in sight. Molly put two dollars on the reception desk and asked the clerk what room Beaufort was in.

When the man held up one of the bills to examine it, Molly said, "Do you believe that some forger would bother with the one-dollar bill?"

Hearing the sharp cutting edge in his voice, the clerk put the money down and began studying the registry. "Fourth floor, number four one eight," he pointed upward. "But we don't want any trouble."

"You'll have not even a pittance," Molly's baleful smile wrinkled the corners of his eyes.

We look around the tiny lobby for a minute.

"No elevator," said the clerk.

"That's a pain in the hole," Molly grumbled as we headed up the stairs.

At the third-floor landing, he paused to catch his breath and then hefted the satchel once again: "Enough here to support a family of seven in County Kildare for five years! We're lucky to live in a land of milk and honey, Lemoyne."

When we arrived at number 418, he knocked, then stood back a couple of feet, balancing on the balls of his feet like a boxer, his right hand hovering over the jacket pocket where Bridget the straight razor lived.

No one answered, and I started back to the staircase, grateful to have avoided a confrontation, but Molly grabbed my arm: "Come on, Lemoyne, don't give up so easily. We've just barely got our trousers off."

He drew a ring of picks out of his back pocket. After looking up and down the hall to make sure we weren't being observed, he tried one after another until he heard the click of the tumbler.

"In like Flynn," he whispered, opening the door.

I had time to sense that the room was dank and fuggy and had the unused smell of single men before I heard Molly gasp.

This body was a savage parody of Val's and might as well have been another species, but it made me think of hers and I was sick with loss again.

Beaufort was stomach-down on the rug, naked except for underpants, with his hands tied behind his back. A rope had been looped from his neck to his ankles and then drawn up taut and knotted, pulling the head and legs up in a way that arched the spine so violently that it looked like the rocker on a chair.

His face was the agonized figurehead on a ship from hell. His good eye stared at us with amazement; the wandering eye seemed to be still looking for the exit; the one thing they had in common was that they were bloody and big as ping-pong balls.

"Just look at that rope, will ya," Molly said. "Tighter than a fat lady's sock."

Then he spit out the word *"incaprettato,"* as if getting rid of a rancid taste. "It's the calling card of those Sicilian gobshites that work for Geist. Like they were slaughtering a goat back in the old country. Rope a poor man's throat to his ankles and make him hold up his legs until he's so exhausted that he can't help but lower them and strangle himself. What I wish for those bastards is that from this day forward they have red diarrhea."

He pulled out Bridget and cut the rope. The crescent of the body's inverted spine relaxed, the toes slowly settling on the carpet and the face following chin first.

After giving the tormented corpse one last look, Molly began to examine the room.

"Looks like the council of pandemonium just finished its annual meeting." He whistled through his teeth. "It's a film canister that we're looking for in case you don't know. Not that there's a fart's chance in a mitten that it's still here."

The sitting room and bedroom both were in chaos—lamps overturned; dresser drawers flung upside down with their contents strewn; gray exposed film from Beaufort's two opened cameras curling on the floor; a check holder without any checks.

"No use." Molly shook his head after we'd searched for ten or fifteen minutes. "This place has been kicked and booted."

He found the phone and called the Old Man. I took a closer look at Beaufort while they talked. His swollen tongue poked out of his mouth as if in a child's taunt; empurpled veins stood out on the forehead like trapunto. The underpants were stained at the seat, creating a fecal bouquet in his immediate vicinity.

I felt sorry for him, but sorrier for myself that I had to see his remnants.

"The Boss wants a word," Molly called to me.

"I don't have to tell you what's happening, Lemoyne," the Old Man rasped when I took the phone, and then he did just that. "Beaufort fucked us by joining Geist and doing these films. Then he decided to fuck Geist by selling them to us after all. Blackmail squared. Geist's guys made him pay. Now Geist's got the film and we've got to get it back. We need to get this thing settled once and for all."

"We?" I couldn't help but ask.

"Yes, we." He was through coddling. "You and Molly. Geist's got the film. You've still got the satchel. I'll call over there and tell him you're bringing it over. I don't mind talking to the bastard. The amount he's going to get from us is penny-ante for him and he'll probably hold out for more. Doesn't matter. Molly will know what to do."

* * *

Molly was somber on the way to Geist's place on Riverside Drive. "Beaufort was a strange-looking creature, God knows. But he was no different from other men in his hopes and his greed. And he didn't deserve to leave this world the way he did. We can only hope the poor soul was scuttered on his gin when the final moment came."

"Hard to believe that he thought he could put one over on both Mr. Kennedy and Geist."

"I guess he believed a little too fervently in free enterprise," Molly gave me a benevolent look.

"But Beaufort was Mr. Kennedy's man. It was Mr. Kennedy who brought him out here in the first place. Why did he go over to Geist?"

"Maybe it was being in sunny California where everything is new and the old rules don't apply. Maybe he got the DGs."

"DGs?"

"Delusions of grandeur. A sad affliction."

"And why is Geist now trying to blackmail us after Mr. Kennedy took up his cause with the studios and helped against Selkirk?"

"I'm just a corporal and we're talking about the actions of generals here, but I'm sure it's a fancier thing than your typical blackmail."

Molly reached for his flask and had another swig. "The Boss told me a little about what's shown on this can of film we're about to get back and I know you've had a look yourself. He says it has value only if he rises again or Johnny does or maybe one of the other kids. Otherwise who cares? Geist is betting on the future. He doesn't need a few dollars now. He wants to put a large deposit of obligations in his account with Mr. Kennedy that he can maybe draw out later on. Men like him are always three steps ahead of the likes of us, Lemoyne. But I'm sure the Boss isn't surprised. He's such a man himself, after all."

When we parked in front of El Verdugo, the bar that served Geist for an office, Molly took his .38 out of its shoulder holster and put it in the glove compartment. Then he opened the trunk of the car and got out the satchel again. When we were about to enter the bar, he told me to stop. Then he stepped behind me and I felt his fingers on my butt.

"Don't worry, Lemoyne," he said, giving me a little pat, "I'm not giving you the glad eye. Just putting Bridget in your pocket for safe keeping. No offense, but I don't think they'll bother frisking a man such as yourself."

The sign in the front window said closed, but the door was open. Stepping in, I saw that the double door leading to the back room had been opened just wide enough to frame Geist sitting with folded hands at a small table, the film canister positioned dramatically in front of him and the Draco twins standing on either side. He beckoned us in with a face as placid as nirvana.

Geist looked at Molly appraisingly: "Kennedy's helper."

"The very same," Molly said, tossing the satchel on the table next to the film canister. He opened both flaps of his jacket, nodding at the empty shoulder holster. Then he gave the Dracos a derisory smile: "We just saw that little rope trick over at the Highpoint. Goat fuckers' way of killing a man, I'd say."

"Appreciate your candor," Geist brushed him off and quelled the brothers' aggressive noises with a sharp look. "Also glad to see that you're not packing in the usual spot, but we still need to have a little pat-down for all the other secret places, so let's get it over with."

"Okay." Molly pointed at Charley Draco. "I'll take Scarface. Greater of two evils."

Charley advanced on Molly with a misshapen smile and began to frisk him gently—too gently, I understood—starting with his chest and proceeding down the front of his leg to check for an ankle carry; then moving around to the back where he did underarms and butt cheeks—brushing lightly, not even patting—before running a hand down the back of one leg, again just caressing the fabric of his suit, and up again and then back down to the ankle of the other. But on the way back up to the knee of the second leg, he suddenly brought the ridge of his hand up hard into Molly's balls.

What happened next I experienced in something like a trance. I've carefully avoided violence all my life, never allowing myself to get in a situation where it was even remotely possible that it should touch me—aside from my brief time driving ambulances in the North African theatre, where the mayhem had at least a small degree of organization and usually was already an accomplished fact by the time I arrived on the scene. What now unfolded before my eyes hit me as a series of stop-action scenes, like those caught in a disco's flashing strobes.

As he was hit in the scrotum, a mournful look crossed Molly's face and he emitted something like a dog's growl, drooping for a second before instinctively raising his elbow and swiveling it around without turning his body to smack Draco's face. The other twin started to advance, but Geist gestured him back: "Stay put, Joe. Charley can handle this."

Charley recovered quickly and threw a hard punch at Molly's neck that dropped him to his knees, followed by a stomping kick to the back that slammed him onto his stomach. Charley was immediately on top of him, repeatedly hitting the back of Molly's head and causing his face to thump the floor with the syncopation of a boxer working a speed bag.

Blood spattered in an abstract pattern on the floor. I thought Molly was out cold, but he somehow managed to throw up his arm without turning over and grab the shoulder pad of Charley's coat. The Sicilian smacked at his arm, but Molly didn't let go. Using this handhold for leverage, he rolled himself onto his side, taking punches on the jaw and ear now. His face looked like it had been dropped from a two-story building.

In a move of pure strength, Molly flipped himself onto his back, but Charley moved up to pin Molly's arms with his knees and began throttling him with both hands. Molly tried to pry the fingers off his throat and bucked as if in sexual ecstasy as he fought for air. Then he sagged and I was about to turn my head so as not to have to see him die, when suddenly he got one arm free and hit Charley with a fierce cupped blow on the ear that caused him to wince and relax his stranglehold for an instant. This allowed Molly to wrench his other arm free and grab the back of Charley's head with both hands, pulling it down hard to smash the nose into his own forehead. As Charley gushed blood with a startled look on his face, Molly, still on his back, seized a fistful of hair with his left hand to hold the head steady while reaching up with his right to jab his thumb into Charley's eye, scooping out the eyeball in one easy, oyster-shucking motion.

Charley shrieked and jumped up with vitreous fluid running down his cheek and the eyeball hanging by bloody threads of tissue. While he danced around trying to stuff the eye back into its socket, Molly rose with surprising agility for a big man. By now the other twin had put his brass knuckles on and was pushing past Geist. Molly sidestepped his rush and lunged toward me. When he spun me around, I thought he was going to use me as a shield, but then he shoved me aside, having pulled the straight razor out of my back pocket and freed the blade in one motion.

Joe Draco's brass-knuckled fist was in mid-strike when Bridget bit under his forearm, slicing through the jacket sleeve and cutting the flesh within. Then the razor kissed the twin's chin, opening a deep gash that showed a whiteness of bone.

"You're a fortunate man," Molly said clinically as he watched Joe try to stem the torrent of blood with his fingertips. "If Bridget had decided to go two or three inches lower, your throat would be cut."

Charley was now on his knees, moaning and crawling around the room. Molly bent over and grabbed him by his hair. I thought he might slash him, but he just used the fabric of his jacket to wipe Bridget clean.

After Molly stepped away, Charley, now holding his eyeball between finger and thumb like a child with a marble, crawled to Geist and looked up at him with his empty socket as he frantically grabbed a pant leg.

"Get the hell away from me," Geist snarled.

When Charley held onto the pant leg harder, trying to pull himself up, Geist drew back his other leg and kicked him hard in the jaw with the heel of his shoe. The scarred face hit the floor like falling fruit.

Molly gave the twins a contented look as he closed Bridget and put her away. He pulled out a handkerchief from an inside coat pocket and began to mop the blood seeping out of the cuts on his face. Then he brushed off the front of his jacket with the back of his hand.

"I'm sure you have some good qualities," he gave Geist a little smile as he nodded at the twins, "but it appears that personnel decisions is not one of them."

"You're right," Geist conceded. "It never occurred to me that one bog trotter could handle two dragons. Congratulations."

Molly picked up the film canister from the desk and pointed at the satchel. Geist looked inside it, picked up a couple of the rubber-banded rounds of bills, then dropped them with a derisive look.

"This might make a down payment."

"The Boss says paid in full, account closed." Molly said, pinching his nose with his thumb and forefinger and then setting it back into shape with an audible snap.

"Not my boss," Geist smiled. "I'll leave the lackey stuff to you."

"Pog mo thoin," Molly said scornfully. "You probably don't know it, being a Jew bastard yourself, but that's Gaelic for kiss my ass. You should be aware that you're still standing only because Mr. Kennedy told me not to send you off to kingdom come today, even though you're an abscess of a man not worthy of God's grace, from my own point of view."

"The honor among thieves we hear so much about," Geist eyed him coolly.

"Whatever. But you should have yourself a hooley tonight and remember when you climb into bed that your guardian angel was fluttering nearby this afternoon."

Molly nodded at me and started to walk out, stopping to look one last time at the Draco brothers, one of them still pinching the bloody furrow on his chin and the other shuffling blindly on his knees.

"Just look at the pair of you," he vaunted. "I hope that poor man you mutilated today will be visiting you in your dreams tonight."

Out in the sunlight I saw more clearly the extent of the punishment Molly had taken. Purple pouches were beginning to close his eyes and small pustules of blood congregated like sweat over the rest of his face. One cut in particular on his forehead that looked like it had been made by a flensing knife was giving him blood bangs despite his repeated effort to sponge it up with his handkerchief.

He saw me looking and shrugged: "Nothing that the styptic and a touch of the little green man can't handle."

Then he brought out the straight razor again and held it up exultantly, showing bloody teeth as he grinned: "Bridget, darlin', you did good work today."

He tossed me the keys and pointed at the car's steering wheel. "You drive, I drink."

We got into the Chrysler at the same time. I was about to step on the starter when motion on the passenger's side caught my eye. I looked past Molly to see the lower torso of someone walking rapidly toward us. A pistol appeared in the open passenger window followed by the face of Niccolo Fortunato.

Molly reached for the glove compartment just as the gunshot exploded. The sound, contained by the cab of the car, spiked my ears. A fine mist of blood drifted over the front seat as if pumped out by an atomizer. In the new layering of smells, cordite was at the top with ferrous just below.

Molly had managed to get his hand on his .38 before he was hit; he now slowly released his hold on it as he slumped onto my leg. A rosette of blood bloomed in right above the cauliflower of his right ear and dribbled down over the back of his head onto my pant leg. His lips twitched and his eyes blinked once before their light went out.

Geist had sauntered out of the bar to watch the denouement with his hands in his pockets and an unlighted cigarette clamped between his teeth. Now he came to the driver's window, nodded at me in a neighborly way, and then looked up at Fortunato over the top of the car.

Fortunato stood back and scowled at him, "What did you think you were going to do, Mone, hold private showings? Sell it to me?"

"Things got a little out of control," Geist averted his eyes in what seemed intended to convey contrition but actually looked more like pure animal terror.

Fortunato allowed the silence to bear down, and then said, "We'll sort this out another time."

Then he opened the passenger door and roughly pushed Molly's legs aside so he could grab the film canister from the floorboard.

"Fear is a pig smell," he shot me a contemptuous glance. "Joseph Kennedy has a favorite daughter about my daughter's age." He was so emotionally destitute that speaking was a chore. "That *strunzo,* he has a son, your friend, who he wants to make into a big man. I will be watching them both and all the others. You know the question I will be asking. Why should that man have children when I don't?"

He pressed the cold barrel of his gun on my forehead. That moment when he finger-shot me in the San Bernardino Mountains now seemed premonitory.

"Why don't I just go ahead and kill you too? Maybe because I have a soft spot for lapdogs. Maybe because you are in their business and I want you to tell your friend and the piece-of-shit father about what I just said, so they won't think the things that will happen in the future are accidents."

Then he spat on Molly's dead torso and pulled back from the car. I could only see his midsection as he shook the film canister violently: "Tell them that if I ever forget my reason for living, I'll only need to hold this in my hand."

He took a few steps away, then sent a ferocious burst of Italian toward me: *"La vendetta di cento anni ha ancora suoi denti de latte!"*

As I lifted Molly's dead bulk off my leg and propped him against the passenger door so I could get out, I saw Fortunato walking away with the film canister in his left hand and the pistol pressed along the side of his right leg.

Geist saw him too. He had finally lit his cigarette and was inhaling through his mouth and exhaling through his nose, with his hands back in his pockets.

"I called you a cab. I also called the cops so they can dispose of the remains," he nodded at Molly. "Let's hope the cab gets here first because a murder scene is not a great place for questions and answers. Anyhow, you've got bigger problems than some dead mick."

We were both watching Fortunato when he stopped about thirty feet away and turned around as if something had just occurred to him. He allowed the pistol to make small nodding gestures like a ventriloquist's dummy. I thought he was pointing it at me, while Geist retreated a few steps toward his bar.

I expected Fortunato to come back again, but the whine of sirens caused him to vanish.

"What was that about?" I asked.

"Who knows?" Geist was shaken. "Don't forget: it wasn't that long ago that the man lost his only remaining kin."

He headed toward the front door of El Verdugo.

"You killed Selkirk," I accused his back.

"I don't even own a gun." He stopped but didn't face me. I noticed for the first time that his right hand was palsied, moving like a small metronome outside his pants pocket.

"Well, you had it done."

"What are you, reopening the inquest?" He took a few more steps.

"I thought you and Mr. Kennedy were friends."

This made him turn, with a thin-eyed smile: "A couple of guys who cooperate once every so often when their interests happen to coincide but don't feel the need to have each other over for dinner. We're both practical men who have learned to look for a little insurance on our walk through life to make sure that the best thing happens."

"Fortunato said something back there in Italian about vendetta," I said.

The false chumminess evaporated from Geist's manner. "Revenge that's a hundred years old still has its baby teeth," he translated for me. "That's been one of his sayings since we were kids. I heard it dozens of times back in the old days. And he means it. He'll wait forever to get satisfaction. *Vendetta* is Nicky's middle name, and every time he says it someone just got his ticket punched for Valhalla. You should tell your people they'd better watch their step, but that probably won't help very much. Nicky's only regret with the people he marks for vendetta is that he can't kill them twice."

Then he disappeared into the darkness of the bar.

TWENTY-FIVE

When I arrived back at the Biltmore, my heart was still bumping. I sat in the car and let the analgesic of exhaustion calm me down for half an hour before going up to the Kennedy suite.

The Old Man answered the door wearing a bathrobe. He was barefoot and I noticed that his ankles were blue with ruptured veins and his toenails yellowed and ridged by fungus. For the first time in all the years I'd known him he actually looked like an old man.

"Where are you hurt?" He suddenly grabbed my shoulders with both hands and gave me a look of genuine concern.

I noticed that Molly had bled out on my shirt and pants.

"Not mine."

"Whose, then?"

"Molly's."

"Where is Molly anyway?"

"He's gone."

"Gone?" The Old Man flinched.

"He got the film from Geist. But then Fortunato shot him and took it when we were getting into the car."

"Molly didn't make it?"

I shook my head and tried to keep my sadness at bay by cleaning the stippling of blood off my glasses with my shirttails.

The Old Man turned so I wouldn't see that his eyes were glistening.

"Molly was a phenom," he said. "I still remember the first time I saw him all those years ago. He could hit a baseball like Tris Speaker. He would have been a star if he hadn't decided to work for me."

Then he made the moment pass and sat down on the sofa, patting the cushion next to him. "Tell me what happened."

I sat too and gave him a blow-by-blow account of what had happened, beginning with Beaufort's hotel room and ending with Fortunato's threat and that odd moment when he had paused in his walk-away to look back at Geist.

The Old Man sat silently for a long time.

The two of us had entered a zone I knew we'd never occupy again, so I seized the moment: "Was Val murdered?"

He scrubbed his face vigorously with both hands, his stubble making a rasping sound on his hands.

When he didn't speak, I did. "I'm asking you if we had anything to do with it."

"*We*?"

"You."

I forced the word out. But instead of the explosion I expected, the look he gave me indicated that he regarded this as a legitimate question.

"No."

He was thoughtful for a moment before continuing: "Ninety-nine point nine that she did it to herself. That woman was a firecracker. All that joy! All that sadness! So alive! Easy when you got to know her to understand why Jack was head over heels. But things aren't always what they seem, and Jack probably didn't see that she was always walking on the razor's edge."

I swallowed my resentment over his presumption in analyzing her: "What about the other tenth of a percent?"

"Such a remote possibility that it doesn't bear examination." He was dismissive, but I could tell his wheels were turning. "Still, if you are desperate for a hypothesis, maybe Geist."

"Geist? He told Jack and me that he and Fortunato grew up together and were close as the fingers on a hand. He still has pictures of them and their friends as boys on his office wall. Why would he harm a friend's child?"

The Old Man gave a weary shrug: "Water is thicker than blood in the world where people like that live. The idea that Fortunato came to Hollywood just to get his daughter in the movies is a fairytale. He was sent out here by his people in Chicago because they felt Geist was losing the war against Selkirk, which meant they might lose their beachhead in the movie business. Remote possibility—Geist might have thought that eliminating the girl was a way to get Fortunato so fixated on this vendetta thing that he wouldn't be interested in taking over. Geist is a smart guy."

He could have been lying, but I always thought of him as someone so beyond good and evil that he didn't mind truths that reflected badly on himself. In any case, he quickly made it clear that the window of rough intimacy he had opened was now closed and that he was back in his pragmatic, what's-in-it-for-me mode.

"But like I say, ninety-nine point nine. The important thing is that Fortunato won't want the stuff about his daughter to get out. What father would want people to see all that? So this is one of those films that will never be seen. He won't use it to blackmail us the way Geist would have. He'll just use it to get a little stiffy of vengeance whenever he's feeling low. But he's got punch and we'll have to be careful. We'll have to find a replacement for Molly. Maybe two. But that's all doable. We'll be fine."

As I watched him convince himself that everything was under control, it occurred to me that the deepest of Joseph P. Kennedy's many character flaws was his belief that no one else could hate as fiercely as he did.

* * *

It was dark when I got home. The house felt dead and deserted—as if Val had carried all its life and vitality with her into the next world.

I was glad there was no light shining out from beneath Jack's bedroom door. Molly was still on my skin and in my hair and I wanted to get him off.

I took a forty-five-minute bath, changing the water twice. Then I drank some warm milk and sank into the sofa. I was exhausted, but the events that had transpired at El Verdugo kept looping through my mind.

I saw first light before I finally dropped off for what seemed a minute or two, when sounds of Jack banging around in his bedroom woke me. It was almost noon. I rooted deeper into the covers, dreading the questions he would ask and the answers I would have to give.

He came into the living room carrying a suitcase and stood at a mirror for a long time as if arranging his features for the future. He was dressed in a blazer and gray slacks, with a starched white shirt and a striped club tie. He was still pale and had thumbprints of shadow under his eyes, but he was already starting to compose his face into that mask of ironic detachment that would one day beguile America.

"I talked to Dad this morning," he said, still looking at himself in the mirror. "He told me what happened so you don't need to give me a replay. He was a little surprised that you survived, by the way."

"They're not supposed to shoot the messenger, remember?"

"Yes, and I know what the message is too. Another thing we don't have to talk about."

"So you two hashed everything out?"

"If we'd done that," he shot me an arctic look, "I'd be a man without a family."

I nodded at the suitcase.

"I'm heading home on the three o'clock," he said.

"The Old Man going with you?"

"No. I'm on my own."

"What are you going to do?"

"I don't know. I've been thinking about maybe having a go at that congressional seat after all."

"That will make the Old Man happy."

"Not really. If I decide to go for it, I'm doing it my way and I'm doing it for myself, not for him. Those days are done."

He didn't say this spitefully; Kennedy DNA was too potent for that. But there was something definitive in the words that made me think he might finally be settling into the driver's seat of his life.

A cab pulled up outside and sounded its horn.

"I've done as much as I can to straighten things up here," he headed toward the door. "Maybe you can take it the rest of the way—dispose of the remnants, sell the Zephyr, do enough cleaning so I get the deposit back, tie up loose ends and all that."

Jack was never very good at asking for favors.

"Afterwards, get yourself a ticket for Boston. I've got a line on a flat on Bowdoin Street. There'll be a place on the sofa for you as usual."

Then he took one last look around and was gone, leaving behind a houseful of things that would forever be left unsaid, the dark shape always submerged just below the tip of our friendship.

I stayed in Malibu for a couple more days, mopping and vacuuming and sifting through everything Jack had left behind, including a closetful of nearly new summer clothing. I called the Salvation Army to come and get it all, including things I probably should have saved, such as the banged-up binoculars he'd brought home from the Pacific War and the equally used portable record player.

I placed an ad for the Zephyr in the *LA Times* and had already gotten three calls by eight in the morning on the day it appeared. A young dentist from Glendale was first in line and had someone drive him out so he could look it over. He offered $700 cash on the spot, which was $15 more than Jack had paid for it, even though we had doubled its mileage in the past two months. I told him it was a deal on the condition that he mailed the painting of Val's mother I'd boxed up for Temple Rose and drove me to Union Station.

He waited while I made one last sweep of the house. There was a manila envelope with cuttings of Jack's articles for Hearst, along with some magazines and records, including Yip Harburg's disc of "Glocca Morra." I decided to throw it all in the trash, then got into the Zephyr for the last time and watched over my shoulder as the Malibu beach house got ever smaller, a fade-out for our brief interlude in Hollywood.

I didn't yet know it would become a forgotten moment—except by me—that would seem never to have taken place, if not for the ripples it created in the Kennedys' lives.

Boston/Washington

✳

Aftermath

TWENTY-SIX

By the summer of the following year I was bunking at Jack's flat in Boston, just as he had predicted, and working as an unpaid aide on his congressional campaign. Aside from providing comic relief, my responsibilities consisted primarily of making New England clam chowder every Friday; holding up a sign with his campaign slogan—The New Generation Offers a Leader—in his appearances at local ladies' clubs and veterans' organizations where he gave earnest speeches in the manner of a high school basketball coach; and building levees around his past to make sure it didn't flood his present.

He had rolled over nine other candidates in the 1946 Democratic primary and was already dancing circles around his doomed Republican opponent in the general election in late August when *Tomorrow Is Too Late* was released. Warners didn't do much promotion and the movie quickly sank into the second spot in double features at neighborhood movie houses.

Jack never said anything, although I was sure he knew about it, and I didn't either. I couldn't bring myself to go see it, but I read some reviews, including Bosley Crowther's in the *New York Times*, which was mostly condescending except for one passage that naturally caught my eye:

> The one bright spot in this sad trifle, which sometimes feels like it was edited in a Sunbeam Mixmaster, is the young French actress Delphine LaReve. Given the thankless task of portraying a character who begins as an idealistic refugee from Nazism and ends as a sadly

> fallen woman undone by the love she cannot keep from feeling, LaReve is a revelation—always believable and above all always beautiful. I can think of no other young actress on the current scene with a screen presence comparable to hers. She shines luminously through the mediocrity of this film and the viewer will keep thinking of her long after *Tomorrow* is yesterday's news.

* * *

In the years following "the events in Hollywood," as I came to think of those indelible weeks, I watched Jack quarantine his heart and adopt the inexorable sense of purpose that would serve as the rebar for the charming nonchalance that had always gotten him by. He had made a bargain with his destiny and understood what it would take to go all the way—employing an assassin's sense of purpose at the same time that he was effortlessly projecting, on cue, that élan vital he had first sensed in himself back when we were kids. He was a natural, just as the Old Man had said, a great actor as well as a great politician, able to transfix voters by the cool intensity of the character he portrayed.

His career was like a forest fire propelled by the wind storm it creates from within. It fed on itself and nothing could stop him, not even the death of Kick a couple of years after he was first elected to Congress, although it was the tragedy that hit him harder than any other he ever experienced, except for Val, of course.

Kick's death became a key moment in the irresistible Kennedy Melodrama just then gaining steam. She was flying with Lord Peter to meet the Old Man in the South of France on a *mission du coeur* to override Rose's refusal to countenance their union, when their plane went down in a driving rainstorm over the Cévennes mountains. The first thing the rescue party found after long hours of searching was one of the red dancing pumps that Kick had been wearing—just one, perched alone on a little hill a couple hundred feet from the smoking wreckage of the crash.

The image of that red shoe would become fixed in my mind, a beacon lighting the search for her remains long after they had been found and disposed of.

Foul weather was the cause of the accident, according to the immediate and unambiguous judgment of the French Bureau of Enquiry and Analysis. At first the verdict had a heavy inevitability for me, as for everyone else, but then I began to wonder. Lord Peter's aircraft was brand new. It was not a light plane. It had two engines and a pilot and a navigator. Shouldn't it have been airworthy enough to break out of that storm?

Up until then, I had always thought of myself as an Occam's razor sort of guy: Demand simplicity in explanations; don't multiply hypotheses, especially those based on the unknowable; choose the most obvious answer first. I always remained deeply committed to these principles with the upper stratum of my mind. But down below was the harpoon of behindness that Val had implanted and I'd never been able to dislodge—the beguiling arcaneness of the alternative truth whose rewards were forbidden to those condemned always to see things through the dark glass of reality.

The idea took shape in my mind like a slow-growing malignancy that Kick might have been the first course in the long meal of vendetta that Niccolo Fortunato had promised me he would savor over time. *I had a daughter and Joseph Kennedy has a favorite daughter about my daughter's age...*

Jack wouldn't have tolerated the thought for an instant, and I would have been forced to ditch it if he and I had still been carrying on our old hero-sidekick relationship with the almost daily contact that had been my stabilizer and compass. But when he married, this long continuity was interrupted for a time as he tried to get Jackie used to the prospect that I would always be, as she eventually referred to me with her ladylike whiff of malice, "the man who came to dinner." So there were a couple of years in the mid-Fifties when I was more on my own than I wanted to be and could not easily whip subversive ideas back into the kennel of my unconscious when they began to prowl on sleepless nights.

The crazy thought took hold when months of free-associating eventually brought up the name Izzy Abramowitz, Fortunato's boyhood friend, the near-midget he had called "Nano" and who, as Solomon Geist once told Jack and me, "would do anything for Nicky." This Nano, I remembered, had worked in aircraft maintenance for Grumman during the war and in its European operations right afterward. Could he somehow have arranged to be in Paris in 1948 and tampered with Lord Peter's highly efficient plane before takeoff?

I kept trying to stigmatize the thought as absurd, but finally gave in and called the Grumman headquarters in Long Island on February 20, 1955, which would have been Kick's thirty-fifth birthday. I asked the operator to connect me with Isadore Abramowitz, expecting her to say that there was no one by that name in the company. Instead, she shuffled her directory, then asked me to hold while she rang his office.

When his secretary answered, I hung up in a sweat. I couldn't sleep that night, and the next morning I called in sick to work and then headed to Penn Station to buy a ticket for the train to Long Island. I stood in front of the passenger-car steps until the conductor blew his final whistle, when I had a failure of nerve and stood back. I should have felt foolish on the way back to my apartment, but I told myself that I didn't really have to make the trip because I had such a complete picture of what would have happened if I did.

I would have gotten off the train and into a taxi that would have let me off at Grumman's corporate entrance. Employees would have streamed out at quitting time, and finally the stragglers and a few harried executives taking their work home. I would have been thinking about leaving when a dapper-looking middle-aged man would emerge from the glass doors—about five feet tall, with graying hair parted in the middle as if by calipers, and carrying an attaché case that resembled a suitcase next to his diminutive form.

I imagined approaching him: "Mr. Abramowitz?"

He would have given an inquisitive look and seemed about to stop before thinking better of it.

"Mr. Abramowitz?" I would have followed as he upped the tempo of his stride. "I would like to ask you a couple of questions."

He would have gone even faster.

"Nano? Isn't that what Nicky Fortune calls you?"

That would have stopped him.

"I was a friend of Kathleen Kennedy's..."

Here he would have turned and come toward me, dropping the attaché case as if preparing to jump up and punch me in the face despite being more than a foot shorter.

"I don't know what you're talking about," he would have said in that high-pitched, helium voice that Geist had described so well. "Stop harassing me. Get the fuck out of my way!"

Then, without another word, he would have turned and quick-stepped away, leaving me standing there flat-footed.

It was such a compelling vision that I caught myself wondering over the next few years if I had actually seen this man Nano or merely imagined that I did.

In addition to plunging me into behindness, Kick's death held Jack down for several weeks at the end of his first term in Congress. Smothered by its uncompromising weight, he sat in his congressional office late into the night after his staff had gone home, staring at the walls with the radio playing in the background. But ultimately the death, so unexpected, hurried him along, making him see once again, as he had so clearly when we were kids, that time was his enemy and that he dare not proceed cautiously in his life or his career. He could not defer to his political elders or stand in line waiting his turn.

When the Old Man at times urged just such an approach, Jack didn't argue; he respectfully heard him out and then continued to move forward at his own chosen pace, which from now on was always full speed ahead.

The unspoken reckoning he'd had with his father after the events in Hollywood led him to create compartments in his life. The one he assigned to the Old Man acknowledged his stature, but reduced his status to that of an engaged adviser—listened to but not automatically obeyed; allowed to offer opinions but not make decisions; no longer the architect of Jack's fate.

It was an arrangement that could have caused an eruption. But Jack handled it with finesse, and surprisingly so did his father. The Old Man was used to working alone and in the shadows, having done exactly that for much of his life. He didn't complain about being kept at arm's length but willingly took on the black work of politics, the jobs usually given to the untouchables, without having to be asked.

One of these jobs was keeping the lines of communication open with people such as Solomon Geist. When I once summoned the courage to ask the Old Man how he could bear to do this, given Geist's treachery in the fall of 1945, he waved me off: "I've got a memory like an elephant. I don't forget and I sure as hell don't forgive. But I also don't throw away people who might be useful to us someday."

That someday came late in 1959, when the Old Man—at what cost none of us ever knew—got Geist to make a connection with members of the Chicago Outfit, among them Sam Giancana, whom I once met briefly when I was in Las Vegas with Jack for a fundraiser and thought of ever after as a gorilla in a man suit.

After a few Geist-mediated sessions with the Old Man, Giancana apparently agreed "to help get out the vote"—as his fellow Chicago mobster "Handsome Johnny" Roselli wryly put it—if Jack got the nomination. In return, the Old Man said that a Kennedy administration would smother the unending federal investigations into organized crime that had become one long national headline in the 1950s and threatened to become even more of a problem in the next decade.

The deal eventually occasioned some harsh words between Big Joe and Bobby, who usually set the gold standard for family loyalty but had made pursuit of the Mob from his time as staff counsel to the McClelland Committee into his manhood ritual, and would turn up the heat even higher when he became attorney general, whatever his father had promised.

Nobody, including Bobby himself, seemed to take note of the fact that his deep animus to Giancana and his ilk was nullified by his central role in the CIA's scheme to use Giancana's crew in its opera bouffe efforts to kill Castro. And as is now well known, the bizarre dance done by the family and the Mob was symbolized most famously by the fact that while Giancana did this clandestine work he was also clandestinely sharing with Jack the favors of Judith Exxner, to whom Jack had been introduced by Frank Sinatra at Geist's behest, thus establishing a circuitry that would have ominous consequences for all.

This ball which Geist helped set rolling into the epicenter of history came to an abrupt halt for him one August afternoon in 1963 when he was stopped on Fairfax Avenue waiting to turn left into the Canter's Delicatessen parking lot and a man in a Dodgers hat and sunglasses who was never identified ran up to the driver's side of his aqua Cadillac and shot him point-blank in the left temple, afterward jumping into a car double-parked across the street and disappearing from history.

Calling it a "gangland hit," the *LA Times* speculated that the murder might have been caused by Geist's alleged support of Crazy Joey Gallo in the war that Gallo was then waging against Joe Profaci for control of what became the Colombo family. Perhaps. But when I heard about it I immediately remembered Fortunato's face that fall afternoon in 1945 when he stopped on a side street near Warners after killing Molly Maguire and gave Geist an indescribable look while his pistol inscribed small, prophetic circles in the air.

* * *

There are many things I'll never know, but one thing I knew for sure was that the Old Man never intended to keep the promise with which he had blackmailed and suborned Val. According to FBI documents declassified in 1976, his effort to get Fortunato deported was eventually blessed by the Truman administration, after heavy lobbying by Hoover, and pursued strenuously from 1946 to 1948. But Italy, not being stupid, refused to take him, so Big Joe's plot ultimately collapsed.

Never knowing exactly where Nicky Fortune was, but often feeling with prickly skin that he might be nearby, I made an effort to keep tabs on him while he lived in limbo in the U.S. and elsewhere. He was a somewhat drab figure in comparison with the real peacocks of organized crime; someone who was a member of no family and who, in Mafia parlance, always "ate alone"; a face typically near the edges of the group photos surreptitiously snapped at the big Mob gatherings that made their way into the tabloids, although it seemed to me that in these shots he always looked anxious to get back to more important business.

Fortunato was at the famous summit at the Hotel Nacional in Havana in 1946 where Lucky Luciano tried to become head of the Commission and Meyer Lansky reluctantly agreed to the hit on his longtime friend Bugsy Siegel because of the skimming that had taken place during the construction of the Flamingo.

Fortunato was called before the Kefauver Committee hearings in 1951, the event that formally introduced most of America to organized crime and also demonstrated the growing importance of television. Large groups of people dropped everything to stand in front of appliance-store windows during lunch hour and watch the perversely telegenic criminals testifying on the small black-and-white screens embedded in the big walnut consoles.

The networks covering the event played up the backstory of Fortunato's wartime service, so his appearance was the most highly anticipated of all. When he reluctantly took the oath and then sat ramrod straight before the Senate committee, regarding the members with sovereign contempt, the gallery in the hearing room—and in the nation as a whole—edged forward in anticipation. But unlike Frank Costello, for instance, who brought the house down by responding indignantly "I pay my taxes!" when Senator Kefauver asked him what he had ever done for his country, or Bugsy Siegel's moll Virginia Hill, who ended her testimony by screaming at the committee members, "I hope an atom bomb falls on all of you!" Fortunato sat as stone-faced as Bartleby in the witness chair for three-quarters of an hour, giving the same anodyne response to all the questions: "I choose to avail myself of the protections offered by the Fifth Amendment of the U.S. Constitution."

Perhaps worried about his ratings, Kefauver finally dismissed him in disgust: "You may step down, Mr. Fortunato. We have other witnesses waiting who understand that all of America is watching these hearings and looking for answers."

Fortunato was glimpsed again a few years later in another group photo, this one taken in Palermo at the 1957 "Pizza Connection" meeting at the Grand Hotel des Palmes.

He was present the same year at the infamous gathering at Joe "The Barber" Barbaro's fifty-acre estate in Apalachin, New York, where a hundred of the top figures in the Syndicate met to deal with Vito Genovese's claim to be *capo di tutti capi* after he sent Crazy Joey Gallo to assassinate Albert Anastasia as he was getting a shave in a Manhattan barbershop.

According to the account in the *Washington Post,* Fortunato was one of a handful of mobsters who escaped the police raid on the estate by running out the back door of the house and tramping through the heavily wooded area behind Barbaro's property to a back road, destroying their expensive suits and alligator shoes in their pell-mell getaway.

It was tempting to see him as a sort of Kilroy of the Mob—always there but never front and center; not complicit in any of the coup and assassination attempts and not a crucial participant in the grand debate that agitated organized crime in the 1950s and '60s about whether and then how to get involved in narcotics, which the more entrepreneurial members of the Commission saw as a hedge against the likely decline of gambling, loansharking, and other of the old ways. But I always thought that Fortunato was content to remain behind the scenes because he had only one real item of business: *vendetta.*

When the news first reached me on November 22, 1963—sweeping through the room like a mistral while I was having lunch at the Cosmos Club—I had only one question: Where was Fortunato when those shots in Dallas shattered America's belief in rationality and made speculations bearing the stamp of behindness into a national pastime?

I didn't get an answer until Bobby was leaving the Justice Department when his feud with LBJ reached a breaking point a year after Jack's death. He invited me to his office one day while movers were packing up, and we chatted about family matters for a half hour before I got my courage up to ask him about Mob involvement in the assassination.

"You too?" he snarled. "I thought you of all people would avoid this shit. Aren't there already enough nutcases out there without you joining up too?"

But I could tell from the look that had crossed his face when I asked the question that he himself was also living under the shadow of a doubt. Possibly because he was willing for me to consider what he could not, either professionally or personally, he called in one of his aides in the Organized Crime Unit at the end of our meeting and told this young man about my historic association with Jack, then ordered him to let me spend the rest of the afternoon in an annex looking at "a few files."

The one on Fortunato that was brought to me was thin, although a few suggestive unknown facts had survived the heavy marker-pen redactions.

One was simply an interesting footnote to history: he was with Lucky Luciano in January 1962 at the Naples airport when Luciano, after meeting with an American film producer and agreeing to cooperate in a movie about his life, collapsed of a heart attack and died.

More to the point were documents showing that in the spring of 1963, when he got in some unspecified trouble with one of the New York families, Fortunato had spent time in New Orleans under the protection of Carlos Marcello, the Mob boss who was later reported by some of his fellow inmates in a federal prison in Texarkana to have bragged that he had masterminded Jack's assassination.

But this brief ray of light was eclipsed by a set of FBI field reports that answered the question I began with: Where was Fortunato when Jack died in Dallas? They provided a definitive answer—with Johnny Rosselli in Beverly Hills, participating in a roast of Frank Sinatra at the Friars Club.

That should have been that. But since Bobby had given me the opportunity, I glanced at some background interviews that FBI agents had done with people who had known Fortunato when he was coming up in Chicago.

Among those mentioned were Isadore Abramowitz, identified by the field agent as a vice president of operations at Grumman, and Jacob "Sparky" Rubenstein—the two people who, along with Geist, had been saved by Fortunato from a beating or worse nearly fifty years earlier, and with whom Fortunato had remained tight ever since. Geist had cashed in his chips a couple of months before the assassination, but I asked Bobby's aide if the other two men had files.

"Nothing to speak of on Abramowitz," he replied, "but a huge a.k.a. file on Rubenstein, as you might expect."

When I gave him a confounded look, he hesitated a bit and then said, "The attorney general vouched for you, so I guess it's okay."

The file he brought was as thick as the Gutenberg Bible. It told how Sparky Rubenstein had kept knocking at the door of the Chicago Outfit throughout the late Thirties and early Forties, desperate to become a made man. But as one mobster later told an FBI interviewer, apparently with a straight face, "He didn't have the mental stability we like to see in our associates."

Condemned always to be one of the small fry looking longingly at the pools where the big fish swam, Rubenstein hung out with his friend Nano before and after the war and was in Southern California playing the horses and staying with Solomon Geist for a couple of months in 1946, a year after Jack and I were there. Afterward he was back in Chicago still orbiting around Fortunato and hoping to be invited to join the club. He finally gave up and moved to Dallas in 1948.

When he got there, Jacob Rubenstein changed his name to Jack Ruby. He ran a succession of sleazy nightclubs over the next twenty-five years, supplying free booze and hookers to off-duty cops and working hard to give everyone the impression that he had juice and was connected.

According to his file, the newly minted Ruby had traveled to Cuba in 1959, where for reasons not clear he paid a visit to Santo Trafficante, then jailed in Havana's Trescora prison. Trafficante had controlled vice for the Syndicate during the Batista years and would be recruited after his release by Johnny Roselli to participate in the CIA's farcical assassination plots against Castro.

The file also showed that Ruby knew Sam Giancana from the old days, and had stayed close to Joe Campisi, lieutenant of Carlos Marcello, who had shielded Fortunato in New Orleans during his time of unspecified troubles.

Chary of raising any higher the lid of Pandora's box, the FBI had trod lightly on these and other coincidences in its investigation of Ruby. Agents did not make much of the unusually high volume of long distance calls that Rubenstein/Ruby made in the weeks leading up to the assassination, nor did they strenuously pursue the persistent rumors that cops on the take had let him into the supposedly well-secured basement of the Dallas Police Department the morning Oswald was being transported. They gave short shrift to informants' claims that he was paying off a Mob IOU when he pulled the trigger.

Left hanging as well were Ruby's comment in his weird jailhouse interview with Earl Warren in June 1964 that he had "been used for a purpose" and the words he employed in his urgent request to the chief justice for a change of venue, "I want to tell the truth but I can't tell it here because my life is in danger."

Instead of seeing the circumstantial as possibly real and diving down into it, the Warren Commission and J. Edgar Hoover himself ignored the banal poseur whose tenuous Mob connections they saw as merely the elevator music of his Willy Loman life; a loony and a loser who was being deeply sincere for once when he said that the only reason he wanted to get Oswald was to pay him back for the pain he had caused Jackie and the kids.

I could see how the FBI and the Warren Commission investigators might have taken Ruby at what they saw as his face value. I understood their reluctance to give the country a reason to sink deeper into the whirlpool of behindness brought on by the assassination, a new and dangerous way of thinking that would challenge all official explanations of everything for years to come.

But I also knew in my gut that Ruby was not just a tawdry bit player in the Dallas drama. He was the Best Supporting Actor, the event's indispensable man who had an even more crucial role than that of the lone crazed assassin himself—creating the silence that drove Jack's death into a dead end, killing the possibility of definitive answers and creating a mystery that was ultimately insoluble and therefore open ever after to a category five hurricane of hallucinatory speculation, like my own, which made all the sense in the world and no sense at all.

* * *

If he had been functioning when Jack was killed, the Old Man would have used all his assets to try to get to the bottom of things. But by then he was mired in vascular catastrophe as a result of a massive stroke in 1961 that left him with skin melted like candle wax on the left side of his face; eyes wandering; hunched and spavined and unable to walk; and robbed of all language except the nonsense word "Nuuu," which he shouted fiercely during his useless speech therapy sessions and at all other times, never again making sense although his around-the-clock caretakers came to believe that they could distinguish a rudimentary language of hatred and despair in the different intonations of this single sound.

On November 22, the family had rushed into the Old Man's room and turned off the television to keep him in the dark about what had happened. When they finally got up the nerve to break the news to him, Big Joe began to scream and thrash around, spittle flying out of his mouth and his face turning purple. He tried desperately to form sounds, and according to what his caretakers later told me, he screamed a slightly different non-word, one they hadn't heard before—something like "Nuuto"—over and over, before slumping down in his wheelchair and falling asleep.

They were convinced that this was an insignificant anomaly, the snap of a synapse brought on by the intensity of the event, resulting in a slight and momentary deviation from the same sound he had been making for so long. But I always thought it was the Old Man's heroic effort to name the man he believed responsible for his son's death: Fortunato.

Nicky Fortune survived the Old Man by several years. Said to be "in retirement" when he was finally subpoenaed by the Church Committee in 1976 for hearings that marked the first and last time Mob involvement in the assassination was ever investigated by Congress, he was by then a stately white-haired figure wearing mulberry-colored linen leisure suits and glasses that darkened when he stepped into the sunlight.

The other aging mobsters snuffled and sniggered as they bird-walked their way through their appearances before the committee. I was on the edge of my seat waiting for Fortunato's turn and anticipated the furor he would create when he took his seat proudly and, now that the baby teeth of his vengeance had grown to their maturity, told the country how he had made the Kennedys pay on the installment plan for the death of his daughter. But he failed to show up on the day he was scheduled to appear, and the federal marshals dispatched to bring him in returned empty-handed.

I concluded that the reason for this anticlimax was that he knew he would be asked about things other than his personal vendetta and decided at the last minute to go into hiding rather than betray the blood obligations of *omertà*. I thought maybe he would surface again with second thoughts. But twenty-five months later Niccolo Fortunato's very partial remains, identified by the one finger not totally decomposed, were discovered in a toxic waste site in Milwaukee, and this story which I have carried with me all these years finally came to an end.

TWENTY-SEVEN

As I've said, Jack never uttered another word about our brief interlude in Hollywood after we left town. During the years of his climb to the summit, when he was becoming a different person from the imp of the perverse I'd first known—his wit scripted; his heart grown lazy from lack of exercise; his sexual appetites now so bureaucratized that he didn't bother to learn the names of the parade of women who serviced him, simply referring to each of them generically as "Kid"—he never once spoke of Val or even said her name. I didn't either, and in time I stopped wondering about what had really happened to her, although the ache of her absence never left me.

At first I thought Jack might have preserved her memory in some secret chamber of his heart, a place he visited in secrecy and solitude. But eventually I decided that he had simply banished her altogether as a heartache and an encumbrance and a drag on his forward motion.

But once, only once, he slipped up and showed me how wrong I was.

After he beat Henry Cabot Lodge Jr. for the Senate in 1952, thus exacting delayed revenge against the Brahmins who had oppressed two generations of his Irish peasant forebears in Massachusetts, Jack, although just thirty-five, was ready to spend the rest of the decade in a final push to the top. But some of his advisers told him that while it might be permissible to be single as a senator, he'd better marry if he didn't want to be derailed on his way to the top by competitors in the Democratic Party who were already concerned enough about his rise to start a whispering campaign against him.

At first he was incredulous. "How can a pussy-mad erotomaniac who gets a headache if he doesn't get laid at least once a day be accused of being queer?" he once asked me, of all people. Then he walked away before I could answer, shaking his head and muttering, "This is total horseshit."

But over the next year, the advisers kept on him and he finally began to think that maybe he should find a woman he could stand being around for more than a few hours at a time. Jackie, of course, was the perfect answer to his problem—someone easy to look at whose rococo personality was able to hold his interest intermittently, the coincidence of their names underscoring the fact that in their collaborative selfhood they were two peas in a pod. He knew she'd be an asset and decided to tie the knot.

His bachelor party in September 1953 was one of those great Kennedy moments. All his friends were there, roaring boys for the evening participating in a choreographed swagger of mead-hall vaunting, jokes sharp enough almost to break the skin, sudden outbreaks of slap-boxing, attempts to give wedgies, and shot-glass mano-a-manos. The Old Man, still functional then, sat on the sidelines with the handful of other elders repeating twice-told tales of possibly apocryphal bachelor parties he had attended in prewar England, where naked call girls hidden by dangling lace cloths roamed around on their knees under the long refectory tables, secretly unzipping the pants of the guests in evening dress and fellating them while they ate.

"It was so English," he gave one of his beaver-toothed smiles. "The idea that nobody was supposed to be able to tell by the look on your face when your custard truck crashed."

A few minutes later, Dave Powers stepped up on a chair and yelled for quiet. Jack's gofer, body man and master of Paddywhackery, Powers also had a decent tenor, and this evening, after clinking a spoon on a champagne flute to quiet the room, he launched into a quavering a cappella version of "Danny Boy."

Jack rolled his eyes and pretended to endure it, and when Powers segued into "Tura Lura" he yelled, "One song's bad enough, but a medley?" Still, he loved the performance and whistled through his fingers while it went on.

I thought Powers would at last stand down after "Red Is the Rose," but he signaled for quiet again. "One last favorite of the groom-to-be," he said.

Then he launched into "How Are Things in Glocca Morra," now a standard as a result of the long-running success of *Finian's Rainbow* once Yip Harburg finally got it to Broadway in 1947.

My heart jumped and I watched Jack closely for a reaction. Under the influence of the sentimental moment and the free flow of alcohol, many were daubing at their eyes as Powers sang with a crooner's dreamy hand movements, but Jack's minimalist smile didn't waver, not even in the verses I thought might break him:

> Is that willow tree still weapin' there?
> Does that lassie with the twinklin' eye
> Come smilin' by and does she walk away,
> Sad and dreamy not to see me there?

After Powers was done singing; after the tournament of toasts, each one pitilessly evaluated after the fact by Jack himself; after the naked girl jumped out of the cake and ran for her life holding her hands over her sweet spot like a chastity belt; after the last champagne bottle was emptied and the last joke told and everyone had filed out—including the Old Man and his thugs, and all the cousins and friends and the hangers-on and poseurs and old Navy pals—there were only four of us left in the room.

Teddy was standing with an arm propped against a fireplace mantel. Bobby, exhausted from organizing the event, had sunk into a Turkish chair, his tux jacket flung on the floor and the ribbon of his black bowtie hanging down on his white shirt front. Jack sat on the floor resting his always aching back against the front of the sofa on which I lay nearly passed out. He was slightly tipsy, a very rare state for him, and smoking a cigar.

"It's not the end of the world, Johnny," Teddy thought his big brother needed to be comforted for what lay ahead. "Think of all the muff you've left behind on the trail of broken hearts. Every one of them a trophy."

"Yeah," Bobby saw an opening for one last fraternal dig. "But also think about the math that lies in your future: not thousands of women, but one woman thousands of times."

Jack seemed lost in his own thoughts as they rattled on. Then, when the brothers momentarily ran out of words, he looked up at the ceiling and said, "There was this one girl."

I waited with my heart in my mouth. When he didn't say anything else for a long moment I thought he'd gotten control of himself and that would be that. But the nature of the event had jimmied the lock on the door I thought he'd never open again. Rotating his cigar slightly with his thumb and forefinger as he blew on its glowing tip, he continued, into the poetry of the memory that he now allowed to rise up within him.

"What I remember most is the heat of her, the kinetic warmth, in those last few days when our time together was ending. We would go off to our room and get in bed and I would feel a sort of panic because of her heat which was beyond sweating, so hot I felt singed by her. She was above me—that's how I remember it—her face like a pale moon dodging in and out of clouds of hair, sometimes dropping tears on my face, always pressing her hands down on my chest as if performing artificial respiration. And her faint humming. It wasn't loud, but it was musical, accompanying the effort to make me live and breathe and come to her. I felt that she was in me, rather than vice versa."

Then he stopped.

His brothers looked at each other, stunned. They had never heard anything like this from him before. Neither had I.

"Sounds like a great lay." Bobby finally gave a nervous grin after a long silence. "But like Teddy says, marriage isn't the end of the world. Consider it a jumping-off point. And don't worry, Johnny, there's more where she came from."

Jack continued looking up at the ceiling, nodding slightly without agreeing, as he blew smoke rings that chased each other furiously but dissolved without ever catching up.

This oral history by Lemoyne Billings was conveyed to the John F. Kennedy Library by a deed of gift dated May 9, 1981. In accordance with Mr. Billings's wishes and the notarized letter of transfer he signed, this document is to remain sealed from public view and usage for no less than forty years after his death, which occurred in New York City on May 28, 1981.

—Daniel Goldman, Senior Archivist